SIGNS OF OBSESSION

A DANA DEMETER MYSTERY
BOOK 3

A. F. WHITEHOUSE

COVER
MARK BURGESS

COPYRIGHT

IN MEMORY OF KAREN BURGESS

WISH YOU WERE HERE

THROUGH OTHERS, WE BECOME OURSELVES.

— LEV VYGOTSKY

1

DANA

12/17 9:00 a.m.

This wasn't going to be an easy meeting. I sat in my car in the law office parking lot having arrived in plenty of time to smoke at least one cigarette before my erstwhile partner, Felice "Nuts" Abandonato, showed.

The first few drags on a Kool calmed me down. My notes for the deposition sat on the passenger seat. I picked them up to scan yet again, wanting to keep the details straight in my mind. We were going to put Alberto Carrera away for a long time.

A few minutes later, Nuts's silent Prius appeared in my rearview mirror. I sucked one last hit of nicotine. A slight lowering of my window gave me enough room to flick my cigarette onto the concrete. A shower of sparks ricocheted at impact. Icy wind whickered through the window crack, bringing the scent of snow. I got out to meet him.

"You're up early," he said, glancing at his phone. "Thought I'd be the first one here."

"Of course you did, Nuts. You usually are. Probably put in ten miles before you left home, too. Right?" My former partner's health and fitness regimens, which included marathons, were well known among the detectives in our squad. But only I got to tease him about it.

He actually ducked his head. "No. Just five." He pointed at my notes with a questioning expression on his face.

"Don't want to make any mistakes in there," I said, nodding at the law office at the far end of the parking lot.

Nuts started to say something but was interrupted when a black SUV pulled in and parked next to my Camry. Our boss, Lieutenant Kozlowski, and another guy got out. Koz aimed a key fob at his car and it beeped. He and the younger guy approached us.

"Morning, Koz," I said. I squinted at the other guy who stood several steps behind our boss. He had a buzz-cut so short I could make out his pink scalp.

"Demeter. Abandonato." Koz was in full dress uniform and carrying his hat. I shrank from his once-over of my only business suit, which had odd wrinkle lines from living on a hanger for a few years since the last time I wore it. Skirts and pantyhose are not me, but I knew enough to don these relics for this important meeting if only to impress on Koz I took it seriously and was keeping my nose clean during my suspension. Nuts tossed a lazy salute at Koz, his own crisp attire earning a return salute.

Koz smoothed his hair back with one hand and put on his hat, its gold shield bright in the sun. He waved his hand in a hurry-up motion and beckoned to the stranger behind him to join us.

"Clint Rokick, meet Dana Demeter and Felice Abandonato." Koz steered Rokick by the elbow to edge the three of us close together in front of him. "You're joining Abandonato here as his substitute partner while Demeter's temporarily out."

Nuts held out his hand and Rokick clasped it.

"Hey," I said, going for a fist bump but getting no response. I lowered my hand.

"Demeter, I had second thoughts on the drive over here about you being deposed this morning," Koz said. "I want Abandonato to handle it alone."

Just like that. No letting me down easy. Nuts squinted at Koz and had the good grace to look as puzzled as I felt, which told me he knew nothing about this new plan.

"Don't do that to me, Koz—Carrera's mine. I'm the one who figured out he was on the take and—"

Nuts grabbed my upper arm and squeezed, hard. I tried to pull away from him but he wouldn't let go. All I could do was glare at him.

Koz took a step closer to me but spoke to Rokick. "The case I was telling you about on the way over? It was Demeter's solve. But she was on suspension at the time." Koz turned to me. "As she still is."

He didn't have to remind me about my status in front of this guy. Twice.

Koz gestured at the law office building. "Carrera's lawyer might make a big deal about you acting outside of my purview. Is that what you want? The media making you out as a *rogue cop*?" His gloved hands had difficulty making air quotes around the unwanted description. Rokick shoved his hands in his pockets and hunched his shoulders as a cold wind picked up and clouds moved in.

Felice let go of my arm. "I can handle it for both of us, Dane." He took my notes and folded them in half.

Koz clamped his hand on my shoulder and applied pressure. "Listen to your partner."

What is it with men trying to physically restrain me? I shook him off but checked my anger.

"Please, Koz. Please let me do this. The lawyer isn't going to put *me* on trial, for god's sake. I want my testimony on the record about Carrera. He's scum." I didn't add Koz obviously didn't want the media to find out I acted outside of his purview, as he put it. He didn't want the press excoriating *him*.

Koz crossed his arms. "Leave it alone. Now. You have plenty to concentrate on instead." His gaze flared over my entire body.

I shifted my attention from one face to the next, encountering Koz's hard stare, Nuts's weary face, and Rokick's slight smirk.

I addressed Rokick and his facial commentary. "For chrissakes, Carrera was going to let Charles Worthy go free by extorting him for two hundred grand! CW murdered two people!"

Rokick mouthed *wow* and shook his head as he dropped his gaze.

Koz blinked but said nothing. It was like talking to the sky, which now held stealthy dark clouds obliterating the sun. Then: "Detective Carrera is innocent until proven guilty. He will be dealt with at his trial."

Koz turned to Rokick. "Detective Carrera lost his job, among other things. It is the reason we have been able to hire you." Rokick nodded, glancing at Nuts and raising his eyebrows.

I pleaded again with Koz to let me give testimony about the result of my hard work, which I performed even though I was suspended. Being cut out of the final resolution to the case felt like the recent dissolution of my marriage: not what I wanted but I had no ability to change it.

"This isn't fair, Koz." I locked eyes with Rokick and stabbed my thumb at my chest. "I'm the one who figured out Carrera was dirty."

"This isn't about you, Demeter. Abandonato has the information necessary for the deposition." He looked at Nuts, who held up my notes and gave them a slight wave. "I want you to attend to your... your issues, so you can get back to doing great work with your partner." Again, the visual once-over of my body.

I took a step back and gave up trying to sway him. "I know. I know." I tapped Nuts on the arm. "I want that, too. Treatment's going well."

"Good, good." Koz flipped up the collar on his wool coat as a light snow drifted down.

One more entreaty. "Yeah. Treatment's going well and I'm losing the weight, too." This last bit was a blatant lie.

All I got was a nod from Koz. He told Rokick to return to the squad and wait for Nuts there, but the two made plans instead to meet at the Elite Restaurant and grab some food on their first day together. I was not included.

As Rokick left, Koz started toward the law office. Nuts called out he'd catch up with him in a minute.

Koz stopped and turned to face me. "One last time: think of your partner."

Nuts patted me on the arm but I flinched away and hissed my frustration. "He's still soft on Carrera! I bet Koz thinks his future son-in-law might skate on this. All because he can't bear to see his daughter hurt. Christ."

"You haven't heard the latest, then. Caitlyn called off their engagement."

I gaped at Nuts and he gave me a lazy smile. Koz's daughter Caitlyn, his only child—make that *spoiled* only child—was my age and worked downtown as a high-powered lawyer and touted a glamour magazine veneer. She and Carrera had announced their engagement not long ago with a splashy picture in the social news. "She keeping the ring?"

Nuts nodded. "All four carats." We both snickered. Nuts glanced at his phone and put my notes in his pocket. "I need to get in there."

This time I grabbed his arm. "Wait. What do you think of Rokick?"

Nuts shrugged. "Koz warned me he's a newborn. There'll be a lot for me to coach him on. He's not you."

The way Nuts said this confirmed the coach role was something he wouldn't enjoy. Of course, Rokick just got assigned, so there wasn't much to appraise about the guy as a partner. But I fully planned on returning to the squad and my rightful place. At my desk. Right next to Nuts. Rokick could find another partner.

"Gotta wipe the baby's ass?" I said this hoping Nuts would get I was joking, but he didn't join me in laughing.

"I'll call you later with the update." He gestured at the law office building.

"Yeah. Okay." I stood in the cold, the snowfall heavier now and matting my hair as my partner of three years walked away, heading to the office to give them *my* chapter and verse on Detective Alberto Carrera's violation of his oath.

Before getting into my car, I bent over and scrubbed at the snow build-up in my short hair and brushed small white mounds off the shoulders of my coat. Inside, I lit a cigarette and checked my phone for the traffic report to decide whether to get on the expressway or not, but a Starbucks drive-thru for some caffeine would come first. While I fiddled with the heat, another car pulled up next to mine.

A muffled tap jerked my attention to the passenger-side window. Alberto Carrera, in person, leered at me through the closed glass. He tapped again. I lowered the window an inch, took a deep drag on my

Kool and blew the smoke his way. He ducked his head back and swore.

"That all you got, Demeter? Blowin' smoke?" He snickered at his little joke. The man behind him—his lawyer, I assumed—looked away.

"I got a lot more smoke than this, Carrera. In fact, my partner's inside building a bonfire just for you. You're gonna choke on that smoke and go up in flames." I grinned at the image, inhaled deeply, and blew more smoke at him.

He pulled back again and then stuck his ugly mug right up to the crack in the window. His voice dropped. "How's your mother, Demeter? I understand she had a little accident."

The quick switch of subjects caught me off guard, but before I could get out of my car and challenge Carrera to his face his lawyer pulled him away and steered him toward the law office.

I lowered the window some more. "Hey, asshole!" I shouted after the two men, but they ignored me and entered the building. I wanted to go after them, grab Carrera by the lapels and bang his head against a brick wall a few times, make him tell me what he knew about the physical assault on my mother last month. But lately what I wanted and what I got were like two strangers passing on opposite sides of the street.

2

FELICE

Noon

Felice Abandonato queued up at the back of the line trailing out the door of the Elite Restaurant. He had hoped meeting Clint Rokick for a late breakfast after the deposition meant they would avoid the early crowd at the popular Greek place, but it looked like everyone in the neighborhood had the same idea.

He stood on tiptoe to see if he could spy Rokick farther up the line, but no luck. Customers leaving, and others in line arriving, brought Felice up to the large plate-glass window at the front of the eatery. Inside, he could see the rookie at a two-top against the back wall. Relieved, he broke from the line and went in.

Chris Sepsakos greeted him, a large menu in hand. "Detective! Come in, come in. I haven't seen your partner yet. Is she late? Again?" He chuckled, the joke a familiar one between them. He gave Felice the menu and held out his hand for a handshake, to which Felice responded.

"Uh, no. I'm meeting someone else, Chris. He's over there." He gestured at the back table where Rokick still hadn't made eye contact. Not exactly hypervigilant, his new partner.

Chris followed him to Rokick's table. "Coffee? Tea? What can I get for you, Detective?"

Felice ordered tea while Chris signaled one of the waiters to bring a refill for Rokick's coffee. Felice asked for the Greek omelet.

"You're having breakfast? It's lunchtime," Rokick said.

Did the guy think he didn't know what time it was? "Didn't have time to eat this morning—except for a banana—after a five-miler and a shower. Wanted to be sure I was early for the deposition."

Rokick shrugged and ordered the lumberjack breakfast.

"I got here twenty minutes ago and there were only three other people besides me. Now look at this place." He tapped the manila folder at his elbow. "Got the prelim field report." He patted the table and grinned. "Also got us a table."

Was there some kind of reward or praise Rokick wanted? Better to ignore the childish angling for a gold star, otherwise he'd end up handing out trophies if this continued.

Felice gestured at the thin folder. "Catch me up on what you got."

Rokick opened the file, murmuring a bit before he read. "Margot Stuckless, dead only a couple hours, happened this morning. Neighbor Janey Foreman found her. No forced entry to the home, although the bedroom where she was found had a sliding door that leads to the backyard. Unlocked. No weapons or obvious cause of death."

He pointed to something farther down the one-page report and looked up. "Her nose was broke. I'm guessing asphyxiation."

"It's okay to guess, but don't let it become fact in your mind. Let's wait for the autopsy to give us more on that."

"How long does that usually take?"

"Depends. For this, probably ten days to two weeks." Felice didn't get into the ins and outs of the Cook County Medical Examiner's Office. Rokick would learn it all later through his own experiences dealing with multiple cases and more complicated causes of death.

Rokick nodded and went back to the report. "Not much evidence, either. Like I said, no weapons found. A baby's picture in a broken frame was next to the body. And those little candy bars, you know, like for Halloween? A lot of empty wrappers from," he ran his finger down the report, "Butterfingers. They were scattered on the ground outside the sliding door to the baby's bedroom. Also around the body. Not much else of interest to point to anything or anyone."

"We'll have to wait for forensic results on those things. Just like the autopsy. At least two weeks."

Rokick looked stricken, like hearing there wouldn't be any cake at his birthday party. Welcome to working homicide. Everything is hurry up until it isn't, especially for the stuff you needed to do your job.

"Look. Don't get too dependent on the forensics or the autopsy. It always takes time. It doesn't give us much right now. If it comes after the solve, it'll confirm what we already discovered."

Their food arrived. Felice dug into an egg-white omelet, Greek style. He flipped through the crime scene photos, but nothing stood out. The photo of the baby came last, a beautiful little girl at her first birthday, gleefully mashing a handful of cake all over her face.

"Look. Once in a while we get lucky early with a fingerprint or blood match, catch them that way. But this isn't a cop show wrapped up in an hour. The work you and I do means witnesses, family, friends, victim's workplace, what the deceased was doing the day she died. Tedious, important work."

Rokick's lumberjack breakfast disappeared quickly. He seemed to barely chew before swallowing and shoveling in another mouthful. Felice clocked the five-year difference in their ages, but he'd never eaten like Rokick either before or after turning twenty-five.

"Is there a husband or partner?"

Rokick swigged some coffee before referring to the file again. "Just getting to that. Let's see. Yes. Husband. But not living in the house and not at work because he was fired. Other than Janey Foreman finding the body we don't have the neighbor list yet. It's a small side street, not many homes. Here's the thing. The baby picture? They have a little girl, almost two years old. Melanie. She's missing. Along with the dad."

If Dana was sitting across from Felice, the baby's disappearance would be the first thing out of her mouth. She would've already initiated notifying the Illinois State Police to put out an Amber Alert. Felice put down his fork. "Is there anything in there about ISP and an Amber Alert?"

Rokick shook his head.

Felice unhooked a pen from his jacket's inner pocket and handed it to Rokick. "Write this down. In capital letters. Abductions of any kind *always* get primary attention." He waited for Rokick to recover from his glare, take the pen, and write. But the guy waved it off and worked his thumbs nimbly on his phone.

"We'll check if ISP's been notified. If not, you copy that baby's photo and forward it to them. That's the *first* thing you do." He leaned in. "Got it?"

"Yes. Sure. Makes sense. I'm sorry I—"

Felice held up his hand. "Don't apologize. Be aware. Learn."

Rokick looked away for a long moment and then studied the report. "Hey. I didn't write this. I'm only reading what the first detective on the scene found this morning." He raised his empty coffee cup and waved it at their server.

Before, he wanted praise. Now, he wanted sympathy. Both expectations grated on Felice. Depending on what they uncovered, he doubted if he'd get in another workout later today, his stress level with Rokick already spiking.

He motioned for Rokick to put down the cup and gestured at the crowded room.

"We're done and they're busy." He had to find a different place to meet with Rokick. Here at the Elite, he and Dana could sit and talk for as long as they needed. Chris Sepsakos blessed them with bottomless cups of coffee and tea delivered at just the right moment. No rushing them out the door regardless of the crowd. Today, the bustling noisy restaurant only raised the irritation quotient Rokick incited in him and made him miss working with Dana.

Felice shook off thinking about his suspended partner. "Let's get out of here. We can take care of the Alert from my car, then we'll figure out how to attack the interviews."

"But we don't know if the kid was abducted."

"Correct. But here's what we have. The father doesn't live in the house and the baby is missing. She's under sixteen. Father is a murder suspect. That's enough for us to confirm with ISP. Doesn't matter if the father has a right to have the baby. They're both missing and that's a problem."

Rokick nodded and jotted on his phone as Felice gave a quick explanation of the process for activating an Amber Alert. Then Rokick flashed his phone at Felice. "Got their website. I'll read up on it, memorize it. Thanks for the info."

The server dropped off the check. Felice snagged it and shut down Rokick's attempt to Venmo him some money. He had no desire to trust his money handling to an app, something he and Dana agreed on one hundred percent.

"Next time, you buy."

"Sure, sure."

At the register Felice handed over the exact change and indicated he'd left the tip on the table. They walked out, a small bell dinging with the door's movement as it closed.

Felice approached his red Prius and beeped open the passenger door. "Ride with me. We can discuss the Alert, see if anything useful has come in from the field, and take a look at the Stuckless house. On the way to the Foreman interview, I'll give you a rundown on how Dana and I work a case. It's efficient." It also gave them the best solve rate in the squad.

"What about my motorcycle?" Rokick pointed across the street at his motorcycle, one of those three-wheeled jobs that mimicked a backwards tricycle.

"I'll bring you back when we're through."

Once in the car, Rokick asked him how long he and Dana were partners.

"Three years."

"Long time."

"Not really. Compared to some of the others we're still considered new." Their partnership was solid from the start. Even though he was furious with Dana for fucking up everything with her drinking, he wanted her back—he wanted *them* back—to what they had. In a New York second.

"How long's she been suspended? I mean, how long before she gets back?"

Felice wished he knew the answer. Dana only had two more weeks in outpatient treatment, but there was the weight loss requirement too. Judging from her appearance this morning, she was nowhere near meeting that.

"I don't know. Buckle up." He snapped his own seat belt in place and punched the power button on the dashboard.

"A couple guys said Koz Breathalyzed her and sent her home. Was she really drinking on the job?"

Here it was. Felice suspected Rokick wanted the inside story, if only to satisfy his curiosity. But he sensed there was more to the question, like whether Felice wanted Dana back as a partner. Or maybe Rokick wanted to find out if he would engage in banal office gossip. And there was plenty to spread about Dana.

Felice signaled and pulled out of the parking space into heavy traffic. "Dana wasn't drinking on the job. Anything else you want to know about her suspension, get it from Koz."

3

DANA

Noon

The marquee sign for Louie's Liquor Palace beckoned me, each large 'L' outlined in purple and blinking on and off, making it hard to miss. Guess that's the idea.

I parked and hustled inside, intent on buying a carton of Kools and nothing else. No booze for nineteen days, if I included today. Cigarettes shouted from the wall behind the cash register and I joined the line as customer number five. Progress was slow. Finally, the guy ahead of me hoisted his twelve-pack of Bud onto the counter and pointed at the wall of cigarettes.

"What brand do you want, buddy?" Louie asked. 'Buddy' loomed over Louie, at least six-six and three hundred pounds, dwarfing the slight store owner.

The hulking man continued to point, and with exaggerated mouth movement said what sounded like "Brrr." Seemed like the guy didn't speak English. I distracted myself and checked the weather app on my phone to see if more snow would show up this afternoon.

Louie frowned at the guy but gave it a go. He followed the direction of the guy's pointed finger and tapped the green Salem carton. "This? You want this?"

The guy shook his head and motioned Louie to scooch a bit to the left.

The twelve-pack of Bud on the counter stared at me. I could easily down the first six and feel little effect except maybe the need to pee. But finishing the second six would be just the thing to melt my anxiety and bring comfort.

Louie moved a step over and touched a carton emblazoned with the red Winston logo. Again, a head shake response.

This played out a couple more times, Louie dancing around behind the counter playing charades with the guy. I sighed audibly, hoping they would get the hint and hurry up. I checked my phone again. Even though I had plenty of time, I started to worry I'd be late interpreting my mother Evie's 2:00 appointment with the police sketch artist. I wanted to get some lunch first. Well, maybe Evie would feed me.

The guy in front of me pulled a small pad of paper and pencil stub out of his back pocket, wrote something, and handed it to Louie.

"Ooooh! I get you, I get you." Louie grabbed a pack of Marlboros from the wall. "Brrr. Am I right?"

The guy made a goal post with raised arms and they both laughed. While Louie rang him up the guy glanced at me and winced an apology, pointed to his ear and shook his head.

This pantomime wasn't new to me. *"Deaf?"* I signed.

His delighted smile and nodding head answered my question. *"You?"*

"No. My whole family is deaf. Me? Hearing."

He indicated we were the same but in the opposite way. His whole family was hearing. He was the only deaf person, a constellation much more common than my family's configuration.

Louie took in our signing while he rang up my purchase. As we turned to leave, he increased his volume several decibels. "THANKS, YOU TWO! HAVE A NICE DAY!"

I waved over my shoulder and exited through the door the deaf guy held open for me. Outside, he asked me to wait a second while he stowed the beer in his car and then asked my name.

I fingerspelled *D-A-N-A D-E-M-E-T-E-R* and added my sign name by tapping the letter 'd' over my heart.

"*R-O-B-E-R-T T-H-O-M-A-S but people call me Bear.*" He signed his nickname, arms crisscrossed over his barrel chest, his fingers arching in a clawed hand shape and lightly scraping his unzipped winter jacket. It wasn't hard to understand the nickname considering his large physique, shaggy hair, and thick black beard.

I copied his sign for *Bear* to show I understood and added a common, worn-out bromide. "*Nice to meet you.*"

"*Are you an interpreter? I need an interpreter. You sign like true deaf.*"

I grew up getting this from the deaf people in my life—and there are many—like my parents, my twin brother, my younger sister, and all of their deaf friends. As the only hearing person in my family, it naturally fell to me to interpret, especially during on-the-spot situations where there was no interpreter, or appointments where one wasn't hired. Happened a lot. And unfortunately continues to happen even though it's against the law.

"*Thanks. Sure, I interpret for my family.*" I briefly considered how much to tell Bear about my current employment—on suspension from my job as a homicide detective—but kept mum. "*I'm not certified but I do some interpreting for Deaf Catholic Office. You know Father M-I-K?*" I fingerspelled the name of a priest in Chicago, well-known to many deaf people, who headed up Saint Nick's Catholic Church. My mother regularly joined its sizeable deaf congregation where Father Mik rendered the mass in ASL.

Bear's face lit up. *"St. Nick's, right? My mother's Catholic. She dragged me to church there when I was a kid."* He laughed. *"I don't go now, want to sleep on Sunday morning. My mother prays for my soul."* He gazed up and imbued his last sign with an exaggerated waver as his hand travelled skyward. He winked at me and grinned.

I chuckled. *"My mother's the same. I'm thirty and she still tries to get me back to church. You need interpreter for?"* I checked my phone again for the time.

Bear read my need to hurry. *"There's no interpreter at P-P meetings. Right now, I record on my phone and mother listens, tries to tell me what they're saying but mostly she fingerspells. It's hard to understand."*

"P-P is what?" My squint and headshake signaled I was asking a question.

"P-O-U-N-D-S P-O-L-I-C-E. To lose weight. My mother got mad when I ate all the Halloween candy."

I smiled as I raised my eyebrows at this confession and nodded. I could relate to overdoing the daily sugar recommendation. As I considered his request, I had to admit I wasn't too busy to help this one time.

During the day I was at loose ends. At night I attended an Intensive Outpatient Program—or IOP—for alcoholism. It met from 6:00 to 9:00 p.m. Mondays through Thursdays and I had just two weeks left. Even though I came into some money from the recent sale of my house, I could always use the cash from interpreting.

I agreed to meet Bear at his PP meeting tomorrow morning for one session and we would take it from there.

4

FELICE

2:00 p.m.

F elice parked in the first place he could find on the small side street and shut off the Prius. Margot Stuckless's house was across the street and three doors down from Janey Foreman's place. He turned to Rokick.

"First we'll get a look at the crime scene." He gestured at the manila folder on the dashboard. "Like the initial report said, there really won't be much to see. But I always observe everything firsthand. People see things differently. People miss things." He waited until Rokick acknowledged this with a head nod.

But the prelim field report turned out to be accurate. Felice took Rokick through the house, pointed out where the techs dusted for prints, even snapped a few photos on his own phone to help with recall when sketching out the scene later. There was no forced entry anywhere, so either Margot Stuckless let her killer in or the unlocked sliding door in the baby's bedroom became the entry point.

On the walk over to Janey Foreman's house Felice mentally lined up how to take Rokick through this interview.

"Listen up. Inside, you observe what I do and how I question Janey Foreman. You have any questions, keep quiet until we're out of there and then we'll debrief." He gave Rokick a hard stare and after a long moment got a verbal agreement.

They climbed the few stairs in the front of Janey Foreman's house, a single-story light brick ranch dating back to the fifties and yellow with age. Before they reached the landing the front door opened. A slight woman greeted them as if she'd been watching for their arrival. "Police?"

Felice held out his badge for inspection and then re-clipped it to his belt, preferring the leather holder to wearing his star on a chain around his neck. He introduced himself and Rokick, and confirmed the woman was Janey Foreman. A few beats behind, Rokick fumbled with and then held out his badge.

"Come in, come in, Detectives. Pretty cold out there." They followed Janey Foreman to a kitchen at the back of the house where she gestured at a round table covered with a blue checkered cloth and surrounded by five chairs. "It's cozier in here, don't you think?"

Felice placed the file on the table and shed his coat before sitting. Rokick copied him.

"I made some coffee cake, so help yourselves." She pointed at a plate filled with healthy-sized portions cut into squares and stacked three high. "I have regular and decaf coffee. Which would you like?" She hovered between them like a nervous waitress.

"I don't drink coffee, thank you. If you don't mind, I'd like to get to the interview."

Janey Foreman glanced at Rokick. "Oh. Of course. I'm sorry. I keep trying to do things to keep my mind off, well, you know. It was horrible finding Margot like that, just horrible." She rubbed her hands down the front of her apron and clutched the folds with both fists.

Felice pointedly gestured for her to sit at the table and waited until she got coffee for herself and then sat across from him. She gave him permission to record the interview on his cell phone.

"I understand you were on the phone with Mrs. Stuckless this morning. Tell me exactly, to the best of your ability, how the conversation went."

The woman's hand flitted to her hair and fiddled with the gold hoop earring in her right ear before settling in her lap. "Yes, well. Margot and I were chatting about PP—that's Pounds Police—and you know she's a leader and all. She was telling me how the women in the meetings complain about not being like her, not losing weight like she did. You know, fast. Do you know, she lost thirty pounds in three months?" She shook her head, then grabbed a piece of coffee cake and held it up. "Are you sure you won't have some? It's fat-free." She said this in a sing-song voice. Rokick started to reach for the cake but Felice touched his hand to stop the motion.

"No. Thank you."

She shrugged and took a large bite of cake, chewed, then washed it down with several sips of coffee. "I just love this recipe. It's Margot's of course. And she made it up all—"

"Excuse me, Mrs. Foreman. You were telling us about the phone call."

"Oh, of course. I'm sorry. I'm so distracted. Let's see. Margot was complaining, well, no, she wasn't complaining. It was more, um, she called the women losers." She put the coffee cake on a napkin and stretched her back to adjust her posture. "Which isn't very nice, I know. Sometimes she can be kind of tough on those women."

Ignoring her second digression, Felice asked if there was more they talked about.

"Yes. Well, no. Just what time she would pick me up because we always go to the meetings together."

"Did you hear anyone else in the background?"

"I was getting to that, yes. Margot told me to hang on because I think she heard the baby or something. I could tell she carried her phone with her when she went to look. All of a sudden, she said something like 'You again' and 'I told you to stay away.' Those aren't her exact words, but you get the idea. It's pretty close. But no one said anything back and then there was a loud crash. I think." She stopped, her eyes filling with tears. "That's when her phone went dead." She swiped at her face with the corner of her apron.

"And you heard nothing else? Not even the baby?"

She dug a tissue from her pocket and wiped her nose. "No. Nothing. Melly usually has a morning nap before we go to the PP meeting. I thought she must've slept through whatever happened. But that was before—" She broke down crying.

"Do you need a break, Mrs. Foreman?" Felice said.

She shook her head. "No. It's just been so scary." She got up and retrieved a box of tissues from the counter behind her chair and sat down.

"I understand. I'd like to take you through what happened next, if you're up to it."

"Yes, yes. Please. I know this is so important." Her voice wobbled but the full-on crying had stopped.

"All right. After Mrs. Stuckless's phone went dead, did you go over to her house right then?"

"I thought it was her husband she was talking to, Detective. I didn't want to interfere." Her voice dropped low, confidential. "She kicked him out, you know."

"If you didn't hear anyone else's voice, what made you think it was her husband?"

Janey Foreman pondered his question for a minute. "Why, I guess it's because she said *stay away*. That could only be her husband, right? Like they were fighting." At this, she teared up again.

"When did you go check on her?"

Janey hugged her arms around her waist. "Margot always picks me up at 9:30. We have a morning meeting at 10. I thought she'd be over to my place, just like always, once she finished with him." She ate more of her coffee cake and pushed the plate toward Rokick. Again he reached for it, and Abandonato stopped him with a minute shake of the head.

"So about quarter to, I got worried we'd be late so I called but the phone just rang and rang. I could see out my window her car was there—she's just down a few houses—so I went over to see what was going on." Janey's voice wavered. "The front door was closed but not latched, so I pushed it open." Her hand made a small pushing motion.

"I know this is difficult, Mrs. Foreman. Take your time."

She nodded and stood, topped off her coffee and brought it to the table. "I feel so guilty. I knew she and Mac weren't getting along. But Margot always had everything under control, and she could handle her husband. Maybe if I had called the police right away after her phone died, she'd still be alive."

Janey Foreman hugged her arms across her body and closed her eyes. "I called out to Margot. The front door goes into the living room. But it was quiet, you know? Too quiet. Like an empty house is. I kept calling her name and went down the hallway to the bedrooms in the back."

Her eyes popped open. "That's where she was, in the baby's bedroom. On the floor." She thrust her arms outward. "Poor Margot." She looked at Felice and started to cry again. "Why didn't I call you sooner?"

Rokick reached out his hand and clasped her forearm. "You did call us. As soon as you found her."

Felice glared at Rokick. There would be a lot of work to do with this guy starting with the obvious: never touch a witness.

"Detective, can you excuse me? I need to use the restroom." She got up and pointed toward the ceiling. "I'll just be a minute," she said, and left the kitchen.

Rokick reached out and nabbed a piece of coffee cake, finishing it off in four bites.

Felice scowled. "You don't take a hint, do you?"

Rokick leaned back in his chair. "She offered."

"This is not a social call. We are not here to make friends. We are not here for a *coffee klatsch*."

Rokick shrugged as if what Felice said didn't amount to much at all.

"I don't get it. It's just a piece of coffee cake."

He put both hands on the table and leaned toward Rokick. "Did it ever cross your mind you have no idea what is in that piece of coffee cake you just inhaled?"

Rokick's smile faltered as he surveyed the crumbs left on the table.

Janey Foreman re-entered the kitchen and sat in her place at the table. The tears were gone and she'd applied a fresh swipe of red lipstick.

"Let's go back to where you found Mrs. Stuckless."

Janey Foreman nodded and squinted at the ceiling. "Yes. She was on the floor in the baby's bedroom. It was so cold. There's a sliding door to the yard in there. It was open partway. I—I checked for her pulse. I remembered that much from my first aid class. But she was gone."

Her gaze dropped to Felice. "I've never been that close to a dead body before. So creepy, you know? But right then I realized I didn't hear Melly. I jumped up and went to the baby's crib, but it was empty."

"Did you check the rest of the house at that point?"

"Yes! I ran around like a crazy person screaming for Melly!" Her voice dropped to a moan. "But she wasn't there. She's gone and Margot's dead."

Felice let her sit quietly for a moment. "You can be very helpful to us if you can get a current picture of the baby for the Amber Alert. In the photo we have, the baby's face is covered in birthday cake. Is there any chance you have a better one?"

"I do! I do!" She pulled her cell phone from her apron pocket and started scrolling. "I watch Melly while Margot gives the lectures at PP and I love taking pictures of them both. Margot sewed these darling matching outfits they wore to the meetings. She said it was to give the women something to aspire to."

She sent several photos to his phone. Felice scrolled through them, then held up his phone. "How old is Melanie here?"

"I took that last week. She's twenty months."

"You said a few minutes ago that Mrs. Stuckless kicked her husband out. Any idea why?"

"Margot said Mac wasn't pulling his weight at home and then she found out he was seeing a woman at work. That did it. She threw him out about six months ago. They were in the middle of a divorce."

"Do you know where Mr. Stuckless is staying?"

She paused for a moment. "No. Not really. It's only Margot and me that are friends. I never liked Mac. When will the Amber Alert be done?"

He held up his phone again and gave it a small shake. "With your photos it's in the works right after we leave. I'm hopeful we'll find her."

He didn't add that missing children not located within the first three hours usually weren't found alive.

5

DANA

2:00 p.m.

My mother is short. At five-ten I tower above Evie. I also probably outweigh her by eighty pounds. My weight soared after my miscarriage, so in order to return to work as a detective a forty-pound weight loss requirement was added to my suspension agreement. One of those *issues* Koz wants me to work on.

Unless I'm unavailable, I am Evie's default interpreter. Like right now.

"Thanks for agreeing to come to my mom's house," I said. "I'm Dana and this is my mom, Evie." I signed this simultaneously for Evie's benefit as I spoke to a police sketch artist standing in my parents' living room, here to make a drawing of the woman who attacked my mother last month. Evie was excited because she had a dream revealing the woman's face, which up until now was only a blank. I was skeptical and hoped Evie's dream wasn't her imagination playing tricks on her.

The cop artist seemed nervous. "I'm James."

I fingerspelled his name to my mom and she smiled at him, lifting her hand in a half-wave.

"Have you ever used an interpreter before?" I asked.

"Just Spanish and Polish, that's all. Like with speaking."

I nodded and explained to Evie it was James's first time working with an interpreter for deaf people. Evie aimed her body language at him and gave a large shrug, as if to say, *this is a piece of cake.* She gestured for James to sit next to me on the couch so she could easily watch both of us while I interpreted.

Evie then mimed drinking something and gave James a quizzical look and pointed at him. He grinned with understanding and asked me the sign for coffee. I quickly signed his question to Evie and she showed him, first stacking her right fist on top of her left fist and then making a small circular motion with it, as if using an old-fashioned coffee grinder. James copied her, getting the idea, nodding the whole time. Evie clapped and went into the kitchen to get us all coffee and a cheese sandwich for me.

Several cups later—Evie teaching James the additional signs for *cream, sugar,* and *thank you*—James had a rough sketch of an African-American woman Evie claimed hewed pretty close to the woman who attacked her. To me it was so generic I didn't think it would ID anyone. James told us he would work on it some more on the computer and send us a copy for final approval and then forward it to the investigating team.

"Tell your mom—oh, I forgot—" He had the grace to blush a little and then faced Evie to address her directly. "Mrs. Demeter, if you remember anything else about her face or hair or anything you think will make it easier to identify her, call me." As he spoke, I interpreted this to Evie.

"*Thank you, James,*" Evie signed, which I voiced for James. She took the business card he offered. He smiled and signed thank you back to

Evie. Beaming at her new student, my mom got up and escorted James to the door, patting him on the back with approval. I carried the cups and my plate into the kitchen and stowed them in the dishwasher.

Evie caught me checking the lock on the kitchen's back door.

"I'm keeping it locked. You don't have to check up on me like a little kid." She went to the fridge, pulled out some bread and cheese, turned her back on me and started to make a sandwich. Leaning against the back door, I watched my mother of sixty-six years, her white braided hair trailing down her back, and wondered why our interactions always seemed to erupt into some kind of argument or challenge.

I went to her side and touched her elbow to get her attention. She gave me a slight glance from the corner of her eye but didn't attend any longer, a sure hint she wasn't interested in talking. I waited for her to finish making the sandwich, and we sat down at the table where she wouldn't be able to avoid looking at me.

"I don't think I'm treating you like a little kid. I'm making sure you're safe, especially when JJ's not here. Like when you didn't lock the door before," I gestured at her head. I felt my anger rising as I reminded Evie of her previous stubborn refusal to lock the back door. And of course, being deaf, she couldn't hear a damn thing when the intruder came into her bedroom. Then it was too late. Knocked unconscious, she suffered a concussion and needed seven stitches.

As Evie put down her sandwich to respond I heard the front door slam, and my father came into the kitchen. I stood and gave him a big smile and hug. He asked how the interview went with the sketch artist. While keeping his gaze on Evie as she described James and the process of questions he asked, JJ retrieved a glass from the cabinet and filled it with cold water, then joined us.

"Do you think it will help the police find that woman?" JJ asked me.

I shrugged. *"Maybe. But Chicago is a large city. They'll do the best they can."* I patted his arm.

"Jimmy could find her. He's the best detective, one hundred percent. When's he coming back from California?" I wasn't fooled by Evie's seemingly innocent question about my ex-husband of ten years currently making his home in L.A.

"I don't know," I lied. I had no wish to tell my parents Jimmy and I were divorced, in the process of separating for good, that he would stay in L.A.

If I told Evie Jimmy wasn't coming back to Chicago it would lead to the question of why. There was only one answer: he thought I drank too much. I had hoped attending the outpatient program would show him I didn't have a problem, but then I lied to him about a drunk driving accident. When he found out, it proved to be the final indignity. He was done.

JJ piped up, explaining things to Evie. *"Jimmy works with gangs. He wouldn't be the right police for your crime."* He turned to me. *"F-A would be the right one, yes?"* He used my partner Felice Abandonato's initials over his heart as a name sign. *"Have you talked to him yet about her attack?"*

Here's the second thing I don't want my parents to find out: I'm on suspension from my job as a detective because of a positive read on a Breathalyzer test administered by Koz. A bogus result, I might add. I hadn't been drinking *on the job*. Some booze still in my system from the night before had yet to burn off. I showed up for work anyway, but that didn't hold sway over Koz or the department's zero tolerance policy.

I slowly raised my hands to respond, waiting for them both to attend, but more to give myself time to figure out what to say without having to lie for a second time. *"I told F-A that you remembered what the woman looked like. I'll send him the sketch as soon as James sends it to me."* Nuts wasn't officially on the investigation team working Evie's case, but I kept him apprised of developments. My parents already knew this. I explained it yet again because JJ, in particular, continued to press me for Nuts to be the one in charge. As if I ran things.

I stood, said I had to get going, and headed into the living room to grab my jacket. If I stayed any longer, I wouldn't be able to continue telling more bald-faced lies. JJ followed me outside to my car. We hugged.

"I gotta go," I signed.

He held onto my arm and signed with one hand. *"Feel okay? You seem..."* He searched for a sign. *"You seem sad."*

Leave it to my father to get me on an emotional level, unlike my mother. Evie needs to be told explicitly, sometimes more than once, when I am upset. She has none of the typical maternal radar allowing her to read her children's signals. I put my hand over his arm and gave it a light squeeze.

"Just tired. Been very busy."

He let go of my arm. *"Are you working tonight?"*

He meant as a cop. I gave him a vague answer. *"I have to go to a meeting."* Not a lie, more like a sin of omission, hat-tip to Father Mik. The "meeting" was at the intensive outpatient program. I hugged him again, always loving his strong embrace, and got into my car. He stood there watching me, then quickly signed he wanted me to tell FA hello from him. I swear on some level JJ knows or at least senses I'm not actively working as a detective.

"O-K," I signed. *"I love you."* I flashed this last one-handed sign with an energetic motion to pump up the inherent meaning.

I kept my nose clean and attended another evening of IOP after leaving my parents' house. A couple of the other regulars talked me into going for coffee afterwards and we gabbed at Starbucks until they kicked us out. After I got home to my third-floor studio and shed my down coat, gloves, scarf and hat, I saw a message waiting on the videophone. I played it back and there was Evie, big as life, signing fast with excitement.

"I remembered more about that—" Here Evie used the slang sign for the N-word, which makes me cringe every time she uses it. I've implored her not to be so crass, but she refuses to back down with her language. Evie went on to describe the woman's hair as black, shoulder-length, with a wide swath of blond starting at her hairline front to back.

"You know, like a skunk!" she exalted. This was something she hadn't told James the sketch artist and I'd need to update him. I sat on my couch as my mother made more crude comments about this woman and I almost turned off her message out of disgust. Then she added one other descriptor: the woman had a sprinkle of purple glitter across her nose and cheeks. That got my attention.

I knew her.

6

DANA

12/18 9:45 a.m.

I waited for Bear, the deaf man I met at Louie's, just outside the room where the Pounds Police meeting was scheduled to take place. Most of the women trooping past me were older and plagued with what seemed to be the inevitable post-menopause weight gain. There were a few women around my age—new moms with their offspring in baby carriers—but I didn't share anything in common with them, either. My sole pregnancy ended in a miscarriage earlier this year.

Minutes before the meeting began Bear arrived huffing and puffing as though he'd jogged from the parking lot. He greeted me and ushered me by the arm into the room, where we joined a line of women who were weighing in.

Before I could engage in any small talk with Bear, the woman about to be weighed turned to the rest of us and moaned in a loud voice, "I've been sooo baaad this week."

I chuckled as I interpreted this to Bear. He shook his head.

Then the woman whipped off her jacket and turtleneck sweater to stand unveiled in a jogging bra. Off came the sweatpants, revealing two meaty thighs encased in spandex biking shorts. "I ate sooo much iiiicceee creeeaam," she said, her voice even louder than before.

I signed this histrionic performance to Bear. He responded. *"Every week she does that. Most of them do. Take off their clothes so they don't weigh so much."* He shrugged as if the behavior didn't faze him.

I asked him if he stripped down too, repeatedly flicking my thumbs underneath my index fingers—as if quickly flipping a coin—as I ran my hands downward from my shoulders to my hips, which I wiggled a bit, as if mimicking a stripper. His eyes widened in horror.

"If I stripped it would scare everyone away. P-P would go broke." We both laughed. When it was Bear's turn at the scale he shed his shoes and stepped on. The woman doing the weigh-in wore a play police hat and a metal star pinned to her shirt. Her name tag read *Captain Janey*.

"Better luck next time," Captain Janey said.

I interpreted this to Bear. He grunted and sat down to put on his shoes. *"Three pounds. Big deal."* I voiced this for her and privately wished I could lose as much in one week.

"Tell him the idea is to lose weight, not gain it. Next."

I held back a laugh at my misunderstanding, told him what she said, and followed Bear to a seat at the back of the room. I grabbed another chair and set it up facing him.

While we waited for the lecture to start I noticed Bear eyeing a young woman. I caught his gaze and tilted my head toward her, raised my eyebrows, and signed *cute*.

Bear made a face. *"That girl? Too fat."*

I recoiled inside, attempting to keep my facial expression as neutral as possible. Was this the way it was with most guys? Here sat a hugely overweight man judging a woman about her weight and apparently not seeing the irony. He lived with his mother. My guess was he didn't date much, either. And the woman he considered too fat? She wasn't much bigger than me.

I shifted in my seat and held up my hands in a non-committal gesture implying I would back off from saying anything more about something so personal.

I interpreted the fifteen-minute lecture, which mostly consisted of warnings about the upcoming holidays and the billion ways they could sabotage a person's food plan.

"Say it again! No! No thank you!" Captain Janey exhorted the group to copy her as she held up her hands, palms out, as if to push away an imaginary eclair being forced on her by the devil himself. Most of the women repeated the words with enthusiasm, but I noticed some barely gave lip service. Bear just stuck out his hands mimicking the Captain. If I used this strategy with Evie offering me a piece of cake, she would copy me and then ask if I was trying to stop traffic.

After the lecture, Captain Janey read a list of the "recruits" who lost weight this past week and earned a "commendation," a silver star sticker. Bear earned a "citation" for gaining weight and had to pony up a dollar for every pound gained. The cop in me rolled my eyes at the appropriating of some law enforcement words, but I had to admit if the faux wordplay got people to participate in order to lose weight, then it was worthwhile.

Bear tossed money in the basket being passed around. *"They donate the money to a food bank, so I don't mind paying."*

The room swelled with chatter as people started to rise and don their coats, but Captain Janey wasn't through. She banged on the podium with her fist a few times but when people ignored her, she blew a loud blast on a whistle hanging from a lanyard around her neck.

"Everyone! Everyone, quiet please!" She beckoned to someone I couldn't see outside the room.

"This is Detective Rokick. He's here to talk with you about what happened to Captain Margot."

It took me a moment to register the guy entering the room and heading toward the podium. My temporary replacement I met just yesterday, Nuts's new partner. I started to flip my chair around to watch Rokick, but Bear stopped me. He wanted me to continue interpreting.

I heard the adjustment of the microphone and a loud squawk of feedback reverberated in the room. Several people, including me, winced and covered our ears. Bear smiled and gaily signed his Deaf Pride by sticking the thumb of his closed fist in his ear, then with a slight twist of the wrist he flared the four fingers upward. Roughly translated: *I'm glad I'm deaf so I don't have to hear that horrible noise.*

"I have a list," Rokick said. The mike picked up the crackle of paper. "Of all the people enrolled in Pounds Police attending meetings here. I want to talk with each of you about Mrs. Stuckless for our investigation."

I signed this to Bear but frowned and added, *"What investigation?"* Normally I wouldn't have a conversation while I'm interpreting because it can be confusing to the deaf person about who's talking. For interpreters, it's a no-no. But I couldn't resist. This was Nuts's partner. *Temporary* partner. I needed to know. Bear quickly signed he would tell me later.

"How many of you knew her?" Rokick asked.

Bear raised his hand in response along with about half the others.

"Uh, okay. Thanks. If you can stay today, I'd like to talk with you. We can do a group interview and it shouldn't take too long. If you can't stay, I have phone numbers and will call you."

Bear couldn't stay. I grilled him for a quick minute. *"Who is Captain M-A-R-G-O-T? What happened to her?"*

Bear formed the letter 'M' with his right hand and tapped his temple, which I understood as a name sign for this Margot woman. *"She was murdered yesterday. She was the leader for this meeting."* He pointed to Captain Janey. *"Like her."*

Bear abruptly changed the topic and asked me to come to PP early next time to interpret a video. I told him I wasn't sure if I'd be coming back, I'd have to find out about PP paying me for interpreting. He seemed so despondent I relented and asked what video he needed interpreted.

"A while ago I recorded Captain Margot's lecture and asked her some things after, but I couldn't understand what she told me. My mother tried to sign it to me but she's pretty lame. Remember? I told you she only fingerspells. I want to know what 'M' said. Can you do it? It's short, maybe ten minutes."

I'm a sucker for this kind of thing. I really didn't know if I'd be coming back to interpret the meetings, but I could always interpret something short over videophone. This is the inherent obligation I carry as a hearing person in my adjacent deaf world. Most of the time it doesn't feel like a burden, only a quirk of fate. We exchanged phone numbers, he sent me the video and then left.

I returned to my seat at the back and flipped it around. Rokick had gathered the remaining members at the front of the room. If he recognized me, he didn't show it. His questioning them about Margot Stuckless didn't take long. The members knew nothing about what happened to her.

One of the women raised her hand. "I'm so worried about her baby. Have they found her? She's so little. Poor thing."

Rokick said an Amber Alert was issued for Melanie Stuckless but so far, nothing. "But it's still early. We're working very hard on this case." He wrote his phone number on the white board behind the podium and encouraged the group to call him if they remembered anything they thought might help.

I stood and made my way toward the podium as the group broke up and headed out. Rokick was chatting with Janey as I approached, and I waited until they finished. I indicated to Rokick I wanted to talk with him but had to talk with Janey first. He seemed uncomfortable but agreed.

"This'll only take a minute. Promise."

Captain Janey wasn't at all interested in paying me for my services as an interpreter. No surprise there. Just as I was about to explain the law she was breaking, she brightened and made me an offer.

"I am willing to barter with you, though. You can join for free, and I'll also waive the weekly fee."

Two immediate reactions: One, do I really look that fat? And two, I *do* look that fat and gotta lose the forty pounds to get back to Abandonato and our work together. I took in Janey's appearance. The woman wore skinny jeans, a huggy cashmere sweater, and had the kind of hair that shouted beauty salon every six weeks.

My own haute couture? Size sixteen jeans and an oversized White Sox sweatshirt, curly hair needing a comb, a face adorned only with moisturizer, and a canvas backpack instead of a woman's purse. If I looked more like her maybe Jimmy wouldn't have divorced me and hightailed it to L.A. "If you don't mind my asking, how old are you?"

Janey blinked a few times but answered. "Why, I just turned thirty."

My age. She wore a fake tin badge emblazoned with her weight loss in PP: forty pounds. Could I ignore the obvious signs any further?

"You have a deal, Captain Janey." I offered a mock salute, which made her laugh, and shook her hand. She gave me her card with the website on it and a code to enter for the starter materials.

I motioned to Rokick. "Come on. I'll walk you out."

He picked up the papers on the podium and we headed for the hallway. "So, how's it going?" he asked.

My snarky side came up with several answers to his innocent question. How's it going? You mean my divorce? My suspension for drinking and being overweight? Let's see. Shitty is the answer to all three. Also, you look sharp, Rokick. Your suit, your hair, even your shined shoes all scream you take care with your appearance. I, obviously, do not. I wouldn't be surprised if Abandonato decided you're a keeper.

I bit my figurative tongue and tried for friendly. "I'm good. So. I'm curious about this investigation of," I snapped my fingers, trying to pull up the victim's name.

"Margot Stuckless."

"Right, right. You and Abandonato on it?"

Rokick nodded in a non-committal way. He folded the papers he carried and slipped them into his jacket.

"What have you got so far?"

We were at the end of the hallway where the doors led outside. "Look, Dana. I can't talk about it." He smirked. "I think you can appreciate that."

I could, but I sure didn't like the side order of condescension. "Where're you parked? I'll walk with you." He might spill with a little more badgering.

"Uh, I took the train over."

"Perfect. Then I can give you a ride. Come on. My car's in the lot behind the building." I pushed open the door and he followed.

At the bottom of the steps, he stopped. "Hey, thanks and all that, but I already got a ride." He gestured toward the street and as I turned, a familiar red Prius glided to a stop at the curb. Nuts. Rokick shrugged at me, got in, and shut the door. I tapped on his window, and he lowered it.

I stooped down and leaned my forearms on Rokick's open window. "Hey, Nuts. Got to see your new partner in action in there. Nice guy."

"Yes, he is." No hello, nothing. Both Nuts and Rokick stared out the windshield. I glanced in the same direction but saw nothing worthy of their attention.

"Yeah. I'm thinking he's a lot easier to get along with than me." That slipped out with no thought. I forced a small laugh, trying for a joke, but neither man cracked a smile. My former partner turned toward his side window, showing me the back of his head, his hand tapping the steering wheel. Ah, body language.

"I mean, Clint here's probably not getting Breathalyzed by Koz and sent home." This had more thought. If Nuts wanted to put my back up freezing me out in front of the guy who was literally between us, I'd troll him about my drinking. But I got no reaction.

Rokick crossed his arms and leaned back against the headrest, his eyes closed.

I pushed ahead. "So anyway, you'll be pleased to hear I'm in Pounds Police and lost two pounds. Only thirty-eight to go." Would Nuts even believe the whopper I just told? I needed *something* to remind him I was invested in returning to our partnership. He hadn't called me, as promised, about the deposition. But I didn't want to bring it up in front of Rokick.

"And what a coincidence, you know? Here comes Clint investigating the murder of one of the Pounds Police leaders."

Rokick sighed.

Nuts leaned toward me, full-face, his hands gripping the steering wheel. "What do you want, Dana?"

"I need a favor." I unhooked my backpack from my shoulder and rummaged inside, pulling out a folder holding copies of the hooker sketch. I extracted two and handed them to Rokick. He gave one to

Nuts while I explained about Evie remembering the face of the woman who attacked her. I'd give Nuts the rest of the story in private.

"In the off chance you see her. Or maybe work your contacts in Vice? I'd appreciate it a hell of a lot." I hooked my thumb over my shoulder at the building behind me. "And if I can help in any way with your case, do any kind of inside work, let me know."

Nuts folded the sketch several times and slipped it inside his jacket, shaking his head as if I had no sense. "We don't need your help. Like Koz said, you have plenty on your plate already. Focus on that."

Hearing this, Rokick's eyes popped open. He took in my hurt expression at Nuts's rebuke. In the awkward silence, Rokick pulled out his wallet and extracted a business card on which he wrote something and handed it to me.

"Here. My address is on there. I'm throwing a holiday party this Sunday for the squad. Early, like one to eight. An open house kind of deal, come when you can. Why don't you come, see everybody?" He glanced at Nuts, then at me, then back at Nuts as if for approval. Nothing.

I took the card and gave it a cursory glance. He lived in one of the condos downtown. I winked at him, which probably looked as fake as it felt, and held up the card with a little wave.

"Yeah, thanks. I'll let you know." Rokick's window raised silently. I stepped back from the curb as Nuts and his Prius slid off without another word.

7

FELICE

1:30 p.m.

Felice sat in his Prius outside the duplex belonging to Kristi Chen, Mac Stuckless's girlfriend. A plastic bowl holding the lunch remains of a fast food salad sat on the passenger seat. He sipped a to-go cup of green tea, the heater blasting to keep the frigid weather at bay.

He hated waiting, for Rokick or anyone. After Felice picked him up at the Pounds Police meeting, Rokick insisted on being dropped off at home so he could get his motorcycle. A waste of time in a schedule Felice had mapped out for today, which hadn't included a side trip to his new partner's home.

Maybe he needed to start thinking of Clint as his partner now, not just a temporary replacement for Dana.

He had no confidence Dana would successfully finish treatment for drinking two weeks from now. Even if she did, no way she could lose thirty-eight pounds in such a short time. She'd still be on suspension because of the weight, he'd still be without her, and still saddled with Rokick.

As if reading his mind, Dana's picture registered on his cell as it rang her familiar chime, the opening eight notes of Beethoven's Fifth, da-da-da-DA, da-da-da-DA; his private joke, a dramatic tune announcing his dramatic partner. He hesitated answering. Was she calling to badger him again about letting her help out on the Stuckless case? Or to check if he had any luck finding the woman in the sketch, the hooker, even though she'd given him the sketch about an hour ago.

"Hey," he said.

"You gotta hear this."

That was his partner, straight to the point. "First, let me tell you about the deposition."

"Yeah. You didn't call me."

He didn't like the accusing tone of her voice. "Been busy. So, the deposition went well. I was able to answer all their questions and your notes were helpful."

"Okay." The one-word response surprised him because of her prior insistence about participating in the deposition before Koz cut her out.

"So, listen," she said. "After you went into the lawyer's office, Carrera accosted me in the parking lot with his usual smarmy crap, which I could ignore. Which I *did* ignore. But get this. He asks me how Evie's doing. Like this." Her voice deepened. "'Heard she had a little accident.' Such an *asshole*."

"Not really surprising. He's in big-league trouble because you nailed him. About all he can do now is try to rattle you."

"I want Evie watched, a car put on my parents' house for a while. Can you do that for me?"

Felice recoiled. He liked Dana's parents, didn't wish Evie any ill, but he wasn't wasting his own capital on something not related to his work. "Not seeing the connection here. Carrera wasn't out on bond when your mother was attacked. And he's not free now to do anything to her."

"No, I know. You're right. But I've been thinking about this since Evie's sketch. Carrera's brother-in-law Fabrizio, the cop trying to blackmail me? He's gotta be involved."

At the mention of Fabrizio's name, Felice's anger at his partner flared. Fabrizio gave Dana a DUI on Thanksgiving and then buried it at her request but for a price—laundering $45,000 for him. Even though Felice believed Dana deserved the DUI, he didn't want Koz to find out about it any more than she did. Dana would be fired, their partnership ended for good.

"Get this, Nuts. Fabrizio and his pal Manny have a fuck pad just off the Gold Coast where they give hookers a choice between having sex with them or going to night court."

When she paused to breathe, he cut in. "Still not seeing a connection."

"Follow me, here." Annoyance in her tone.

"I got about fifteen minutes before I interview someone."

Throat clearing on her end. "Right. Okay. I think Carrera's way of getting back at me was to have Fabrizio set up the attack on my mom. Evie's sketch I gave you and Rokick? I recognized her. She looks like a hooker who was hanging around Fabrizio's fuck pad when I was there."

"I think you're giving Carrera too much credit for creative thinking. Besides, he's in enough trouble with the case against him. Which reminds me, Charles Worthy won't testify against Carrera unless the charges for kidnapping Rameeka are dismissed. Since there's no case without him, Koz ordered the charges dropped."

"Rameeka's gonna go ballistic when she finds out."

"Maybe knowing CW's being charged with two murders will mollify her. We have him cold. He'll never get out."

"Yeah. Still, being stuffed in CW's trunk knowing he was going to kill her wasn't exactly a joy ride for Rameeka. Hold on a sec." The click of a cigarette lighter sounded, followed by a deep inhale and exhale. "So, you're not going to help me out here?"

He had to admire his partner's persistence even if he didn't appreciate being badgered. "Carrera's threatening Evie to rattle you, and I'd say message received. Even if he did order the attack before, he wouldn't do anything right now before going on trial. The guy's crooked but he's not stupid." Felice finished his tea. "What did you mean before about Fabrizio blackmailing you?"

Long pause. "I went ahead and deposited his 45K. You wouldn't help me with it and I had no choice. He would've sent the DUI to Koz."

His anger flared again. He crushed the empty cup with one hand but held his voice steady. "Again, I don't think Evie's in any danger here or I would help. With her. But you have to be delusional to think I'd have anything to do with helping you launder Fabrizio's money."

Silence on the other end. Felice waited a beat, thinking she was trying to process his rejection, when his cell phone automatically disconnected. She'd hung up on him. He stuffed his cell in his jacket. He missed their work together, but he didn't miss the bullshit she toted along with her.

Rokick was late. There were still five minutes left before the scheduled time to interview Kristi Chen this afternoon, but Felice had instructed Rokick to be there fifteen minutes before the 2:00 appointment. He didn't have time to waste, especially with other cases vying for his attention along with a last-minute meeting Koz set up for right after this interview.

A text from Rokick dinged on his phone. *Five minutes away.* That's all he'd give him, then go serve the warrant and do the house search and interview alone.

With one minute to spare, Rokick pulled in and parked front of Felice's car. Abandonato got out and locked his car, not stopping to talk to Rokick but heading for Kristi Chen's duplex.

"Sorry I'm late! I got stuck—" Rokick called out as he hurried to catch up.

Felice held up his hand. "Save it. Come on." He ignored Rokick's continued apology and explanation as they climbed the staircase at the front entrance.

A young woman answered the door. Felice indicated his badge on his belt and introduced himself. "And this is Detective Clint Rokick." Rokick fumbled with the star on a chain around his neck, finally managing to hold it up for inspection. Felice handed her the search warrant after ascertaining she was Kristi Chen.

"If you're looking for Mac Stuckless, he doesn't live here anymore and I have no idea where he is." She tried to hand back the warrant, but Felice showed her his palm.

"Okay. But the warrant covers a complete search of your house regardless. And we need to talk to you, too, Ms. Chen. Stuckless is missing and so is his daughter."

She gave him a look he couldn't decipher but was decidedly unfriendly. "Wait here." She waved the warrant. "I'm going to call my lawyer about this." She closed the door.

Rokick tried explaining his tardiness again, but Felice waved him off. "Don't let it happen again. Give yourself plenty of time to get some-where—this is Chicago. There's traffic. Deal with it. We want witnesses to be cooperative, which means we don't keep them waiting."

"Sure. Okay." Rokick flipped up the collar on his leather jacket.

"And you'll ride back to the squad with me so I can catch you up on some things before we meet with Koz."

Rokick gestured at his motorcycle. "But I gotta have it for after. You're gonna bring me back, right?"

"Look. Yesterday I cut you some slack but I'm done chauffeuring you around. You want to look cool riding your," he gestured at the motorcycle, "whatever that is, your business."

Rokick shoved his hands in his leather jacket and looked away.

"But if we're going to work together we need to *be* together. There's lots to discuss. So, no. You find your way back here from the squad."

Rokick hunched his shoulders and shuffled his feet, his gaze still toward the street. "Fuckin' freezing out."

"Again. Chicago. Deal with it." And maybe don't ride a motorcycle in winter.

"So, yesterday." Rokick spoke to his feet. "Demeter always that pushy? Wants to get in on this job even though she's suspended?"

Felice didn't reply right away. He didn't know where to start with Rokick. So much to learn, this guy. There wouldn't be any squad gossip from him about anyone, especially Dana.

"Here's what you're going to do in there." He gestured at the closed door. "Watch me. That's all. Don't eat anything, don't touch anyone. Observe and formulate your own questions, write them down if you want. We'll talk after. Then we'll split up the remaining interviews. Got it?"

Rokick half-turned toward Felice and held up his hands in surrender. "Sure, sure. Look, I didn't mean to get under your skin about Demeter."

Felice shook his head. "Anything to do with her suspension? That stuff's up to Koz."

"Understood. Except it does affect me." Rokick waved his hand back and forth between the two of them. "And us. If she doesn't come back then we're partners, right? Which is great."

Before Felice could reply the door opened again, and Kristi Chen waved them in.

"Okay, okay. Do what you have to do. My lawyer says I have to comply but I'm staying with you the whole time."

She sounded pissed but he didn't care. "We'll start down here and then go upstairs. Do you have a basement?"

"No."

"This will go fairly quick then." He turned to Rokick. "Remember what I said." Rokick stuck out his bottom lip. Felice leveled him with a squint.

True to her word, Kristi Chen followed close behind them as they searched. They found nothing in the living room, kitchen, or a small room tricked out as an office. Upstairs was also unremarkable with one exception.

They searched the first bedroom together. Felice sent Rokick to search the bathroom while he took the second bedroom.

"Done," Rokick said, joining him to finish the search.

Before they returned downstairs, Felice checked Rokick's work in the bathroom. A pile of laundry lay on the floor next to the hamper, which was still half full. He snapped on a pair of latex gloves he always carried for this kind of thing and placed each extracted item on the growing pile of clothes. At the very bottom lay an open package of disposable diapers for toddlers. He plucked them out and sent Rokick to retrieve three evidence bags from the Prius.

Kristi Chen hovered in the doorway. "I can explain those diapers. See, they're—"

"Hold on, Ms. Chen. We need to finish up here and then we'll talk." He replaced most of the dirty laundry in the hamper. Rokick returned, and Felice showed the rookie how to bag and tag the diapers. Next, he pinched a pair of men's briefs from the pile and jiggled them for a second in front of Rokick's surprised face before bagging them.

Felice's final protocol was rolling off his latex gloves from his wrists to his fingertips, balling them up inside-out, and placing them in the third evidence bag. He then washed his hands.

Downstairs again, they settled in the living room.

"So, I know what this is about. Margot Stuckless's murder. Am I right? I mean, I watch the news, read the paper. Especially now that I'm out of work because of that bastard Mac. *Plenty* of time to keep up."

Felice held up his phone. "Okay if I record instead of taking notes? A lot easier." He smiled at her, trying for some kind of rapport. She nodded her approval although no smile was returned. While he fiddled with his recording app, Kristi Chen pulled her waist-length hair into a high ponytail using an elastic band from around her wrist, then draped it over her shoulder so it cascaded down to her lap.

After noting the date, time and person being interviewed, Felice asked if Mac Stuckless had ever lived in the duplex.

"Like I said. He lived here 'til we both got fired. I kicked him out after that."

"Tell me what happened."

"Stupidity happened. We had sex at work, got caught, got fired."

"How long were you seeing him?"

Kristi Chen performed a silent count on her fingers. "About six months. His wife found out we were screwing around and threw him out, so I let him stay here. But god, he was a slob." She indicated the room with a wave of her hand. "You can see I'm a neat person. We were far apart on that subject."

"And you haven't seen him since..."

"Last month. That's when I had enough. Thanksgiving, to be exact. I wanted to go to my parents' place. They're in New York. But he didn't want to and we just lost our jobs and this guy was such a loser I had to get away from him. So, I went to my parents for a week and told him not to be here when I got back." Her hands folded around the ponytail.

"And the diapers?"

"From his kid. He had this big idea his wife would share custody with him. He's nuts about his daughter. Their divorce dragged out for a while, and she had to agree to share the kid while the court decided. He brought her over a few times before I broke up with him."

"Why were the unused, disposable diapers in the hamper?"

She leaned back into the couch's overstuffed pillows, crossed her legs and then her arms. "Look. I don't have much storage space here. I put them in the hamper to keep 'em out of the way and out of my sight."

"And the men's briefs?"

Kristi Chen took a long pause. "You're not going to believe this. I found them yesterday. I was flipping my mattress over, which I do every six months, and they were wedged between the mattress and the bottom frame." She shook her head. "You see what I had to deal with?"

Felice nodded. "Did Mac Stuckless ever talk to you about his wife? He must've had a reaction to her kicking him out."

She laughed. "You could say that. But it wasn't what you think. He was thrilled. He hated his wife, wanted nothing more than to get away from her."

"He told you that?" Rokick blurted this out. Felice pushed a flat palm at him and got a frown in response. Add *maintaining a straight face during an interview* to the rookie's list.

"Ms. Chen, please tell me everything Mac Stuckless said to you about his wife. Anything and everything."

And she did. Mac hated his wife, realized his mistake in marrying her soon after the honeymoon. She was always on him to make more money even though he brought home plenty from his job as a day trader and worked fifty to sixty hours a week.

"She was one of those women who was never satisfied, period. And then she got pregnant. I don't know if it was hormones or what, but according to Mac she became insufferable. No sex, more demands for money. That's when we started seeing each other."

"Since Thanksgiving have you had any contact with Stuckless? Did he want you to take care of his baby after his wife was killed?"

She avoided his gaze and grasped her ponytail again.

"Look. That's not what I signed up for. Besides, if I wanted a baby it wouldn't be some white baby." She straightened and massaged her neck. "I'm proud to be an Asian woman." Her stare sent Felice a silent challenge. Then, she muttered something.

"I didn't catch that last thing."

"I said, *asshole* cost me my job." Enunciated perfectly.

Rokick snickered at this, but Felice cut it short with a side glance.

"Have you seen baby Melanie since the break-up with Stuckless?"

"No. Nope. Not interested in the little ones. My own or other people's." She shook her head. "I can't..." Her voice trailed off.

Felice waited. She seemed on the verge of saying something else, but she pursed her lips in a tight line and said nothing more.

"Did Stuckless tell you anything about where the baby is or if he had anything to do with her disappearance?"

Kristi Chen shook her head again, setting her ponytail to a slight dance. "Like I said. I kicked him out of my place and my life after we got fired. Haven't seen him or his kid, haven't talked to him, or thought about getting back together with him."

That was pretty thorough. "Anything else you can think of that you'd like to tell me?"

Her head bobbed in assent. "Sure. Mac Stuckless told me once he wished his wife would just die. Said it maybe a couple of times. How his life would be so much easier without her. Seems like he got his wish."

8

FELICE

4:30 p.m.

On the way back to the squad offices Felice reiterated what he expected from Rokick when they worked together.

"Keep it professional and play it straight. Blurting out a reaction to something a witness says isn't acceptable because you don't want them to know what you think. Kristi Chen gave us good information about Stuckless. And no eating."

He noticed Rokick kept quiet and didn't argue. Well, it was a start. He'd have to work with the guy longer to discover if their partnership had legs.

"Why did you stop searching the hamper halfway through?"

Rokick fidgeted with a leather wristband he wore but was silent.

Felice glided to a halt at a red light. "Also, I buy my own latex gloves. The department's stingy about reimbursing for them, so it's up to you." The light turned green, and he accelerated.

"So. The hamper. You missed the diapers."

"She's on the rag. There was blood on some panties. I couldn't—I didn't want, you know—"

"Exactly. One of the reasons I wear gloves. And you don't want to compromise any evidence with your fingerprints."

"Yeah. Got it."

Rokick's too-quick response triggered Felice's curiosity. "Something else?"

"Yeah. Blood makes me puke, okay?"

Rokick's defensive tone was understandable. But aversion to blood wasn't a good sign. There was plenty to be seen every day on the job. Felice knew other homicide detectives squeamish at the sight of blood. But he also knew they didn't last long, something he would keep to himself.

"Sure. Still, the search has to be thorough. Here's why. In the clothes you left in the hamper—"

"I know. I know. The guy's shorts."

Felice pulled into the squad parking lot and parked but left the engine running. "Right. So, she had reasonable explanations for the diapers and the briefs. But they could also point to her harboring Stuckless and the baby."

"That's what I thought, too. I mean, why keep that stuff? Seems to me if she dumped the guy, she'd just pitch 'em."

Felice gave Rokick one point for deductive logic. "And because she didn't, we have to consider them and take a closer look at her."

Rokick unlocked his seat belt and turned halfway in his seat toward Felice. "Yeah. Yeah! Because she said Stuckless was crazy about his kid. He offs the wife—who he hates—and steals the kid."

Felice made a calming motion toward Rokick with both hands, patting the air. "It's only one theory. We're just starting to pull ideas together. Keep an open mind."

"I got a question about the Chen chick. I think the diapers means Stuckless *did* hide the kid at her place."

"What's the question?"

"You didn't tell her it's a crime to harbor a suspect who's got a warrant out."

Okay, two points for logic and showing some thought process. "No, I didn't. Good catch. I don't think she was lying about breaking off with Stuckless and kicking him out. But I'm leaving the option open for Stuckless to come back and hide out there. Who knows what he might promise her if she lets him? Like a cut of the insurance money."

Rokick smiled and nodded. "Okay, yeah."

"If she doesn't know it's a crime, then we have a possible chance of catching him there. But if she knows she'll get in trouble harboring him, my guess is she'll steer clear and not take him back."

Felice cut the engine and they made their way to the squad room. Felice checked in with Veda, Koz's assistant.

"The Lieutenant said about an hour from now, Detective."

He made his way back to the side-by-side desks across from the elevators and sat, Clint Rokick now ensconced in Dana's place. "It'll be another hour before Koz can meet with us. Let's review the file and see what we need to do and how to split up the work."

Felice uncapped an erasable marker and went to the white board nailed on the wall near their desks. Dana had set it up when they were new together. Back then he scoffed at the idea of using something he relegated to a housewife's to-do list.

But like many of Dana's ideas, he came to understand the sense in it, came to trust her way of working in the world—so different from his, at times—which made them successful as partners and detectives. Trust he would need to rebuild now with Rokick, and the very idea exhausted him. He wanted Dana and their comfort zone, not this baby rookie.

On one side of the board Felice wrote their names to list the jobs they would each shoulder. On the other side he listed the victim, Margot Stuckless, and the missing husband and baby.

"I can handle the list of people I got from Pounds Police. Probably won't show much," Rokick said.

"I'm going to work the insurance angle. And the neighbors." Felice dutifully noted the tasks. He didn't think anything in his assignment would yield much, but he would do the work and close that particular book.

The Butterfinger wrappers teased at him. He doubted they came from the victim because they were scattered on the ground outside the back bedroom's unlocked sliding door. Pretty clear someone stood there a while before entering. And then that same someone discarded more wrappers around the body.

He'd have to wait on forensics to determine who left the evidence, but with a murdered wife and a missing husband and baby, the most viable suspect couldn't be clearer. He was holding out for Mac Stuckless.

Rokick flipped a few pages on a list and flicked the paper with his finger. "Hey. I wanted to ask you. This guy here, one Robert Thomas, is deaf and dumb. How am I supposed to call him?" He handed the list to Felice. Next to Thomas's name Rokick had underlined the word *deaf* and added several question marks after the phone number.

"Did you try the number?"

Rokick furrowed his forehead. "No. I told you—"

Felice cut him off with a raised palm. "First, don't believe everything you read. Always check it out for yourself. But let's say he is deaf. There's a phone number there, so call it. Maybe he lives with someone who can hear and would sign to him for you. Same as if the person spoke Spanish and you got someone in the family to translate."

Rokick leaned back in his chair, and Felice could tell he wasn't happy with the lecture.

"With me so far?"

"Yeah. Sure."

"Okay. Here's the thing. Technology has come a long way for deaf people. They have videophones, which is just what is sounds like. They can call anyone, people who are deaf or who can hear, and we can call them."

"But I don't have one of those things, videos...phone. How's he gonna hear me?"

Felice hated to admit it but he missed Dana right now. He didn't want to have to explain the ins and outs of Deaf Telephone 101. And she would be able to call Thomas directly on her videophone—the way she did with her parents—and communicate directly in ASL.

"You don't need a videophone. You use your phone to call the number," he pointed to Thomas's name. "It'll ring at a call center staffed with American Sign Language interpreters who have video-phones. They'll be a go-between in your conversation. You talk, they sign to Thomas. He signs back, they tell you what he's saying."

"Wow. That's amazing. I never knew any of that. How—"

"You met Dana. Her parents are deaf. I learned it all from her." Felice doubted he would learn anything of such value from Rokick. He sagged a bit inside at the heavy lift Koz was asking of him in training the rookie. He handed back the PP list.

"Call Thomas. I doubt he'll be of any help but you never, ever, assume anything about people you interview. Again, we're always thorough." Except Rokick wasn't, not with those diapers or men's briefs.

"And while we're on the subject, it's *deaf*. Not deaf and dumb, not hearing impaired, not anything else. Just deaf. Unless they tell you different, that's what deaf people use." His cell phone buzzed with a text from Veda. "Let's go. Koz wants us now."

They stood. "He always like that? Tells you an hour then calls you in fifteen minutes later?"

Felice ignored the question and headed for Koz's office.

"Don't bother sitting," Koz said. "I have a quick update for you two. Rokick, you're taking lead on the Stuckless case."

Felice started at this. "Koz, I don't think he's quite ready—"

Koz held up an index finger. "Hold on, let me finish. This has nothing to do with your work so far. What about the little girl? Anything yet?"

Felice winced. "No. Nothing. No tips, no leads from family." He ran down the interviews with Janey Foreman and Kristi Chen.

"Doesn't look good," Koz said.

Felice took this as criticism directed at him, but before he could respond Rokick piped up. "She's a dead end."

Felice joined Koz in staring at Rokick. "Poor choice of words there," Koz said.

Rokick mumbled something unintelligible.

"We're going to pull some other strings today; interviews, canvassing the neighbors, insurance," Felice said. Laying out these things for Koz felt pointless, almost a lie or smokescreen to hide what little they had. He was sure finding Mac Stuckless was the key to solving what happened.

Koz stood and came around his desk to stand in front of them. "Okay. Rokick handles it from now on."

Rokick hooked his thumbs on his pants pockets and grinned. Felice started to object again. Koz tilted his head toward him.

"The leaders of the three largest gangs in Chicago have been murdered in the past month. The mayor's scared we're going to have a large-scale gang war if these aren't solved soon.

Koz tilted toward Rokick. "There's something like fifty-nine known gangs in Chicago and over a hundred thousand members belonging to those gangs. The mayor fears increasing rumors about the murders will escalate the situation."

"Doesn't sound good," Rokick said.

Koz aimed a grim smile at Felice. "I'm appointing you to the city-wide cohort the mayor has set up to solve this. You're the best we've got."

Felice's earlier rankling at Koz's criticism morphed into adrenaline, both from the praise and the excitement of such a challenge. "Will do, sir. And thanks. I'm sure Clint can handle the Stuckless murder." He was not sure of this at all; in fact, he thought Rokick would screw up and the result would be the first unsolved case of his nascent career.

The Stuckless baby, by all statistical measures, was dead and lay hidden somewhere never to be found. And Mac Stuckless would get away with murdering his wife.

"You'll work from City Hall. That's where the murder room is set up. You can go over there now, settle in, meet the others." Koz turned to Rokick. "Since we'll be short one man, you're on your own with this case. Any problems, questions, call me. Not Abandonato. He's got one job, 24/7."

"Sure, Lieutenant, sure. I got a question." He gestured back and forth between Felice and himself. "Since the two of us are partners now, what with Demeter out, we'll still be partners after this gang thing's over, right?"

Felice cringed. What the hell was wrong with this guy? How many times did he have to tell him to lay off talking about Dana.

Koz returned to his desk and sat in his high-back leather chair. "Demeter's not out, Rokick. Stop listening to gossip. It only makes you look stupid for believing it. You are *temporary* with Abandonato until she returns, which I have every reason to believe will happen." He jabbed his thumb on his own chest. "Get your information straight from this source. Clear?"

Although not a physically demonstrative person, Felice could've hugged Koz right then. Rokick straightened up and saluted.

Back at their desks, Rokick engaged Felice in discussing the case again. "So, you'll give me everything you've got, right? The insurance angle's a good one. If there's insurance on the wife, Stuckless or the baby might get it. I bet if the kid dies, he gets all the dough. Plenty of motive there, right?"

Felice unearthed his backpack from under his desk. He took in Rokick's expectant expression. He had enough of talking to this guy and wanted to get over to City Hall to immerse himself in what promised to be big. The Stuckless case came first, though, even before his personal animosity.

"Plenty. Remember what we discussed about Kristi Chen and what might pop from that." He stood and began organizing what he should bring to City Hall.

"Got it. I thought of something else about her. Chen. Suppose she didn't kick Stuckless out, was trying to stonewall us, make us believe it."

Felice paused in packing his laptop. "Okay. What if?"

"She gets Stuckless to kill the wife so *she* can have the baby. A ready-made family. She said herself she didn't want to have kids. But maybe she meant the carrying part, like the kind that makes chicks go all fat and ugly."

Okay. It was a plausible theory, one Felice could sign onto, except he had been at the interview with Rokick, and seen and heard Kristi Chen in the flesh. The anger the woman displayed regarding Mac Stuckless was real, as was her rejection of having children. He believed her. Before he could point this out, Rokick continued.

"So, there's that. And I'll check out the deaf guy. And what about Janey Foreman? She found the body, right? There might be something there."

Might be. As in never.

Rokick ticked his fingers. "So: money, mommy, dummy, Janey. I'll work 'em in that order. A little poem to help me remember."

He looked so pleased with himself. Felice wanted to smack the smirk off Rokick's face but stifled the urge. Koz's unexpected gift assigning him to the task force meant he wouldn't have to work with the guy anymore, and he couldn't wait to get away from him. In spite of his irritation with Dana, missing her struck him like the sting of a bullet graze.

"Look. I'm in the dark about what to expect with this task force. Anything more you need help with or want to talk about, do what Koz says and ask him." He waited for Rokick to look up at him. "Got it? Koz. He's your source. Not me. We're done." He hadn't mean for that last bit to slip out.

Rokick jumped up. "What the hell does that mean? I know Lieutenant said Demeter's not done but she sure looks baked to me." He grinned at his own joke.

Felice quickly added his external drive and then closed his backpack for the trip downtown. He lifted his winter jacket from the desk chair, slung the backpack over one shoulder, and leaned in close enough to Rokick to get a whiff of truly awful aftershave.

"She's still my partner. Like Koz says, you're temporary. Focus on what you've got with the Stuckless case. Solve it and Koz will notice."

9

DANA

6:00 p.m.

During Intensive Out-Patient tonight, Marvin, the lead counselor, lectured on 12-step programs and showed a short video titled *What is Self-Care and How Do I Do it?* He then announced a surprise urine drop. The surprise came from the frequency. We had a drop just five days ago. When I complained, Marvin gave me the standard answer.

"If you're clean, Dana, then you have nothing to worry about."

"I *am* clean, Marvin. That's not why I'm objecting." I started to tell him more, but he cut me off with a shushing motion of his hands and went to talk with a new woman in the group. I lined up with the others, got my pee cup, and waited in another line at the women's bathroom for my turn. I made a mental note to harangue Marvin later during our one-on-one session.

Hades sauntered past me, one hand holding his winter jacket slung over his shoulder and the other hand repeatedly flipping and catching a coin. I grabbed his upper arm and he stopped.

"Nice going," I said. "Six weeks done and you're outta here."

He grinned. "Dana, Dana. Dana with the nice name. You got what, three more weeks?"

"Less. Two. More than halfway through."

He showed me the coin he'd been flipping. "You'll get this, see?" He held his palm closer to my face for inspection. The light overhead reflected on the brass and highlighted the number six in Roman numerals, the word *weeks* in small print below. The treatment center's name and phone number were stamped on the other side. Hades put on his coat, and I handed back the coin.

"Congrats, Hades. Been good to know you." And I meant it. He was one of the few upbeat people here projecting a positive outlook, a commodity in short supply. Our group tended toward depression, low energy, and negativity. I harbored the same disposition. Attending group therapy felt like a chore and something to avoid. I didn't want to hang out with more of me. But Hades made group enjoyable to some extent. I told him I was going to miss him.

He leaned in close and whispered, "That's real nice of you and all, but I am done with this shit. Don't need it. Never did, never will. I got a connection soon's I get outta here." He winked at me, stuck the coin in his pocket and sauntered on.

I was briefly surprised but somehow not shocked at his revelation. Maybe Hades put forward a happy face only to please the treatment staff and never showed his true self. Hiding is what addicts do best: hiding a stash, hiding in relationships, hiding pain. All that hiding until the drugs and booze don't work anymore, often resulting in a wrecked brain, or prison, or death. I don't know the stats about how many of us get straight or sober and actually stay that way. I'm guessing not many.

My turn to pee in the cup. I locked the bathroom door, did the deed, and addressed my reflection in the mirror as I washed my hands. "You are not Hades." My gut told me different.

Because of the coin ceremony graduation earlier, Marvin and I were meeting one-on-one in his office for only half of the usual hour. As soon as we sat down, and Marvin asked me how I was doing, I blurted out Hades's secret.

I covered my mouth with my hand even though the words had already escaped. I glanced at Marvin. He nodded but said nothing, just waited. I took my hand away from my mouth and leaned forward. "Look. I don't consider myself a snitch, not by anybody's measure."

"Okay. Why do you think you told me about Hades?"

"I don't know. I'm not sure. I liked Hades. He was upbeat, you know?" Why *did* I tell? And why was I talking about Hades in the past tense? Marvin let me stew a few minutes in silence.

"Dana, earlier you complained about the drop—"

"Yeah! I wanted to talk to you about that. How come so soon? We just had one."

"We vary the timing so people can't game the system."

"Okay, sure. But I could've gotten drunk since the last drop and today's test wouldn't have showed anything."

"Well, first, our test can detect alcohol up to five days after use," he see-sawed his hand, "so it might've shown up. Sure, you could've gotten drunk right after the test five days ago, but who's to say we wouldn't have tested you again the next night? See? The whole idea is built-in uncertainty. We surprise you."

It seemed so juvenile to me. "So, we live under the threat we might be discovered? How's that supposed to keep me sober?" I thought of Hades. "I mean, where's personal responsibility in all this. Look at

Hades. He's going right out from here to get high." I stabbed my index finger on Marvin's desk. "*Tonight.*"

"Actually, a little bit of the theory behind the surprise testing *is* about keeping the idea of not drinking foremost in your mind. You might think twice before picking up if there's a chance you might be found out."

"That's two *mights* in once sentence, Marvin." Which made me highly skeptical of his theory. All I know is, when I went to Brau Haus recently with the intention of drinking only pop with my dinner, I ended up staggeringly drunk. Rosie, who was the bartender and my friend, drove my Camry to her house. Because I was passed out in the back seat of my car, she left me there to sleep it off the rest of the night. A surprise urine drop at IOP never, ever, crossed my mind.

Marvin shrugged. "The theory says the person starts to own the idea of not drinking or drugging as a choice instead of the threat of being found out through a drop."

I crossed my arms. "Doesn't seem to be working for Hades."

Marvin laughed. "Maybe not this time. But we might have at least planted the seed in his mind."

"There's that *might* again."

Marvin actually winked at me.

"You said first. What's second?"

Marvin showed a moment of confusion and then smiled. "I'm impressed, Dana. Shows your ability to concentrate has improved. You took in and remembered what I said. See how four weeks without booze has cleared your mind?"

I couldn't help returning his smile and then ducked my head at the compliment. Of course, Marvin didn't know I did drink twice since starting IOP.

"*Second*," he said in a dramatic voice, coaxing another smile from me, "and this is way more important in my view. If someone can't stay straight or sober for the six weeks in IOP, then it's a red flag, you know, for us, the staff. Tells us the person needs to get evaluated again, probably needs a higher level of intervention."

I frowned. Marvin added, "You know, needs inpatient treatment."

Later, while I drove home, I replayed Marvin's compliment about how clear my mind seemed to him and I had to agree. I also had a delayed realization about Hades. He was a leader in our group, no question. We all looked up to him and his optimism. But it was now clear to me he was scamming not only the staff but the rest of us too, which made me mad.

As Marvin noted, my mind had cleared. So, it seemed, had my emotions. I was unable to submerge my anger at Hades as it flapped to the surface. But the fuel for my anger was gut-wrenching fear. If Hades could walk out after six weeks of IOP with the sole intention of getting high, what would happen to me when I graduated? Would I have the same impulse, or worse, the cocky assurance he seemed to have about using again?

I parked across the street from my studio and sat for a minute repeating my familiar mantra about what I want: to return to my job as a homicide detective alongside my partner Felice Abandonato. I've lost most everything else having any meaning for me: my baby, my husband, our home of ten years. The job is all I have left between me and some unknown but frightening abyss.

No. Drinking was not an option. And it sure as hell wasn't because I was afraid of what a urine drop would expose.

Inside my studio I shed my coat, sat at my desk and considered calling Felice. I was still mad at him. He wouldn't supply any protection for Evie. He embarrassed me in front of Clint Rokick. Blew me off about Evie's sketch, told me he didn't want my help with Margot

Stuckless's murder, and echoed Koz's barb that I *had enough on my plate.* All in one day.

I wondered if Koz and Nuts purposely used the phrase as a not-so-subtle dig at my overeating, the double-meaning some kind of sick humor. Did they talk about me in disparaging terms? I rejected the self-pity but postponed the call until tomorrow. I didn't trust myself in my current state of tiredness and free-flowing anger. I might tell Nuts what I really thought.

I got under the covers of my futon and assumed my usual comfortable position on my right side, and then realized my comfort extended to my insides. I felt better after my session with Marvin. Less keyed up. Until now I didn't see much worthwhile in meeting with him. But up until now I hadn't offered anything revealing, either. My inadvertent blurt about Hades was real, was what I felt, and not censored to please anyone. Marvin didn't try to fix me, just left it to me to figure out on my own.

10

LOUISE

The little girl wouldn't hold still. If it was this hard to cut her hair, she'd have to think twice about the plan to dye it. Louise Conway clamped her legs around the toddler to tighten her hold. Soft, fine blonde curls lay in tiny puffs on the chair's arms and on the floor.

"Almost done, Angel." She was a little angel, too. Louise liked to think of her that way. "Hold on, almost done." She crooned this over and over trying to soothe the child.

"No! No!" The little girl's voice was at once urgent and on the verge of crying. She wriggled her tiny body uselessly against the vise grip of Louise's legs.

"Shhh, shhh." Louise would have to wrap Angel in a blanket when they went out. This brought some calm to her racing thoughts. She startled at the in-room phone's loud ring. As she stood to answer it, the little girl squealed with glee, released from her fleshy prison.

Angel chugged around the hotel room on unsteady legs, her hair chopped off in front but longer in the back. A baby mullet.

"Pizza's here," announced the voice on the other end of the line.

"Come here, Angel. Lunch time." She cornered the little girl and scooped her up, then pulled the plaid coverlet from the bed and draped it around the small shoulders. The baby began to whine in a now familiar cadence Louise knew would lead to outright crying. She jostled the bundle and made shushing sounds.

"Mmmaaa-maa! Mmmaaa-ma!"

"I'm your mama now, I'm your mama now," she said, bouncing the baby up and down in a rough rocking motion, hoping to bring quiet. But the crying got louder. Stumped at how to retrieve the pizza downstairs without drawing unwanted attention, Louise carried the screaming child into the bathroom and deposited her in the tub, still wrapped in the bed cover, then left and closed the door. For good measure she propped the desk chair under the bathroom doorknob before going downstairs to get the pizza.

11

DANA

2:00 p.m.

Before viewing the video Bear sent me, the one he wanted interpreted, there was the small matter of securing my mother's safety. Since Nuts wouldn't help me by ordering my parents' house watched, confronting Fabrizio seemed like the only option.

My anger at Nuts had cooled a bit since I hung up on him yesterday. Some of my aggravation stemmed from him thinking I was asking for help with Fabrizio's 45K. I wasn't. I've already done that laundry myself and without his help.

As partners, we've always had each other's backs, right from the start, and not solely at work. Like when his fiancée didn't show at their wedding, Jimmy and I brought Nuts to our home where he nursed his wounds for the week that would've been his honeymoon.

But he wasn't holding up his end on Evie needing protection, which he could've arranged, so I'd have to do it myself. I got his point about the attack sending a message: if they wanted to kill her she would be one dead deaf woman, instead of a live one with a slight concussion and a scar from seven stitches. I still wanted her safe.

I needed to find out if Carrera ordered the attack on Evie. Convicting him of the additional crime would add to his certain prison time for extorting CW and give me added pleasure witnessing his steep fall. I also harbored a bit of glee about Carrera getting dumped by his fiancée Caitlyn, Koz's daughter. Koz was quick to suspend me but took his sweet time acknowledging Carrera's perfidy.

I cruised around the block where Fabrizio and Manny's fuck pad was located, hoping against hope I might again see the woman in Evie's sketch. But the wind gave the normally cold winter air a biting sting and not many people were out. I didn't even know if Fabrizio or Manny would be around and if they were, would I be interrupting them during the intended purpose of their little hideaway?

I parked a block away and dawdled along the sidewalk, dragging on a Kool while trying to quell my anxiety and squelch memories of Fabrizio's assault on me last time I was here. As I approached the building the front door opened, and a woman exited intent on zipping up her full-length down coat. She had on heavy makeup and death-defying stilettos, but there was no way to tell if she was a recent visitor to my destination.

Inside, I rang the doorbell set below the mailbox and waited for a response, both hoping and fearing one of the two stooges would answer. Nothing happened. I stood there a moment considering my next move. Starbucks sounded like a good option, get some coffee—no calories as an added incentive and a nod to following my PP food plan—and maybe watch Bear's video.

I left the warmth of the foyer and braced myself for a burst of cold, hunching my shoulders and ducking my head against the wind as I walked the block to my car. Halfway there I heard a familiar gruff voice.

"Demeter! Over here!" Fabrizio, his car window lowered, yelled at me as he parked his cherry red Jeep across the street. Obey his summons or make a break for my car? I wanted to warn him off Evie but seeing him re-ignited my fear from his previous assault. He was already out of his Jeep and exerting a lot of effort at what he probably thought was a jog but looked like what it was: a fat guy who couldn't get his body coordinated enough to go any faster than a slow-motion shuffle. Made me glad I'm losing weight.

"What do you want, Fabrizio?"

He stepped from the street onto the curb a few feet from me and stopped, bent over, hands on his thighs, panting. He held up an index finger signaling me to wait while he joined the living again.

"What you doin' over here? Lookin' for me? I was gonna call you. Never got the receipts for them CDs." He straightened up. The pudgy fingers on his oversized hands made a beckoning motion at me as if I had the receipts ready to turn over.

"What're you talking about? I dropped them off the day I deposited your grift. You weren't home but someone buzzed me in, and I slipped them under the door to your place. About two weeks ago." I glanced at my phone for the date. "I was close. Almost three weeks ago. December second, to be exact."

He lowered his hands. "No shit?"

I shook my head. He muttered, "Fuckin' Manny. How many times I gotta tell him?"

Several times, apparently. "Yeah. Ask Manny where he put your mail. Listen, I want to ask you something about Carrera." I described what happened in the parking lot of the lawyer's office. When I quoted Carrera's line about hearing Evie had a 'little accident,' Fabrizio snickered. It set me off.

"What the fuck's wrong with you two? Why would you hurt an old woman? Wait, I think I get it. You only attack people too weak to fight back. In a word, you're *pussies.*" I picked the word I knew would have maximum sting for Fabrizio, whose whole persona was macho with a capital M.

He sputtered. "Wise-ass bitch."

"You want to send me a message, send it directly to *me.*" I had to quell the urge to slap him on the back of his head.

Fabrizio held up his hands in mock surrender. "Hey, lighten up. Who said anything about me? Carrera does what he wants. Ain't nothin' to me." He shrugged his shoulders.

"Then what's with the chuckle about my mother being attacked? Come on. You're Carrera's brother-in-law. You two mopes are cut from the same cloth; on the take, on the make, doing anything you can to fuck someone over."

Fabrizio pulled the lapels of his thin jacket together and held them closed with one hand. "I'm fuckin' freezing. Let's get inside outta this fuckin' wind. Come on." He turned and started walking toward his building.

As he retreated, my stomach lurched and quivered. I couldn't go back into that apartment with him. I flashed on an image of a drunk Fabrizio, his pants around his ankles, his erect cock waving in my face as I knelt in front of him, my hands cuffed behind my back, him waving a gun and ordering me to blow him. A quick headshake cleared the memory.

I jogged and caught up to him. "Not going upstairs. We're staying here." I gestured at the foyer as we entered.

"Okay, okay, Demeter. Never thought of you as a scaredy-cat." He hunched and shook his shoulders, mocking me.

"Christ, Fabrizio. You cuff me, hold a loaded gun to my head to force me to blow you and that makes me a *scaredy-cat*?"

He gave me a blank look, as if what I described was the first time he'd heard it. He sidled over to the wall and leaned against the embedded heating grate. Arms crossed, he squinted at me.

"I ain't never done nothing like that, Demeter. You're crazy." But his eyes stayed focused on his feet as he said it, the name-calling trailing off into a question. I recognized the denial. He was unsure of his behavior because he'd been drunk. But somewhere inside he knew it was a possibility because in trying to retrieve the memory of what I described, all he could summon was a blank. I bet this wasn't the first time, either.

I was intimately familiar with the squeamish feelings of embarrassment, chagrin, and disbelief when friends told me of the outrageous things I did while drinking—things I had no memory of. Fabrizio really didn't have a clue what I was talking about. His attempted assault on me happened while he was in a blackout, which I'm learning in IOP is different from passing out.

A drunk in a blackout can carry on conversations, walk around, hell, even drive a car. Problem is, booze causes the brain to snuff memories of those things. If he can't remember what he did, then it's as if it never happened. For a moment I felt kinship and pitied him.

I waved my hand in a dismissive motion. "Not what I want to talk to you about." I dug into my backpack and pulled out the sketch of Evie's attacker and described what happened. "My mother remembered what the woman looks like."

I stepped over to him, handed him the sketch of the woman I recognized, and recapped my brief meeting with her the last time I was here. "She told me she knew you and Manny. I watched her go into this building. You must at least recognize her."

Fabrizio glanced at the sketch, then held it at his side and avoided my gaze. In a quick motion he balled up the paper and tossed it back to me. "Never saw her before."

I caught the balled-up sketch. "No?" I appraised his gaze, which was still directed at the floor. He was lying. But I needed his intervention with Carrera. "Okay." I stepped back a few paces. "I'm gonna assume you're telling me the truth and the attack on my mother was orchestrated solely by Carrera. Maybe he had Manny's help. Either way, talk to your brother-in-law, get him to back off." As an afterthought I added, "You've got forty-five thousand reasons to do what I'm asking."

His head jerked up and he pointed an index finger at me. "You better not screw with my dough. I still got the DUI report, and it goes straight to your Lieutenant unless I get my forty-five K back." He leered at me with a self-satisfied smile.

"You know what? You can go ahead and send that report. You got zero leverage, you don't scare me, and here's why. If Koz fires me because of you, you'll never see that money again. When the CDs mature I'll donate the money to a good cause."

Fabrizio's mouth hung open in a perfect picture of disbelief. "You can't do that!" His surprise quickly morphed into a threat. "I'll come after you, Demeter. You know I will."

I laughed, enjoying the upper hand with this clod who tried to rape me. "What, you gonna kill me? Think this through. You kill me, how're you gonna get the bank to give you those CDs? They're in *my* name, stupid. Besides, you didn't name a beneficiary, so I took the liberty. You kill me and the money goes to the priest at St. Nick's."

As soon as I said this I kicked myself for being so cocky—who was stupid now? Fabrizio would just as soon threaten a priest as he did me.

"You gotta change that to me, Demeter. I'm the bene—benefit—that's *my* money."

I held up one hand in a mollifying motion and signaled with my index finger. "One, be nice to me and help me find this woman." I tossed the balled-up sketch back to him and raised a second finger.

"Two, get Carrera to leave my mother alone."

I flipped open my thumb to sign ASL for three. "And three, do those things and you'll get the forty-five K back." This last bit was never going to happen. Never.

Like dimwits everywhere Fabrizio stuck to his demand and upped the menace in his voice. "Change it to *me, my* name."

I shook my head. "Do you really want your name attached to this dirty money? Isn't that why you gave it to me to clean up?" I tapped my temple.

"Also, and follow me on this one, Fabrizio. After you blackmailed me with the forty-five K and then assaulted me, I wrote a memo of our interactions and took pictures of the money, every bill, and sent the whole thing to my lawyer. If for some reason I end up dead, Ms. Crouch will happily send it all to internal affairs, along with the info about your little fuck pad here you and Manny run to keep a personal supply of hookers in line."

His eyes widened with each revelation of what I hadn't actually done but sounded plausible in the moment. He sputtered and tried to come up with a response but had nothing. Lucky for me he's stupid. Also lucky for me he was filthy drunk when he came up with his supposed foolproof plan to launder his dirty money. He never considered the consequences.

At the time, neither had I. At least not at first. Fending off his sexual assault and almost losing my thin, hard-won sobriety at his hands didn't leave much time or space to figure out how I could outsmart him. Adrenaline during an assault tends to focus the mind on one thing: survival.

But after some thought I realized I had the upper hand, one which held $45,000.

I worried all the way home about my loose lips naming Father Mik as the beneficiary of Fabrizio's CDs. It could become a big problem.

Even though Fabrizio finally agreed to find out who ordered the attack on Evie—and I was still convinced it was Carrera—I wasn't sure he'd follow through. He was royally pissed off at me for outsmarting him. To get his money I wouldn't put it past him to kill me and then go after Father Mik. I doubted he would kill Father Mik, though. If threatened, the old priest would turn over the money.

I couldn't stand the idea Father Mik would discover I willingly participated in money laundering, though. But I would be dead and couldn't explain I intended the 45K for Mickey—a deaf boy I rescued —my attempt to make something good out of bad.

At home I put it all in an email while I ate late lunch, every last detail of the money's origin. I described how I came to own the CDs and named Father Mik as beneficiary in order to make sure Mickey's family got the money. Then I sent it to the priest. Even though I wasn't on my knees in the confessional at church, I found some relief.

12

LOUISE

4:00 p.m.

L ouise surveyed her work. Angel's transformation into a little boy was convincing because most people saw only the shell, not the person. Angel wore boy's pants and a miniature Cubs sweatshirt. Getting the hair right took a while, short all around and dyed dark brown, but now Louise felt confident she could go out in public with no problem.

Dressed up in a winter jacket and hood the baby passed for a boy, not at all like the girl with golden curls in the two pictures they kept showing on the news. In the first, the the baby grabbed a handful of cake from a huge slice with a number one candle at the center. Adorable.

The second shot was really recent. Margot the Monster held Louise's Angel. She could tell it was taken in the PP meeting room, a large sign behind them read *Happy Holidays!*

Angel ran around the hotel room, going from the bed to the desk to the television, stopping for a few moments here and there, intent on the toys and bits of paper at these stations and strewn on the floor in between. After several days of trying to keep the room straight and neat, Louise was frazzled from running after Angel. The mess the little girl created—any mess, really—made Louise nervous and uncertain.

Being stuck in this room with an almost two-year-old was a lot harder than she first imagined. Her home offered solace and calm because everything was orderly: paper booties at the door for guests to don once they shed their shoes, furniture covered in plastic to ward off dirt, plug-in air fresheners for any possible invading odors. It all gave her a sense of pleasure and peace, which she had a hard time finding otherwise.

Ironic that even though she tried to provide a welcoming shelter, her husband stayed away for longer and longer periods of time. He thought she didn't know about the gambling in Joliet. Had he forgotten she managed the household finances? He gave her his paycheck every two weeks, for crying out loud. Did he think she didn't notice the checks he wrote for cash or the cash advances on the credit card bill?

She didn't say anything, though. He earned the income, and she was supposed to concentrate on becoming pregnant. Once that happened they would be a family, and he would stop the foolishness.

But all of that was behind them. After all the trying, naturally she ate to quell her frustration and anxiety. Of course, she gained weight. Who wouldn't? The doctor suggested she try and lose some weight because it might make conceiving easier. And wouldn't you know it, three weeks after joining PP her monthly visitor was late, very late, missed altogether.

So she quit trying to lose weight. Even though the drugstore test showed negative, she paid no attention to it because those things were faulty. Made in China, right?

Never mind the gyne woman telling her she was starting menopause. When Louise grilled her, the doctor had to admit there could be other reasons she was late and offered a blood test to make sure. But it turned out wrong, too. She would somehow have a child. A real family would make her life perfect.

Angel picked up the ball sitting in the corner of the room and began throwing and chasing after it. Louise flicked on the television and tuned in to the local news while she brewed coffee in the two-cup pot on the counter next to the sink.

The Amber Alert flashed on the screen at the beginning of the program with a follow-up report on Melanie Stuckless, still missing along with her father, Herman "Mac" Stuckless. Next, a short film clip of the detective in charge of the investigation into Margot Stuckless's murder. Louise had seen it twice so far.

She figured there wouldn't be any tips about her—they were all out there looking for a *man* with a baby *girl*. And she was sure she wouldn't be connected with the death of Margot the Monster. The Monster was dead, deserved to be dead, and no one would be sad she was gone, especially the women in PP.

The Monster wouldn't bully any of them again. Really, she'd done all of them a favor. She had to wait it out now, here at the hotel, until the police didn't care anymore and it became—what was the name of that show? Oh, yes. A cold case. Yes, the Monster was a cold case all right, a hard case and now a cold, dead case.

Smiling at her own little joke, Louise stirred a hefty dose of sugar into the coffee and put it back on the burner. When this was all over, she would return home and present her husband with their child.

Her pocketbook on her lap, she counted the cash left from her original four thousand. Thirteen hundred and forty-two dollars. Without a credit card, the hotel was charging her a thousand a week. Now it was the end of the second week. Tomorrow she'd have to hand over another thousand. She doubted it was safe enough to return to the condo and present Angel to her husband so soon. She could stick it out here for at least a few more days. After that, she might have to make other plans.

Louise heaved her ponderous body from the chair and trod to the bathroom to sit on the toilet. She caught glimpses of Angel stutter-stepping around the room, throwing the ball up in the air, her little legs chasing after it as it descended and bounced along the floor. The baby's giggle and gurgle of delight filtered into the bathroom.

Suddenly, a sharp smack followed by a short silence, then a loud scream pierced through the television's background drone. Louise finished up as quickly as she could and hurried out of the bathroom.

The little girl's head was soaked with steaming coffee running down her neck and onto her shoulders, her shirt blotched brown. She continued screaming one loud, piercing note. The noise scared Louise. She scooped up the baby and rushed into the bathroom, thrust her into the tub, and turned on the shower. The baby's screams intensified at the cold water's impact.

"Stop! Stop! Angel, stop it! Quiet!" The volume of Louise's voice escalated with each command, but the baby continued crying.

"You're okay. You're okay. It's over." The baby's clothing was soaked from the cold water, the coffee imprinting a stain on her shirt like an overgrown birthmark.

Through the bathroom door Louise spied the overturned coffee pot on the rug and grew anxious at the mess. She shut off the water and left the hysterical Angel in the tub, and rushed into the other room to clean the carpet with a wet towel. After she draped a dry towel over the large, damp spot on the carpet, she retrieved the baby and cleaned her up.

Angel hiccupped and gulped sobs as she quieted down. Louise phoned the desk and asked the desk clerk if there was a crib available. She couldn't let Angel run around loose anymore.

13

DANA

4:00 p.m.

In order to meet with Rameeka Hartmann I had to leave my coat, backpack, and cell phone at the front desk of the inpatient treatment program. Then they checked all of my pockets. The counselor assured me it wasn't personal. Everyone had to follow the same protocol.

"We can't risk outsiders bringing in anything that might compromise a patient's progress," she said, smiling at me.

I understood her message loud and clear. "Makes me glad I left that bottle of gin at home." She had the grace to laugh at my awkward humor. We walked down a dank hallway reeking of an unfortunate combination of B.O. and piss. Marvin's words about needing inpatient treatment if I wasn't successful in IOP reverberated in my head. This place might make me think twice before screwing up again.

We turned a corner and entered a large room similar to one in IOP. Tables and chairs were scattered here and there. Some women were eating from dingy beige trays, and a large-screen TV hung on the wall, but instead of programming from the outside world it played a familiar video. Some of the women formed a half-circle and watched listlessly. Some slept.

Rameeka reclined on a couch in the corner of the room away from everyone, wearing green scrubs like the other patients, her arms crossed against the room's chill, and a book propped open on her lap.

"I can take it from here," I told the counselor.

Rameeka looked up as I approached but didn't register any welcome or even recognition, which frankly pissed me off because I saved this hooker's life not so long ago. I tried to rein in my anger. I needed her help. I grabbed a nearby chair and dragged it over to her couch.

"How the heck are you, Rameeka? You're a hard woman to find." I smiled at her and sat down.

She glared at me but said nothing. I continued, trying for light-heartedness. "Yeah, I trolled your old stomping grounds but no Rameeka. The other women said they didn't know what happened to you. Of course, they probably wouldn't tell me because I'm a cop." During my conversational gambit, she sat stone-faced and without response. "Took me most of today to finally get the scoop."

"Rhonda." There was no mistaking the venom in how she pronounced her sister's name. "Am I right?"

"Yep. Told me you wouldn't stop doing drugs in her condo and kicked you out. Then you were arrested, and the judge gave you the opportunity to get clean or go to jail. And miracle of miracles, you chose treatment. Those are Rhonda's words, by the way, not mine. How long you been in here?"

Rameeka closed the book and put it on the table between us. *I Know Why the Caged Bird Sings.* She sat up. "Halfway through. Gotta do twenty-eight days."

It was easy to tell from her grudging remarks Rameeka was not happy to be in treatment. I swept my hand around the room. "Beats jail, though."

"Barely."

Well, she would know the difference. I wasn't sure how to cajole her out of her sullenness. In her current mood she would not be eager to help me. "If it makes you feel any better, I'm in treatment too. Won't be done 'til—" I had to count to be sure. "Well, I'm about halfway through, too. Like you."

She leaned forward at this. "If you in treatment, how you get to go out? We don't."

"Oh. I didn't—it's not inpatient like this. I go four nights a week for six weeks. It's the same stuff you get, though." I pointed to the video playing on the TV. "Saw that one already. Plus, counseling and group therapy." Where I was headed right after this visit.

She mulled this over. "Drugs?"

I shook my head. "Booze." I was about to launch into my lament over being wrongly Breathalyzed by my boss and forced to choose between my job and treatment when Rameeka piped up.

"Lemme ask you somethin'. You payin' for treatment? Police insurance pretty good, I bet." She folded her arms over her chest.

She was right. I never analyzed the quality of my health insurance or the outpatient program at all. Here she sat in a treatment facility on Chicago's West Side, which mostly drew its clients from the area. The majority of the faces in the room were brown and black.

"It is, you're right. The hospital I go to is pretty nice. On the North Side, lots of restaurants, and of course Starbucks every other block." I paused and patted my hair like a movie star. "Only the best for us white people." At least this garnered a snicker from her.

I waved my hand around the room again. "I wish this place was nicer, Rameeka. I really do." I lowered my voice. "They sure could do something about the smell, don't you think?"

She met my gaze and nodded. "I been all worried up here about how I'm gonna pay for this. My Medicaid don't kick in 'til next month. I'm gonna have to go back to the streets to earn money and that means right back to the drugs. No point bein' here if that's what it takes." She picked up the Maya Angelou book and hugged it.

She was right again. I doubted Rameeka went as far in school as her sister Rhonda, who graduated from University of Chicago Law, but there was nothing wrong with her thought process or understanding of the irony she faced.

"Your sister's covering your treatment. As long as you stay the whole time."

Rameeka laid the book on her lap, her scrunched-up face visibly relaxing at this news like she'd been holding on tight to the fear of cycling back into prostitution. But the worry crept back in a hurry. The fingers of her right hand picked at the short, kinky ringlets of her bright magenta hair, pulling and twisting in deft, quick motions.

"Rhon told you that?" Her face opened up, vulnerable with hope, like a little girl learning her lost dog had been found.

"Yeah. She also told me not to tell you, make you squirm a little. So, keep it to yourself." Rameeka chewed her bottom lip. "And act real surprised when she tells you."

Rameeka rewarded me with a genuine smile. "Actin' is my middle name."

I was unsure if she was willing to give up The Life, but her sister was a high-powered lawyer who lived in the Hancock building downtown and tried periodically to get Rameeka clean and straight. Maybe this time it would work.

I scooted my chair closer to her, plucked a folded piece of paper from my shirt pocket and handed it to her. "Take a look at this. I'm trying to find this woman. Recognize her?"

Rameeka studied the police sketch of Evie's attacker. "What she do?"

I gave her the short version of my first visit a few weeks ago to Fabrizio and Manny's fuck pad, ending with Manny interrupting Fabrizio's assault on me.

"When I got out of there, a woman," I reached over and flicked the sketch with my finger, "this woman, was sitting on the curb next to my car. She asked me for a square. I was so rattled from being assaulted I sat down next to her and we both smoked my Kools. She said she knew Manny. 'He do me a favor, I do him a favor.' Short. Like that. Then she got up and walked toward the fuck pad. I didn't think anything of it."

At least not until Evie's sketch provided the telling details. I wanted to find out the mystery attacker's identity and charge her with Evie's assault. I didn't trust Fabrizio to follow through with Carrera, or to even find out if Manny orchestrated Carrera's dirty work using one of his hookers. But Carrera's gloating outside the lawyer's office didn't dead-end with Fabrizio. I realized Rameeka was another possible avenue of discovery.

Rameeka handed back the sketch, nodding in a tired way as though she heard stories like this all the time. "Ain't seein' any connection here, this woman and your story."

Not pleased to hear Nuts's refrain from a different source, I continued. "I was getting to that. My mother was attacked at home, knocked unconscious, had to have seven stitches in her head. This is the woman she remembers attacking her. She's a hooker. I thought you might know her."

Rameeka squinted her eyes at me, and I got the crossed-arms treatment again. "You think all us hustlers know each other? Is that what you think? Like we in a gang or somethin'?" She made a loud, huffing sound. "This ain't no movie."

She stood, went across the room to a mini-fridge, and retrieved a small carton of orange juice. She made a grand display of shaking the carton, opening it, and taking sips while ignoring me.

I went over to her. "Look. I hoped you might be able to help me with this. Okay, so you're not a big fan of Evie's, but I think you owe her. She let you hide in her home when CW was hunting for you."

Still not looking at me, Rameeka chugged the last of the juice and tossed the container in the trash. She faced me, hand on hip, and spoke in a clipped tone. "First, let's get it straight. You stuck me in her house, remember? Without telling her. There wasn't no *letting* me stay there from your mother. Second, she called me the N-word. Don't know why I should help her, her bein' so hateful and all. Third, CW *did* find me, *did* kidnap me, and *did* almost kill me."

All true things. Logical reasoning clearly runs in this family. I held up my hands in a surrender pose. "Okay, okay. You're right about Evie." Then I leaned in, inches from her hazel-colored eyes, my voice a tight whisper. "But you're forgetting one important detail. No, wait. One major fact. My partner and I rescued your ass and put CW behind bars. At least you owe *me*." I put aside telling her about CW's kidnapping charges being dropped. No sense in adding to her disgruntlement.

Rameeka pulled back. My hot reply seemed to mollify her. She snapped the fingers of her right hand in quick repetition. "Lemme see the picture again." I handed it over. After a long gaze at it she snickered and pointed at the swath of blond—front to back—in the middle of the woman's dark hair. "Think that her real hair color? She look like a skunk with that thing."

Should I tell her Evie made the exact same comment? Instead, I looked askance at Rameeka's neon magenta hair and raised one eyebrow.

She got serious. "Okay, okay." She rattled the sketch. "Nope. Still don't know her. Besides, I can't help you none 'til I get outta here and that's two weeks from now. Fourteen days."

I nodded. "Got it."

"January first."

Just in case I didn't get it. "The new year."

"Mm-hmm," she hummed.

Good news for me she agreed. None of the hookers I buttonholed when trying to find Rameeka would cop to knowing the woman in the sketch. And of course, they wouldn't try to help me because I had nothing to give them in return. I wanted this smart woman's help. Rameeka was the key, my key, for info.

"Sounds good, Rameeka." I paused for a moment to lodge the date of her discharge in my brain so I could enter it on my phone when it was returned at the front desk. "But you will help me?"

She frowned at me. "*Said* I would."

I held up my hands in a pacifying gesture. "Okay, okay." I asked her about some possible areas where I could search for the woman in the meantime, but Rameeka put a damper on the idea.

"She ain't gonna be trickin' right now. She safe. She got money from the job on your mother and sounds like some cop's watchin' out for her. He ain't gonna want her found 'cause it leads back to him. Yep."

I took a step back in admiration. Rameeka came to a conclusion that not only made sense but also saved me further wasted time searching the streets of Chicago. I like to think I would've figured out what she surmised, but in all honesty it wouldn't have been as quick.

"Right. All excellent points."

She tried to return the sketch but I told her to keep it, to study the face of this woman with the blond streak in her black hair and dusting of purple glitter across her cheeks and commit it to memory. Rameeka understood. "You and me, we find this bitch when I get outta here."

I held up my hand for a high five, but she frowned and shook her head. "Nobody do that anymore."

Guess this white girl has to catch up. "Where are you going after you get out?"

"Rhon told me I could stay with her."

I heard hesitation in her voice. There was more to the sentence she didn't complete. "But?"

Rameeka flipped her hand in the air, as if her next statement was of little consequence. "I gotta stay clean."

I touched her arm. "You and me both, Rameeka. You and me both."

14

DANA

10:00 p.m.

After IOP some of the group went out for coffee but I declined, just wanted to get home and eat the dinner I missed because my visit with Rameeka went longer than I planned. I was also worn out from the long day, and my default unwinding mechanism—a beer or six—currently not an option.

Marvin taught me the cheesy acronym *HALT* to identify how I was feeling if the tug of a drink made itself felt. Am I *H*ungry? Starving! Am I *T*ired? Beat! Tonight, those two bookended questions were easy to pinpoint. The *A*ngry and *L*onely in-betweens, not so much.

I wanted to eat something my PP food plan would approve, new behavior for me. I had to admit following a food plan made eating simple with meals already figured out. The structure did seem to help me. There wasn't anything in the PP reading materials, though, about how to ignore the package of chocolate chip cookies in the cabinet.

The fridge yielded a leftover roasted chicken breast, some carrot and celery sticks, and half a cantaloupe—my favorite fruit. *You have enough on your plate.* The irritating phrase reasserted itself, triggering my resentment at Koz and Nuts all over again. I made quick work of my dinner, dumped my dishes in the sink for washing in the morning, and started getting ready for bed when Bear texted me.

> no pp meeting next week cuz xmas. can u
> come to tmw mtg instead? come early for
> video interp?

I agreed to the PP meeting and signed off with an emoji of a girl waving her hand, and he sent back a thumbs up.

I settled on my futon, which snugged up against the wall under the three-window panel of my studio, and opened the attached video from Bear. I wanted to get a look at Margot Stuckless, the woman who was murdered.

Captain Margot held a little girl—I assumed her missing daughter, aged somewhere between one and two—and stood next to the podium chatting with another woman. In the treacly way some women dressed, Margot and her daughter sported matching outfits: pink and white-striped pants and magenta cardigan sweaters over white turtlenecks. If I ever have a daughter I will never, ever, subject her to this horror.

Margot was slender, late twenties, probably around five-eight, and looked as though she never had a problem with food or her weight. My guess? She gained some weight during her pregnancy, went to PP and lost it, and they recruited her as a poster girl for the program. She had *the look.*

I pressed the pause button. Her haircut was a perfect, chin-length bob with blond highlights, her makeup flawless, and she completed the outfit with tasteful jewelry at the ears, neck, and wrist.

My clothing choice earlier today was grabbed from the chair where I threw it the night before: jeans and a light blue sweater with a small hole under one arm, appropriated from Jimmy when he left for L.A.

It was a gift I gave him ten years ago on our first Christmas as husband and wife.

I raked my fingers through my short, curly hair, which hadn't seen a comb since this morning, and studied the freeze frame of this woman. Only a couple of years difference between us.

With this second example of PP perfection—first Janey and now Margot—I again interrogated myself without hesitation. Would Jimmy have stayed had I paid more attention to all this high maintenance stuff expected of women? Hard to ignore the incriminating evidence.

I stabbed the play button. Two women who must have been sitting close to Bear were discussing a recipe for low-cal pizza. It sounded hideous. Captain Janey, who I recognized from the first PP meeting, approached and took the little girl from Margot and retreated to the weigh-in table. The lecture was short and ended with an easy quiche recipe, which actually sounded good.

After the lecture some of the members left, others stood in small groups chatting, and Bear approached Margot Stuckless, his camera still recording. I assumed this was the part he wanted me to interpret and let the video play on, curious how he would interact with a hearing person and even more curious how she'd interact with him.

Captain Janey showed up again and handed off the toddler to Margot. Bear waited a moment while mother hugged daughter and repeatedly kissed her head and cheeks. Margot then seemed to sense Bear was waiting for her and beckoned him forward. He handed her a piece of paper, which she read. She smiled at him and nodded, and he held up the phone closer to her. Margot shifted her daughter onto one hip and took the cell phone, her face looming large on the screen.

"IF YOU'RE STILL HUNGRY ON THE FOOD PLAN, YOU SHOULD EAT MORE PROTEIN!"

I jerked the phone back and quickly reduced the volume. Great. Another hearing person who thinks upping the volume will make the deaf hear. She handed the phone back to Bear. There was more on the video, but I'd seen enough for now and sleep nudged me.

I changed into an extra-large T-shirt, got under the comforter on my futon, and turned out the light. The city's tangerine-tinged street-lights bled into the room's darkness, a reminder to complete some unfinished details of my recent move into the one-room studio. I needed curtains. I closed my eyes and drew the covers over my head.

Even though Jimmy and I had been apart almost six months this soli-tude at night continued to sting. In IOP tonight Marvin brought up my divorce, wanted me to pinpoint the hardest thing about being alone. Trying to get me to talk about it really put my back up. Way too early for dispassionate, rational discussion.

I made up some bullshit I thought he'd like to hear, something along the lines of how my future was so uncertain now, all the plans Jimmy and I had were gone, my job in jeopardy. All true things, safe things, to discuss in therapy, but nowhere near the rage I have at Jimmy for giving up on us, on me. All because he thinks I have a drinking problem.

Marvin fed me some pablum about taking it a day at a time, that this too would pass, blah, blah, blah. What was it with these self-help people? Did they *all* think a few words or catchy phrases would change you or stop you from doing something self-destructive?

If I had been real with Marvin, I would've told him the hardest thing for me to swallow in the divorce was discovering how quickly Jimmy replaced me with a sleepy-voiced bitch in California, my imagination serving up a blond who earned her bikini body by working out—in every sense—with my husband. It took him only four months to dissolve our ten-year marriage. Four months.

Here's what I couldn't tell Marvin: I loved Jimmy from the moment I met him, married him at twenty when we both graduated from the

Police Training Academy, wanted only him as the father of my kids. He pissed on all of it. Four *months.*

I discovered then Jimmy was a lazy coward. Not willing to do the hard work we both needed to do after I miscarried.

I guess the most important thing to know about a person is the thing you don't know.

One of the main reasons I craved getting back to work with Nuts was the familiarity of being in a partnership. For ten years Jimmy and I were a team, a great match.

I drowsed. Match. Matching outfits. Margot's seeming perfect life. But she was dead and her daughter missing. Not so perfect after all.

15

DANA

The next morning, I assembled the six ingredients needed for Margot's quiche—which I dreamt about last night—and propped up my cell phone by the stove so I could follow her cooking instructions. I've never made quiche before, always considered it an ultra-fancy and difficult dish to assemble, certainly nothing I would've made during my ten years as a cop. But it all came together quite easily, especially because this low-fat version had no crust and minimal cheese. Really, it only seemed like baked eggs. I delivered the pan to a hot oven, and someone knocked on my door.

"Miss? Miss? You are home?" Sandor, my landlord and manager of our three-flat building. He and his wife lived in the first floor apartment while I surfed the third floor. We sandwiched a couple of college students on the second floor. I opened the door to Sandor standing in the hallway with a newspaper clamped under one arm.

"Good morning, Miss. You are doing well? A beautiful morning, yes?" He tilted his head up a bit for better eye contact and tipped his battered Cubs cap.

"Hi, Sandor. Hold on one sec." I flipped back to the start of Margot's recipe description to get the baking time and set the timer on the oven. I let Bear's video continue to play. Back at the door I leaned on the frame and asked Sandor how he was doing.

He drew the newspaper from under his arm and unfolded it, showing me the front page. "This here bad news. Bad. Sandor afraid this people will, will—" He made swooping motions with one arm. I took the paper, unsure of his gesture and curious about what worried him. In a picture on the front page a city crew power-washed gang insignia from the wall of a building.

"They will be coming here to make confetti," he said, his voice rising in pitch with excitement.

"Con—oh, you mean graffiti?"

"Yes, yes. Can you the police stop them?"

I handed back the paper. "Look, Sandor. Streets and San is completely different from the police, different city services."

Confused look. I resorted to gesture to make the point. In the space in front of my body I opened my arms wide as if I was going to hug him. "Police here," I wiggled my left hand, "and Streets and San here," I wiggled my right hand. I shook my head. "Not the same. Different."

Before he could respond, I heard raised voices coming from my cell still propped up next to the stove in the kitchenette a few feet to my left. I held up my index finger. "Hold on." I retrieved my cell, but Bear's video had ended. I returned to Sandor, still waiting at my door, still sporting a worried expression.

"Please, Miss. What is streets and sand?"

I couldn't help smiling at his misunderstanding but tried to make it pass for being friendly. I didn't want to alienate Sandor, he was a nice man, but I didn't need to prolong this either.

"Not sand. San is short for sanitation. Like making things clean." I mimed using a broom and he lit up with understanding. "If someone tags our building you call Streets and Sanitation to come and clean it." I grabbed a sticky note and wrote the name of the department for him. I could smell the quiche and my stomach growled.

Sandor took the note and thanked me. "But I must tell police. This is wrong." Again with the swooping motion.

"Yes. Right." I imitated his swoop. "It's called tagging. You can call police but," I took the sticky note back from him and jotted down '311' and handed it back. "Call this number if it happens and tell police."

He read what I wrote. "But 911?"

Navigating the ins and outs of a large city is hard enough, and it must be all the harder with Sandor's patchy English skills. "No, don't call 911 for tagging because that's for big, bad problems." I opened my hands wide and exaggerated my frown. I touched the sticky note. "This, 311, is for small problems." I brought my hands close together. "Like tagging." I swooped one more time.

A smile creased his face. He tipped his cap. "Thank you, Miss. You helped Sandor a big lot." He opened his arms wide, mimicking me.

I returned his hat tip with a two-finger salute. "Good. 'Bye, Sandor." I closed the door and went to peek at the quiche. Ten minutes to go. It was puffy in the middle with a caramel sheen on top, really pretty. Something I never took time to notice in the years of marginal cooking I did for Jimmy. We subsisted mostly on carryout, fast food, and whatever we could grab at a convenience store while working a case.

Another stab of guilt. Had I done more cooking for my husband would it have made a difference in his wanting to stay? I had no idea, but where else could I lay the blame?

I restarted Bear's video at the spot where Margot screams at him to eat more protein. She hands Bear the phone. A woman stands to

Margot's side as if waiting for Bear to finish, then pushes closer and begins talking to her. Bear steps back but keeps recording. Either he was interested in knowing what the woman and Margot were discussing or he wasn't finished talking with Margot.

The woman exemplifies the weight-loss blues. She's overweight by at least fifty pounds, wears a shapeless black shift, tights with Birkenstocks even though it's winter, and her haircut looks like someone put a bowl on her head and trimmed around the edges. Although she seems only a few years older than Margot the difference is striking. I can't make out their conversation until the woman reaches out as if to take the baby from Margot.

Stepping back, Margot gets loud. "Don't touch her!"

The woman recoils and ducks her head as if avoiding a slap, but then she straightens, puts both hands on her hips and makes a snide face, saying something I can't quite make out. Her body language is easy to read, though. She's telling Margot off. The woman waves her index finger between Margot and the baby, who hugs her mother tight around the neck and pushes her little feet against Margot's body as if trying to get away from the woman.

The volume swelled and the woman's voice came through. "You think you're so perfect with your daughter and your stupid matching outfits! You make me sick!" She whirled away and stomped out of the frame. I had to agree with the woman: comparing my outsides with Margot's made me sick, too. Janey hurried into the picture toward Margot and the video ended.

The oven timer dinged. I pulled the quiche out of the oven and set it on the counter to cool for a couple of minutes. I measured one teaspoon of butter for one piece of toast, resisting the urge to make another, and set it up on a plate. While waiting for the eggs to cool I replayed the last bit of the video of the woman shouting at Margot.

What got me was her reaching for the baby. Almost a grab. How odd. Especially in the circumstance presented. I'm not a mom, but I have enough sense not to take a woman's baby from her arms without at least asking permission. Clearly that didn't happen. Part of me, though, could relate to the woman's anger at the seeming perfection of Margot and her baby. Same shit, different woman.

My hunger made quick work of the quiche. I texted Bear. He didn't know the name of the woman in the video but did have a list of names and numbers of the meeting members willing to be contacted for ongoing support. He took a picture of the list and sent it to me. I knew it was a long shot for her to be one of the contacts, but the list was a start to do some of the inside work on this case.

The one Nuts didn't want my help with.

16

LOUISE

8:00 a.m.

Louise couldn't stand the noise. How could such a little thing make such a big ruckus? Even though Louise wore earplugs, Angel's screaming woke her up. The clock radio registered 8:00 a.m. She reached for the small lamp on the nightstand and flipped it on. It made no difference in the screaming level.

She rolled over and there was her baby, standing in the crib, little hands gripping the railing, eyes closed and mouth wide open. Angel vibrated with outrage. Louise kept her in the crib for her own good, though, and she wouldn't change it only because the little sourpuss didn't like being confined.

Louise waited for the noise to abate. After a few minutes someone started banging on her door and yelling for her to quiet down. Angel continued to scream even louder—if that was possible—and Louise pushed up off the bed and trudged to the crib. What would happen if the person banging on the door reported her? Would they kick her and Angel out?

Angel took a deep breath between screams and opened her eyes. Seeing Louise put an abrupt stop to her noise. But when Louise did nothing but stand in front of Angel and stare at her, the baby started blubbering, sobbing, and gulping, spouting what sounded like gibberish.

She wouldn't free the baby from the crib but searched for something to eat for the little one. After two weeks of staying at the hotel, there wasn't much food left in the mini-fridge and nothing to put in the baby bottle other than water. Louise didn't think water would satisfy Angel.

Louise's purse yielded two Butterfinger candy bars, her last two, and she hated to give up even part of one, but with Angel jeopardizing their temporary home Louise gave in. She unwrapped one, broke off a piece, and held it out to the baby. Angel turned her head away and ramped up to a moaning cry. Louise made shushing noises and pried one of Angel's hands off the crib railing, then placed the candy in the baby's fist.

"See? Good candy. Yum. Look." Louise took a bite of the candy bar. Angel began to copy Louise's movement but when her fist reached her mouth, she reared back and threw the candy in Louise's face.

"No!" Louise's loud reaction reignited Angel's screaming and crying. Louise bent over and scooped up the candy from the dusty floor, wiped it on her pants, and popped it in her mouth. "Bad little girl! Bad little girl! No more candy for you. Only me."

More awake now, Louise realized Angel's prolonged crying might mean a needed diaper change. After all this time, she was beginning to understand the differences in Angel's crying jags. At first, they all sounded the same. But now she could distinguish between the hunger cry and the fussiness cry when Angel was tired.

She picked up the baby and laid her on the bed, unsnapped the onesie and checked the diaper. Soaking. Cold. Now that Louise was addressing the origin of her discomfort, Angel was quiet.

When Louise laid Angel back in the crib, the baby rolled over and was out immediately. Louise told herself to check the diaper first next time and avoid all the noise. The baby was asleep but now Louise felt wide awake, her thoughts straining at the idea they were almost out of food and needed more to drink, too. Yesterday she paid another thousand dollars for a third week's stay. She wanted to go back home, back to her husband, present him with this baby, start their real life as a family.

This room was a godawful mess and smelled worse than a garbage dumpster, while her own home was an oasis of comfort, order, and cleanliness. Louise did not allow the housekeeping people in, afraid they would recognize Angel in spite of her disguise and call the police.

She lined up the full garbage bags at the door but didn't allow them to be hauled away, sure someone would paw through the bags, find the diapers, and discover her identity. And because the room had an overpowering stink, Louise kept a window cracked open for some air. The only problem with that? The winter wind in Chicago kept the room cold, adding to Louise's overall anxiety. She would have to get back home soon.

17

DANA

9:45 a.m.

When Koz suspended me he took my badge and gun, but my official CPD lanyard still held my ID, and I stuffed it in my pocket to take to the PP meeting. I also considered wearing my beat uniform but rejected the idea as over-the-top. Bad enough I was impersonating an active-duty cop, I didn't have to advertise it.

I arrived at the PP meeting early, as promised, interpreting the *YOU SHOULD EAT MORE PROTEIN* part of the video for Bear. He didn't stay for the meeting, having just weighed in two days ago, and left.

I didn't weigh in either but stayed for Captain Janey's lecture on "Oil: Friend or Foe?" I didn't know that was a thing—so much to learn about this weight-loss business. She then handed out stars to the members who lost weight in the past week and citations to those who gained.

I waited while the basket was passed around to collect money for the Chicago Food Depository. When it was handed to me I experienced an unexpected swell of gratitude. Here I was trying to eat less and lose weight while many people in Chicago—hell, the world—had nothing and counted on food pantries for their next meal. I wanted to help but only had a couple of bucks on me, which I tossed in the basket wishing there was more I could do.

Then I remembered Saint Nick's annual holiday party for the congregation happened around this time. Evie and JJ have helped Father Mik set up the popular event every year starting when I was a kid. I could stand to do some volunteer work, too.

As most of the women filed out of the meeting I went to the front of the room and waited behind two women talking with Captain Janey. She was describing some kind of dessert.

"I can't believe it's made without any sugar at all," one of the women said. Full rapture.

Why can't I get as excited about this kind of thing? Janey handed the recipe sheet to both women and then to me. Sugarless Christmas cookies. Oh boy. But I smiled and thanked her as the two women donned their coats and left.

I made sure my police ID was visible when introducing myself in case Janey didn't remember me.

"Oh! I had no idea you were with the police," she said, eyeing my lanyard.

"Yes, well. It wasn't important until now."

"I already talked to them once. No, twice. The one who was here, he came to my house before with the other one." She snapped her fingers a couple of times. "He had an Italian name."

"Felice Abandonato."

"Yes! That's him. I told him everything already."

I nodded. "More things have come to light in the investigation." I pulled out my cell and brought up Bear's video. "I want you to watch this clip and tell me if you recognize the woman in it."

She came to my side and I held up my phone so we both could view it, then tapped the *play* icon.

"Oh! Oh, Margot." Janey's voice shook and she let out a big sigh.

I paused the video and touched her elbow. "Are you okay?"

Her eyes brimmed with tears. "I—it's hard to see her like this." She gestured at the phone. "I mean, she's alive and, and—" She hiccupped and then full-out cried.

I steered her to one of the folding chairs and we both sat until she finished sobbing. She dug a tissue from her sweater pocket and mopped up. "It was so shocking. I found her, you know."

No, I didn't know, not being privy to the actual investigation information. This was doubly good news for me. "Would you care to tell me about it? It might help you process the trauma." I had no idea if this was true, but it sounded logical or at least maybe comforting.

She nodded. "Okay." She related that while she was on the phone with Margot Stuckless, an unidentified person showed up. Margot seemed to know this person and got angry. "She said, 'You, again!' and 'I told you to stay away!' Something like that."

"The other person say anything? Could you identify if it was male or female?"

"No. I told the other detective it was probably her husband Mac." She gave me a gossipy version of the Stuckless divorce, none of which I found helpful because I wanted to get back to the woman in the video, but I let her ramble. Besides, if the husband was a suspect, I assumed Nuts and Rokick already had him in custody.

Finally, I nudged her back to finding Margot's body and how the scene appeared.

"Margot usually picks me up for the PP meetings. I watch little Melly while Margot lectures." At the mention of the baby, she teared up again and asked the status of the Amber Alert.

"I'm not handling that part of the investigation." Technically true, because I wasn't handling any part of the investigation, at least not on CPD's payroll. "But I can find out and get back to you, if you like." Not true at all, most of the case information was confidential, but I wanted to mollify her by promising a vague future connection.

"You were telling me Margot usually picks you up for the PP meetings."

"Mm-hmm. It was getting close to that time. I could see from my window that her car was still there, in the driveway, so I just went over. We did that sometimes, but usually she'd call me first, you know, like if she was running late."

I waited while she blew her nose and took a deep breath.

"I found her in the back bedroom—the baby's room." Janey's expression was a mix of misery and sadness, a needed reminder for me as a homicide detective who has seen countless murder victims, bodies in morgues, and the indignities performed during autopsies. None of it fazed me anymore. For her, finding a dead person was shocking enough, but discovering her best friend laid out cold morphed from shock into permanent trauma. I needed to go easy.

"I'm so sorry this happened to you." I patted her shoulder.

She placed her hand over her heart. "I mean, I'm *young*. My parents are still alive. Heck, so are my grandparents. You never expect someone your own age to, to—" She couldn't bring herself to say the word.

"No. You're right. You never do. And it's always a shock, no matter if the person's been sick or really old or whatever. It's funny. We all know dying is a part of life but for some reason it has the power to catch us unawares when it happens."

Janey's smile had a wry twist. "Exactly. I guess I'm being a little immature."

I assured her that was not the case and her reaction completely normal. And gave her kudos for being willing to talk about it again. I wanted to probe for more details about Margot's body, if there was any obvious trauma or indication of how she was murdered, but I didn't need to make Janey relive it. Besides, it would alert her to the fact I didn't already have the info as part of the investigation team.

She pointed to my phone and asked to see the video again. I cued it up and as soon as Margot began yelling at the woman Janey said I could turn it off.

"Oh, yes, of course, I know her. Louise Conway. She's been in and out of PP several times."

I asked for the spelling of the woman's name, which turned out exactly the way it sounded, nothing fancy. She lived on the North Side. I checked the date of Bear's recorded meeting—four weeks ago —and asked Janey if she'd seen Louise Conway since.

"I haven't, but I can check the attendance records. Maybe she's been in meetings with other leaders. Just take a sec." I followed her to the back of the room. While she spent a few minutes on the computer I checked the PP member list Bear sent me. No Louise Conway.

Janey turned the computer monitor toward me. "See? She hasn't attended meetings since then," she said, pointing at my phone. She touched the monitor's screen. "And here, she canceled her autopay. She's not an active member anymore." She jotted down Louise Conway's address and phone and handed it to me.

"You've been very helpful. I appreciate it." I gave her a business card with my name, crossed out the squad number, and added my cell. "It's a lot easier to get hold of me this way."

"Something's been bothering me since after I talked to those other detectives. Something I forgot to tell them. You know those little bite-sized Butterfingers? The kind they sell for trick-or-treat? There were lots of those wrappers all torn open around Margot. Like someone stood there over her body eating candy and throwing the wrappers on the floor. Margot never ate candy."

"Okay. Then it's a strong possibility they're from the person who killed her."

"But that's what I mean. So, it can't be Mac, can it? Her husband? He's highly allergic to chocolate."

BITTER COLD ASSAULTED me as I walked to my car. I hate wearing hats, gloves, scarves: all extraneous outerwear I inevitably lose every year and have to replace the following winter. As a result, my down jacket is really all I wear during the winter. My ears were smarting by the time I slid into my Camry and hit the ignition.

Louise Conway lived in a condo on the North Side, not too far from me, in the Ravenswood neighborhood. Parking was a bitch, but I finally scored a spot next to the Northwestern train tracks.

I lit a Kool and fingered the scrap of paper displaying her phone number and address, info Nuts and Rokick didn't have, so I didn't have to worry about them scaring her away. More important, would I scare her away? Would she even be home? But if she was home, another worry: I had no way to effect an arrest and take her into the squad for questioning if she wouldn't cooperate.

I needed Nuts for this. I called and when he didn't answer, left a message to call me. I assumed he let it go to voicemail because he was equally pissed at me for hanging up on him before. The one thing we both agreed on, though, was the case came first regardless of our personal differences.

I chain-smoked a couple more cigarettes waiting for him to return my call, then texted him stressing it was urgent. I lowered my window and flicked my spent cigarette into the street, mad at myself because I didn't better think through how to approach Louise Conway.

I tried Louise's phone number, ready to impersonate a salesperson for kitchen flooring if she answered, and was surprised to find it disconnected. Evidence she was on the run? I popped a breath mint, aware my smoker's breath could be horrible, and hurried the two blocks to her condo.

Once there I leaned on the doorbell, but no one responded. I waited a minute and rang again. No luck. A manager was listed for the first floor. I rang and was buzzed in. The foyer had an intercom system; a woman's voice greeted me and asked me my business.

"I'm from the Chicago Police Department and I'm looking for Mrs. Louise Conway. She doesn't answer when I ring. Do you have any idea when she'll be back?"

"No. Listen, can you wait a sec? I'll be right down."

A minute later the foyer door opened and a woman about my age, clad in a green chenille robe and pink fluffy slippers, emerged. She clutched her cell phone in one hand and a pack of Salems in the other, depositing both on a decorative table below the mailboxes.

She cinched her robe belt tighter and approached asking for ID, which surprised me. When I identify myself as a cop or detective, very few people ask for proof. I fingered my lanyard, told her my name, and then made a hopefully distracting show of retrieving a pen and notepad from my backpack, flicking the notepad open a few pages and clicking the pen.

"And you manage this building, Miss—?"

She nodded. "Bonita. Most people call me Bonnie." Diversion successful. She ran her hands down her robe and did a shuffle-step with her slippers. She smiled sheepishly. "I also live here. Obviously."

I smiled back, asked for her last name and number, which she hesitated about giving but then relented, and went back to my original inquiry. "I need to speak to Louise Conway. Any idea when she'll be back?"

"Like I said before, no. But I have to tell you I doubt she'll be back at all."

When I asked for clarification, she took a step closer to me and dropped her voice, as if wanting to keep what she had to say from being overheard. Beats me who that would be. We were alone in the foyer.

"They fought, the Mister and Missus. More than once I had to bang on their door and tell them to keep it down. That's how loud they could be."

"Annoying," I agreed. "Any idea what they were fighting about?"

She shook her head. "It was loud but muffled, you know? I couldn't make out the words. But one time when I banged on the door and Mister answered, Missus was nearby and she was crying, real hard, like, sobbing."

I scribbled on my pad, pretending to write this down. "So why do you think Missus won't be back?"

"Not hard to figure. Mister told me. About two weeks ago he gave me his mailbox key and a different address, asked me to send his mail there. He didn't want to put in a forwarding address at the post office until he had a permanent place. Said his wife left him and went to live with her mother. He was moving out and selling the condo."

She panted a little, breathless from the excited telling of the dissolution of the Conway marriage. She retrieved her pack of Salems from the table. "Mind if I smoke?"

"Not if I can join you." I dislodged my Kools from my backpack. I held my lighter for both of us. We inhaled, smiling at our shared addiction.

"So, you haven't seen Louise Conway for two weeks?" That would be before Margot Stuckless was murdered.

Bonnie stopped, counted on her fingers, then shrugged. "Something like that. Like I said, Mister asked me to do the mail a couple of weeks ago. Yeah, sounds about right. And I haven't seen her since then. Not sure exactly when she went to her mother's house."

She tapped her ashes on the floor. I raised my eyebrows at her. "It's okay. I'm washing the floor today. Feel free." She waved her hand downward.

The manager didn't have the location for Louise Conway's mother, but gave me Gerry Conway's temporary address, way south in suburban Maywood. She had no phone number for him.

"He told me he was getting a new number so his wife couldn't contact him." She snapped her fingers. "I do have a number for her, though. Come on up."

She ground out her cigarette on the floor but picked up the spent butt. I copied her. As I passed the table, I pointed. "Don't forget your phone."

She shook her head. "I'm always doing that." She grabbed it and I followed her up the stairs to the third floor. "Their place is across from mine," she said, pointing down the hall.

"I'd like to take a look around her condo."

Bonnie hesitated long enough I knew she wouldn't allow it. "You have a search warrant?"

I shook my head. "How about a peek inside? Won't touch anything."

Her eyes lit up. "Oh! Like to get a feel for her personality?"

"You got it."

She relented, retrieved some keys from her condo and opened the door to the Conway home. She entered first and stopped inside the door. "Just here."

"Got it." The room showed signs of someone moving out, packed boxes lining one wall, an empty bookcase, but no personal effects—pictures, an empty coffee cup, opened mail—on display.

To the left of the door a plastic tray for shoes lay on a brilliant white carpet. A small basket full of paper booties nestled against it. The only furniture in the room—an overstuffed couch and chair—were encased in clear plastic, and the scent of vanilla emanated from a plug-in air freshener.

"I do like how neat she kept this place," Bonnie said. "Of course, she didn't work, like I do. Staying home all day would make that easy for her. Me? I got this building to take care of and I bartend at night." She gestured at her robe and slippers. "So I sleep late."

"Sure. Of course."

The room creeped me out. It was too perfect. Antiseptic. How could anyone live like this? She must've been on constant alert for any speck of dirt or dust trying to find a way in. And I sure couldn't picture any guy putting up with a woman who had to live in such surroundings; at least, not any guys I knew.

Bonnie gave me Louise Conway's phone number, but on inspection I saw it was the same useless one from Janey. I handed over my card and thanked Bonnie for her help.

"You never told me what this was all about. Did Missus do something? Are you going to arrest her?" Again, excited breathiness.

I shook my head. "I only need to talk to her about something connected to a case we're investigating. She's not in any trouble." In the off-chance Louise showed up at the condo again, I didn't want Ms. Nosy Manager blabbing to her. "In fact, if Louise does come back, would you do me a favor and give me a call?"

I pointed at my card in her hand. "Use the cell number. Don't say anything to her about my visit. I don't want to scare her, you know, like she might leave."

Bonnie nodded sagely as if she was asked this all the time.

18

DANA

1:00 p.m.

Before driving down to Maywood to talk to Gerry Conway, I FaceTimed Evie to find out when she and JJ were helping set up Father Mik's holiday party. Turned out they were going later this afternoon and I told her I'd pick them up.

I headed south on Harlem to get on the Eisenhower Expressway, but even this early in the afternoon traffic on the Ike crawled like it was rush hour. It took an hour to arrive at an unkempt six-flat in Maywood. Near the entrance a wooden sign advertising furnished apartments by the week or month hung from a post stuck in the ground. Inside, the apartment 3C mailbox had Gerry Conway's name taped to it. I rang the bell and the door almost immediately buzzed back.

As I climbed the stairs I craned my neck to see if anyone waited for me on the upper landing. No. I knocked on the apartment door and it opened, a short length of security chain halting the door's progress. The horrid smell of burnt cheese wafted out.

"Hi. I'm looking for Gerry Conway. Is that you?" Through the four-inch opening in the door I could make out a short guy, his face sidewalk gray, gazing up at me with a worried expression.

"Who're you?" he said.

I held up the ID card at the end of the lanyard around my neck and introduced myself. I asked his name again. Instead of answering he asked what I wanted.

"Before I tell you that I need to know if you're Gerry."

He sighed, apparently tired of our back and forth. "I'm Conway."

"Do you mind if I come in, Mr. Conway? I'd like to talk to you about your wife."

At the mention of Louise Conway, he grimaced. "She's not here. She went to Gary to live with her mother."

I tucked away this bit of info, already supported by Manager Bonnie, to remember to ask Conway for his mother-in-law's address. "I actually wanted to talk with you. Mind if I come in?"

He scraped open the chain and I entered a studio apartment not unlike my own, with a kitchenette built in along one wall and a twin bed in the opposite corner next to a small dresser. The room was humid and overheated. Gerry waved me over to a card table with three folding chairs. The origin of the unholy burnt smell sat on a paper plate, a half-eaten grilled cheese sandwich the color of tar.

We sat.

"Bonnie give you my address?"

I smiled and nodded. He frowned but said nothing.

I unhooked my backpack from my shoulder and set it on the floor, then shrugged off my jacket and pulled out my notepad again, this time for real notes.

I ascertained his full legal name and phone number in order to hand over to Nuts any helpful information Gerry Conway might share. "Sorry to interrupt your lunch," I said, gesturing at the plate.

A small smile from him. "I let it go too long." He picked up the plate and ditched the offensive sandwich into a garbage pail underneath the sink.

"Want a Coke?" he said.

"Sure. Sounds good."

He pulled a two-liter bottle from the mini-fridge next to the sink, filled two plastic cups and served us, leaving the bottle in the middle of the table.

"Thanks. So, when I spoke with Bonnie she mentioned that you and your wife are separated?"

"I guess so. Lou, uh, Louise—I call her Lou—we haven't been getting along for a while. She decided to go live with her mother. At least I think so. I have no idea where else she'd go. She left without telling me." Conway was a small man, shorter than me, but at this admission he seemed to shrink.

I cocked my head. "Did you consider filing a missing person report?" I leaned forward. "Most people, their husband or wife goes missing, that's what they do."

He folded his hands on the table. "I—we're not most people, Detective. My wife has problems." He touched an index finger to his temple. "She's—you know." His hands resumed their prayer position.

"Can you give me a little more than that?" I tapped my temple. "I'm not sure what this means."

He picked up his cup of pop, leaned back in his chair, and spoke to the table. "I didn't file a report because I didn't want to find her. We've been married for ten years. The last five have been hell." He took a long drink from his cup and set it back down.

I waited in silence for him to continue, not wanting to badger him. His claim of hell was reflected in his demeanor and appearance. It was hard to gauge his age due to what seemed like premature balding, remnants of hair a scraggly fringe above his ears. His winter-grey complexion implied poor health although, judging from the burnt sandwich, lousy cooking might be a factor. Or maybe it was all because of Louise.

"After our first five years, when we got settled and a little money saved, we decided to have kids. So, we tried. And tried and tried and tried. After a couple of years, I found out I have a condition called azoospermia." He wouldn't look at me while he related this, so I attended to my notepad, jotting down what had to be a difficult admission.

"That means no sperm. None. Doesn't happen very often. The doc had me take vitamins, zinc, C, D. I exercised. I did everything, but nothing worked." He sat with his arms cradling each other, more like a self-hug than a defensive posture.

"I understand. I'm sure it put a stress on your marriage."

His head snapped up and he locked eyes with me. "Stress! That's not even the half of it. A major instruction from the fertility doc was *no stress*! But my wife was on me all the time to try everything she could find on the internet to, to—" He stopped.

"Not too relaxing."

"Right. So, then her next idea was to try, you know, like a test tube baby. But Lou was overweight, and the doc ordered her to lose fifty pounds before she could be considered."

"More chance of miscarriage?" I knew this from my own pregnancy.

"Exactly. She wasn't happy about it but she went to that weight loss place," he snapped his fingers and frowned.

"Pounds Police?"

"Yes! She always calls it PP, so the name escapes me. Anyway, she did lose the weight. It took a year. We started IVF treatments." He shuddered. "I had to give her the shots. Never got used to that."

"From what I understand about IVF it can be pretty expensive."

He nodded. "I was lucky. My insurance covered some of the cost, but you're right. The insurance capped the amount. We couldn't keep at it forever."

"From what you've told me so far, Lou sounds like most women who are trying to get pregnant, so they cover all the bases. Not," I touched my temple, "you know."

"She got depressed about not getting pregnant. But that's not what I meant about her. About a year ago she started eating all the time. A lot of it mostly junk; cake, ice cream, cookies, chocolate. Especially chocolate."

Bite-sized Butterfingers.

"And she ballooned up, way past her original weight when she went to PP the first time. We had to stop the IVF treatments. Then about six months ago the doc told her she was in menopause."

"The last straw?"

"Among many. But here's the odd part," cueing me again with a tap to his temple. "She went back to PP saying she would lose the weight again and everything would be fine, she would get pregnant, we could be a 'real family.' As if the past eight years hadn't even happened." Conway drank the remainder of his pop, and after pouring another cupful held out the bottle to me.

"No, thanks. Still working on this one," I said. I hadn't touched it, remembering too late regular Coke wasn't on my food plan.

"When she started in on me again with the whole vitamins, exercise stuff, and her crazy insistence the baby be at least part of her or me, her eggs or my sperm, I just checked out."

"Makes sense." And it did. Louise Conway sounded like a woman obsessed with her own quest to have a baby. Dysfunctional hormones, failed attempts with science, and the final ignominy of menopause must have been hard enough to bear. Then her husband wanting a separation tipped her over the edge. It all added up to a woman out of options.

Until an answer appeared at the Pounds Police meeting: Margot Stuckless and her perfect baby. Bear's video clip ran through my mind, the part where Louise reached for Margot's daughter. Just four weeks ago.

Gerry Conway retrieved a Costco-sized bag of potato chips from a cabinet and placed it on the table. "I'm hungry," he said, grabbing a handful and pushing the bag across to me. "Help yourself."

Only my favorite snack in the world. "I'm good. Okay. I appreciate all the info on your wife. Really helps me understand her better. When did she leave?"

"What's today? Friday?"

I nodded, puzzled he didn't know. "What do you do for a living?"

"I'm an IT guy for the regional hospital system of northern Illinois. I work on the overnight shift. Twelve hours. My usual schedule is four days on, Monday through Thursday, and three days off. The weekends kind of blur for me." He finished the chips he held and scooped more from the bag.

"When did Lou leave?"

He stuffed more chips in his mouth, holding up one finger as he chewed and then swallowed. "Two weeks ago I finally got up the nerve to tell Lou I wanted a separation."

"How did she take that?"

Gerry Conway considered this for a moment and then drained his cup of pop.

"She didn't seem mad, more like defeated. Hard to know with her. We didn't really talk after that. I went to work the next day for my twelve-hour shift and when I got home the next morning she was gone."

"And you haven't seen her since?"

He shook his head. "That's when I made kind of a hasty decision to sell the condo."

"Because she left?"

He frowned. "No. Well, I mean, it's mine. I own it. I rented this place and hired a realtor for the condo. I was going to tell Lou she could stay there until the end of the month, that's when it's going on the market. But the realtor thinks it's easier to show empty."

Yes, easier on the realtor. And on you, Gerry. Much easier to avoid facing your wife after telling her you want a separation. "Any possibility she could be staying at the condo?" I recalled the living room Bonnie showed me. If anyone was living there, it wasn't obvious.

"No. I've been in and out over there, moving things, cleaning. There's no sign of her. Her largest suitcase is gone, too. That's why I assumed she went to her mother's." He paused for a long moment and then stood, clearing the table of our cups, the two-liter bottle of Coke, and the giant bag of chips. Lingering at the trash can, he cleared his throat. "I, uh, changed the locks on the condo."

It is hard to be privvy to another couple's lousy communication abilities. Gerry Conway was adept at throwing up a smokescreen and then at the end slipping in a key piece of info, which left me to discern what was most important when all this went down.

So, was Louise Conway really gone? Was she at her mother's house in Gary, Indiana? Or was she lurking somewhere close by, possibly with baby Melanie, hoping to get back into the condo even though Gerry changed the locks? Did he even tell her he changed them?

Further questioning revealed Louise Conway didn't have a car, had never been employed, and was probably existing on credit cards because Gerry closed their joint checking and savings accounts.

"What about her friends? Would she stay with any of them?"

Conway shook his head, and his sorrowful expression deepened. "This is probably hard to understand, but my wife has no friends. She was an only child and blamed her loneliness on that, claimed siblings would've helped her learn how to relate to other kids. Maybe she's right, I don't know. I guess I was her only friend."

Somehow this information didn't surprise me. Louise Conway, cut off from regular human interaction, with the exception of her husband, hadn't developed coping skills that came from mixing with a variety of people, didn't have a close girlfriend she could unburden herself to.

I thought of my friend Rosie driving me home when I passed out drunk in the back of my car, and her direct way of talking to me about my drinking. She didn't judge me but still told me how it affected her. Louise didn't have that kind of regular give-and-take with others. Kidnapping a baby—and possibly killing the mother—might start to seem like a reasonable way to achieve what she wanted.

Gerry Conway gave me his mother-in-law's address and phone number. He hadn't called Lou's phone directly to check if she was in Gary. I told him her cell was disconnected.

He shrugged. "Don't tell me if you find her. I know it sounds cruel, but we've been through a lot and I'm done." He drew his index finger across his throat. "Maybe early next year I'll get up the nerve to actually file for divorce, but right now I just need to be alone. I don't want to know where she is and I don't want her to find out where I am."

"I think I understand, Mr. Conway. Everyone needs space." For a moment my own statement struck a personal nerve. At least this man's logic for wanting to distance himself from his wife was the result of her persistent negative behavior. Jimmy made his distance from me permanent, and I was still trying to understand how much I was responsible for that.

"You mentioned Louise is probably living off credit cards. I'd like to track down recent expenses she might've made to get a general sense of her whereabouts. Can you help me with that?"

He motioned for me to follow him to a laptop on a small desk set in the corner next to the kitchenette. He sat and I stood next to him while he logged on and accessed the first of three credit cards in his name, but Louise was an authorized user.

All three cards showed cash advances in the first four days after Louise left home, for a total of four thousand dollars. The transactions took place on the North Side at their local bank, which housed the now-closed checking and savings accounts. Her last withdrawal was December 9.

Since then, only Gerry's activity showed on the cards. It was obvious Louise knew she could be traced through the cards and stopped using them, pointing up her guilt even more clearly to me. At the very least she kidnapped the baby, and she might have killed Margot Stuckless. I was on the right track.

I stood, thanked Gerry for his help, and gave him my card. "If you notice she's made any new transactions on the cards, give me a call. Oh, and if she happens to show up here, don't let on I'm looking for her. Again, just call me. Okay?"

"I never asked you why." Worry etched his face. "What did she do?"

"I can't say she did anything, Mr. Conway." I modulated my voice to be as soothing and warm as possible. "We're at the beginning of investigating a case and your wife's name came up as a person who could possibly help us, that's all." I hoped my lie satisfied him.

19

DANA

2:30 p.m.

Triggered by Gerry Conway's huge bag of chips—really, I wanted to eat the whole damn bag—I paid homage to the *H* in *HALT* and pulled into the closest fast-food place I could find. I got a turkey sub, diet pop, and feeling victorious at resisting the chips at Conway's, allowed myself a small bag.

While I ate, I called the number for Louise's mother. I hesitated at first. If Louise was there, it might spook her into taking off. And her mother might lie to protect her from my search.

A decidedly southern accent answered. After introducing myself, I ascertained the woman on the other end was not Louise's mother but a live-in caregiver. The mother had dementia.

"As for Louise, that one never calls, and I have yet to meet her." It had been less than a year since the caregiver started working for Louise's mother, so it didn't strike me as strange Louise hadn't visited. I asked again if Louise had contacted her mother as recently as two weeks ago or made any plans to visit soon.

"No siree. Such a shame. Children, nowadays."

I hummed my agreement. Of course, if Louise was desperate and on the run, she wouldn't be logical in her desire to escape with baby Melanie, wouldn't be planning a nice little getaway to Gary.

The caregiver gave me the same disconnected phone number I already had for Louise Conway and nothing more. I wished the woman a nice afternoon and put aside the idea of driving to Indiana unless I ran out of other options more likely to yield results.

No return call from Nuts about my earlier call and text. After talking with Gerry Conway, it was clear to me Louise had baby Melanie. I couldn't be positive she killed Margot Stuckless, but she seemed like the best bet. At the very least, a BOLO on her should go out.

I tried Nuts again. This time he picked up. "Hey."

"Listen. I've got the goods on this Stuckless case." I described my interview with Louise's husband, her obsession with having a baby, and Bear's video. "She's somewhere on the North Side, as recently as two weeks ago."

To Nuts's credit, he listened. At least he didn't cut me off or hang up on me the way I did when he wouldn't help me with Evie's protection.

"We got Mac Stuckless. Actually, Clint got him. I'm off the case and he's lead. Koz has me at City Hall with a gang task force, so I'm not even at the squad."

This was news. Rokick was a baby detective, not even broken in yet. "Koz put him on *lead*? That's ridiculous."

A slight chuckle on the other end. "Maybe. When Koz did it, I thought the same. But Clint nailed the main suspect here."

"How'd that happen?"

The gist of what Nuts relayed was simply good detective work. He and Rokick found some evidence of Stuckless and the baby at his girlfriend's place. Clint did the footwork and in interviewing Kristi Chen's neighbors and former co-workers, discovered she and Stuckless were still an item even though she had denied it in their interview.

Rokick's theory came to this: Kristi Chen and Mac Stuckless conspired to kill Margot Stuckless for the million bucks from the wife's insurance. Money was a strong motivator—in addition to Mac hating his wife—since they were both out of work.

"Clint picked up on something I suggested and ran with it. Chen told us she kicked Stuckless out a month ago, but Clint and I both agreed she should be watched and he followed up. When he staked her out, Stuckless returned, thinking they were in the clear after our interview with Chen. Got to admire Clint's work."

Admire Rokick? Since Nuts didn't hand out praise lightly, I found it galling he'd roll over so quickly and dismiss my work in favor of his temp partner. And when did he start calling him Clint?

"But Stuckless didn't have the baby, right? What about the baby? Louise Conway seems much more likely for it."

"That's the kicker. The baby was insured for another mil. She dies? Daddy and girlfriend get more money."

I lit a Kool and inhaled deeply. I had to admit money was a primary motivation for a lot of the crime we encountered. And the Amber Alert hadn't turned up anything so far, so maybe there was no kidnapping and Stuckless did kill his wife *and* his daughter. Crap.

I inhaled again, holding the smoke in deep for a long beat. My effort was useless at quelling the sudden pain in my stomach, which triggered an unexpected reminder of my miscarriage.

My next question erupted in a choppy stream of smoke. "Is the Alert cancelled?"

"No. I told Clint to keep it. In the off chance something might turn up we haven't considered."

A bit of relief there. If Louise was on the run with a baby in tow—my fervent hope—the Alert would keep the kidnapping in the news. Surely someone would spot them. Then I realized the Alert was for the baby and Mac Stuckless, not *Louise*. A city the size of Chicago teemed with women carrying babies. She had the perfect camouflage. Double crap.

"Look, let me send you this video and you'll see how deranged this woman is. You can at least get the Alert changed to her. Or put out a BOLO. There's something there, I'm sure of it." Sure of it? I sounded pathetic.

"Send it to Clint so he can decide if he wants to follow up. I'll text you his number."

"I have it," I said, picturing the business card Rokick gave me along with the invitation to his holiday party.

I had to try one more time. "I don't think the baby's dead. I still think this woman is the key. Her husband says she gets whacked out on chocolate—what about that? You know, the candy wrappers. So she just wants Melanie, somehow gets inside the house, and Margot Stuckless interrupts the kidnapping and—"

Nuts cut me off. "Look, Dana. I appreciate, uh—make that understand—your worry about the baby. But stay out of this. Don't screw things up. I think the reality is the baby's dead. Clint's pressing Kristi Chen to come clean about their plan. If she's only an accessory he can flip her about Stuckless in exchange for some leniency."

I hated how logical it all sounded. And accurate, damn it. I sucked hard on the last inch of tobacco left in my cigarette, lowered the window, and flicked it onto the street.

My partner was rarely wrong and he knew me pretty well. Maybe I was too close to this.

Nuts interrupted me right before I could reveal my most convincing fact—Stuckless's allergy to chocolate. But it's possible the information from Janey Foreman might not even be accurate, only her faulty memory. Hell, for all I knew, maybe Stuckless interrupted *Margot* bingeing on leftover Halloween candy and killed her, which meant Louise Conway was not involved. At all.

Since Nuts wasn't interested in what I'd found so far, my shiny fact would stay under wraps. For now. It was just one possibility. Sending the video to Rokick might jolt him enough to question Mac Stuckless further and maybe then he would uncover the chocolate allergy. Or at least consider Louise Conway as a suspect.

"Anything else you want to talk about?" Nuts asked.

"Just working hard on losing the weight. Treatment's been good. I'm dry. Two more weeks and I'm done." Pat me on the head.

"Good. That's what I want to hear. Gotta go."

On my way to pick up Evie and JJ, I wrestled with myself about whether or not to send Bear's video to Rokick. I had convincing arguments on both sides. I could admit being jealous of what he'd accomplished and not wanting him to succeed. Self-preservation kicks in when my own job is on the line. But...the missing baby nagged at me.

Evie, JJ, and I put in six straight hours at St. Nick's helping the other volunteers ready the gym for the holiday party. I didn't get home until a little after midnight.

Just before sliding into my futon, I listened to my better angel and sent the video to Rokick. I included the corresponding identity of and information about Louise Conway, including the woman's fragile mental state and her penchant for chocolate. I also added her husband's info, even though there was little chance Rokick would pay attention to any of it because now he had Mac Stuckless in custody.

In a burst of *what the hell*, I sent it to Nuts, too.

20

LOUISE

12/21 11:30 a.m.

Angel had been fussy all morning. She stood in the crib, her typical stance now, gripping the rail raised to keep her safe and out of trouble. She whined, sucked on her fist, cried a bit. Louise couldn't figure it out. She kept checking the little girl's diaper, but it only needed changing the one time.

Angel gnawed on the crib's rail making Louise think she was hungry, but when Louise tried to give the baby a cracker or bottle, the response was always the same: more crying. When Angel worked herself up from a crying jag into a full-blown scream, Louise relented and picked her up. Freed from the crib's confines the baby's screams subsided, and she sobbed and moaned in Louise's arms.

Up close, Louise located the source of Angel's discontent. The little one was teething. Her lower gums were red and swollen, two buds of white blooming where her bottom teeth would eventually push through. Louise hugged Angel and rubbed her back as she walked in a continuous circle around the room in an effort to sooth her. It provided small comfort.

Louise got the idea of taking Angel outside and going to a fast-food place where they could get some soft-serve ice cream. The cold would feel good on the baby's gums. And getting outside would be a welcome relief after being cooped up for so long in this stinking room. Louise wanted some chocolate in the worst way. Her candy stash had given out. Ice cream with hot fudge on it sounded like heaven. She might even find a convenience store to load up on more candy.

Louise peered out the hotel window and pointed. "Look, Angel, look. It's snowing." The baby was momentarily distracted, but then started fussing and broke into a tired cry. Louise gently guided the baby's head to rest against her shoulder and to her surprise, Angel acquiesced.

Louise gazed at the flurries whipping around in a gusty wind. Her daughter yawned amid her crying. Louise would put the baby in her crib for a nap and then they could go out for the treats.

21

DANA

Noon

E vie sat in front with me, and JJ sat in the back of my Camry so he could tease me and call me his chauffeur. Evie kept trying to engage me in conversation on the way to Saint Nick's, and even though I'm pretty adept at signing while driving, she was making me crazy. I ignored her questions about the investigation into her case. She assumed once the sketch was completed the entire Chicago Police Department would make it their mission to comb the city, 24/7, until they found the African-American woman who attacked her.

Amping up my annoyance at my mother's harangue was the fact she continued to use the sign for the N-word. I could not get her to stop using the ugly slur. I pulled up to the front of Saint Nick's, parked, and turned to my mother.

"Finish! When I know something, I'll let you know!"

Evie started in again with some vulgar signing. I raised my hand and slapped hers. She howled. From the back seat my father put a heavy hand on each of our shoulders. We both turned toward him.

"Please don't fight. We should get inside for the party." With that, he squeezed our shoulders and exited the car. I glared at Evie and she glared at me, but we retreated to our respective corners, gloves lowered. For now. Even though I couldn't see the content of her spirited signing with my father as they walked ahead of me, her movement was enough to tell me she was badmouthing me all the way.

Inside the parish hall lots of noise emanated from upstairs. As we climbed the long staircase to the large gym, my phone buzzed. Nuts. I shooed my parents to continue without me and went back outside to take the call.

"Hey. So, what'd you think when you watched the video?" I hunched my shoulder to hold my cell to my ear while I lit a Kool.

The pause on his end was long enough to make me think we'd been disconnected. "Nuts? You there?"

"I'm here. I'm trying to decide how to tell you to butt out so you'll actually *do it.*"

I jerked the phone away from my ear, his bark surprising. It takes a lot for him to be so loud. Nuts usually communicates his displeasure in a quiet but deadly manner. There's no mistaking it. Our last phone call meant we were friends again and he was talking to me; now, a day later, he was yelling at me.

"Message received, sir," I said, aiming to jostle him with some humor.

He wasn't buying it. "You will not interfere further with this investigation. Don't contact me or Clint about it. Don't talk to any of the people you've decided are involved, no matter how tangential. Do not think you can win Koz back with some fancy footwork so he'll hit his forehead and say, 'Your suspension was all a misunderstanding, Dana. All is forgiven. Please come back.'"

Even in the midst of his tongue-lashing I had to give Nuts kudos for a spot-on impression of Koz. Sounded just like him. But my admiration was momentary. His sarcasm and imperious orders, not to mention psychological analysis of my behavior, really pissed me off.

"I'll take that as a negative on the video. It's a huge help but you and *Clint* can delete it and struggle on your own."

"I deleted it as soon as I got it, and no, I didn't watch it. You want to help me? Finish treatment. Lose the weight. Get back here. That's all you have to do. And I'd say it's plenty."

I took a deep drag and exhaled the smoke in a quick rush. "Does spouting Koz's mantra give you a hard-on? Make you feel like a man telling a woman what to do? Fuck you." I stabbed the disconnect icon with my extended middle finger.

I finished the rest of my cigarette as I stood on the sidewalk outside the church. Heavy traffic blurred as cars whizzed by. Halfway down the block several cars came to an abrupt stop behind a car double-parked in the right lane. Honking and yelling ensued.

The last blocked car escaped around the offender, revealing a cherry red Jeep. It was too far to identify the driver, but the car had Fabrizio written all over it. I started to jog toward him, but he pulled into traffic and disappeared.

I returned to Saint Nick's and entered the parish hall just as Father Mik descended the long staircase.

"Dana! Hello!"

I gave a small wave but said nothing and sat at the bottom of the stairs. He joined me. I glanced at him sideways and then looked away.

"Your parents said you were here but I didn't see you up there."

I gave my cell a shake to indicate the call and then shoved it in my pocket.

"What's going on?" Father Mik's voice evidenced real concern, which

I appreciated, just not at this moment. I didn't trust my voice to respond to his question and signed instead.

"Got some bad news. Nothing important, just disappointing. How's the party going?"

He didn't sign back. "Lots of busy people having a wonderful time. Are you going to join us?" Father Mik trying to fix something when he had no idea what was wrong. But trying.

"Yeah, sure. I'll be up in a minute."

He put his arm around my shoulder and gave me a side hug, which I leaned into, because it was better than any words or signs right now.

"By the way, I got your email. We should discuss it," he said.

I started to explain but he cut me off. "Not now, of course. Whenever you're ready." He stood and climbed the stairs.

I silently fumed some more about Nuts's wholesale rejection of my minor assistance, which not only baffled me but hurt like hell. He didn't even get I was turning the information over to the active investigators instead of working it myself. Well, other than checking out Louise Conway's whereabouts. I hadn't planned on doing anything further. Truly. As for thinking Koz would dismiss my suspension, I no longer deluded myself about the possibility. A hard-won perk of not drinking.

Noises from the upper room drifted down. I put aside Fabrizio's brazen appearance here, mentally tucked Nuts's blanket rejection into a box marked *do not open*, and went upstairs. When I arrived at the large gymnasium, the party was in full swing. A huge Christmas tree greeted me at the door where I stopped for a moment. I breathed in the fresh pine scent, which felt calming, and then breathed it in some more.

My favorite event at Saint Nick's was the Thanksgiving Day feast, but this party came in a close second. The room radiated joy as deaf and hearing people arrived in droves. The party was primarily for the children of Saint Nick's, but it was obvious the adults were having at least as much fun as the kids. Games were set up around the perimeter of the gym. Little kids played Duck, Duck, Goose, while tweens favored Twister. The oldest kids congregated at the buffet tables piled with food, intent on eating and socializing like the majority of the adults.

Some of the deaf men played a spirited competition with bean bag toss while some of the deaf women, my mother included, teamed up for shuffleboard, all traditions since I was a kid. One young woman in front of Evie held a baby who looked about a year old. Evie was signing to the baby and mom at the same time, saying what a pretty girl she was and trying to elicit a few signs from the little one.

Next thing I knew the woman handed the baby to Evie, clearly thrilled to be the recipient, and headed for the bathroom. The little girl was momentarily stricken and started winding up to cry, but my mother managed to jolly her out of it by unhooking one of her jangly earrings and using it as a distraction.

Evie caught me watching and pasted me with an eyebrow raising question—no signs needed—her expression roughly translating as *well, when are you going to produce one of these*? I didn't respond. No surprise she wants grandchildren, as does JJ. Neither my twin brother or younger sister are married or even in relationships, so no children in the offing there. No. Somehow, it's always my responsibility to provide for my parents' wants and needs, whether as the only hearing person in the family or because I exhibited a penchant as the reliable one, even when I was young.

Seeing Evie bouncing the little girl in her arms, so happy, so fulfilled in the grandmother role, my earlier aggravation with her evaporated, replaced for a moment with an image of three generations of Demeter women: Evie, me, and my daughter.

A couple arrived at the door and jostled me out of my daydream. They hesitated. Several children behind them ran into the room and scattered toward various games. I smiled at the couple and only then noticed the woman held the hand of a boy who mostly hid behind her. His other arm was casted up to his shoulder and supported in a sling. Mickey Maitland.

I signed hello to the couple after ascertaining they were deaf. *"Come on in. Lots of food and games."* I gestured at the room with a wide wave of my arm and then pointed at the buffet tables heavy with food. *"And lots of socializing, of course."* The couple chuckled, agreeing it was the most important aspect of any deaf gathering.

Mickey gazed at my face, but he gave no indication of recognizing me as the person who found him locked in a closet where he'd spent the first ten years of his life, put there by Flora, his biological mother. I squatted down to his level.

"Hi. Hi. My name," I tapped the letter 'D' over my heart several times but not fingerspelling it out. Mickey was deaf but had no language— ASL or otherwise. He looked at me and then up at his foster mother. She encouraged him to copy my introduction, showing him how to substitute his name sign, which turned out to be the letter 'M' on his upper arm. I asked about this placement of his name sign.

"We're trying to give him the idea he's strong," his mother said, smiling at her husband, who raised his eyebrows at me and then glanced at Mickey, a cue for me to watch their interchange.

He touched Mickey on the shoulder to get his attention. Instead, the boy looked at the floor. The mother squatted in front of Mickey and placed her hands on his cheeks, gently positioning his head to turn his gaze toward his father. The father struck a he-man pose and pointed at Mickey, repeating the sequence several times. Mickey watched but did nothing. His mother stroked his cheeks and then formed the letter 'M' on her hand and tapped it on Mickey's upper arm. After a long moment he placed his fingertips next to hers.

His foster parents smiled and nodded, signed *yes*, and we all signed a hearty *thumbs up* to Mickey. The trio headed into the room, taking it in slow steps so Mickey could shuffle along, his legs atrophied and bowed from his imprisonment.

At the buffet table Father Mik welcomed the foster couple and knelt down in front of Mickey, taking the boy's free hand and holding it to his own cheek for a long moment, letting Mickey pat his beard. Then Father Mik signed *eat* several times and waved his hand at all the food. Mickey immediately copied the sign. The couple smiled and laughed, signed *yes, food, right, good boy.* Father Mik stood and the trio inched toward the stack of plates.

I jogged over to the priest. I gestured at Mickey. "Amazing to see him." The last time, the only time really, was when I lifted him from the floor of his closet prison, his legs too weak to support his body. Hard to believe it was only a few weeks ago.

"I'm heartened the Sampson family is willing to foster him. You could not ask for a better placement, African-American parents who are deaf taking in a mixed-race child who is also deaf. I expect Mickey will thrive in their home," Father Mik said.

"Will Flora lose custody?"

"That remains to be seen. Her other children are in foster care while the criminal justice system sorts out her case."

I teared up at the mention of those children, in particular Emma. At five, she was the youngest of Flora's six kids. She captured me with her innocence, eventually leading me to where Flora stowed Mickey. An unfortunate result of Emma spilling the family secret meant she was separated from her mother and her sibs. I still couldn't shake the image of the hysterical little girl, her arms outstretched to me, as the social worker struggled to secure Emma's seatbelt in the emergency services van. I wiped my eyes on my sleeve.

Father Mik patted my shoulder. "I understand how you feel. Children are most often the victims and bearers of suffering in the world."

"Gee, Father Mik. Thanks for cheering me up."

He laughed. "Well, the rest of my pitch includes hope." He gestured at Mickey and his foster parents. "As long as there are people in the world who follow what Jesus teaches us, the suffering will not be in vain."

I didn't know or care much about the Jesus part, having quit the church as a teenager, but I could agree with the people part. Father Mik pulled a folded paper from his pocket and handed it to me.

I opened it. A crude drawing of a lone tree with three black branches and bright green scribbles at each end suggesting leaves. "What is this?"

Father Mik smiled. "Mickey drew that. His foster mother gave it to me yesterday because she wanted me to know he was happy. She said that's all he draws, picture after picture, of the same tree."

I studied the picture by a boy locked in a closet for most of his ten years, let out only at night to sleep on a bare mattress with his other brothers and sisters. What would a tree mean to him? I started to hand it back but Father Mik told me to keep it. "You're the reason he sees trees now."

I folded the paper and slid it into my back pocket.

Someone flashed the gym lights on and off several times to garner the crowd's attention. The adults gathered the children and teens to begin the traditional festive whacking of the piñata, which hung from the ceiling in the center of the room. I didn't recognize the shape.

"What's with the weird shape? Don't we usually have a donkey?" I asked Father Mik.

"Yes. This year the piñata was made by one of our parishioners from Mexico. She taught me something new. That shape," he indicated its roundness with short, pointy spikes emanating around the surface, "can be one of two types. If it has seven points, they represent the seven deadly sins." He arched his eyebrows at me. "You do remember the seven deadly sins from your confirmation days, don't you?"

I chuckled. "Sure. PALE GAS. Pride, Anger, Lust, Envy, Gluttony, Avarice, and Sloth."

"Bravo, bravo. Good to know my catechism class had some lasting effect. So. Here is where it gets interesting. The baton we use to break open the piñata represents love. And the candy that pours from inside is the sweet reward for overcoming those sins."

"What's the other type? The donkey?"

"No. The shape is basically the same as this one but has ten points. I am sure you can guess what they represent."

I only half-listened as Father Mik continued, my attention drawn to what was transpiring below the piñata. Two deaf men formed the fireman's seat with their hands and Mickey's foster father lifted the boy onto it. Mickey grasped a small baton in his good hand, his thin arm unable to support a larger baseball bat one of the teenagers held. The two men lifted Mickey within striking distance of the piñata. Mickey did nothing. He looked at the crowd below as if to say, *okay, what do you expect me to do here?*

The teenager with the bat waved his hand to get Mickey's attention, which didn't work, so he positioned himself in the boy's line of sight and began jabbing at the piñata with the bat in short, punchy shots. When he pointed back and forth between Mickey and the piñata, Mickey kind of woke up and raised his arm holding the baton. He stroked the piñata with several small thumps.

Everyone watching—everyone—held up their arms and quickly twisted their open hands back and forth at the wrist. Deaf applause. The fluttering hands grabbed Mickey's attention. He held up the baton for a moment as if conducting a symphony, and keeping his gaze on the crowd beneath him tapped the piñata again. The applause was visually overwhelming and interspersed with people signing *good! Right! Finish! Again, again!*

The two men lowered Mickey onto a chair placed in the circle of kids so he could watch the rest of the custom. When the piñata finally cracked open and the candy cascaded onto the floor, Mickey struggled from his chair and joined the other kids, grabbing candy with his good hand and stuffing it in his pocket.

Later, driving Evie and JJ home, the conversation revolved around excitement at Mickey's small but real progress. I half-wished I could tell my parents about my plan to donate Fabrizio's 45K to Father Mik to help support Mickey's foster family. But opening that can of worms, especially with Evie, would subject me to her inquisition. I had no wish for my parents to find out about my DUI, job suspension, or treatment for drinking. Hard to admit, even at thirty years old, but a tiny shred of me still wanted my parents' approval.

22

LOUISE

With the baby bundled up, cap on and scarf hiding the bottom portion of Angel's face, Louise threw on her own winter jacket. She stowed the baby in the stroller—one she guessed was a high-priced gift at a baby shower for the Monster—and made her way down to the lobby.

The girl at the desk gave her directions to the closest ice cream place, which turned out to be more than two miles away. There was no way Louise could walk there. She swore at the girl and then abruptly burst into tears because her plans were stymied.

Louise's crying set Angel off, both of them sobbing uncontrollably. Louise hefted the baby from the stroller and tried to soothe her.

"There's a bus that goes right there," the girl said. She gave Louise explicit directions on how to catch the bus, which stopped right up the street and would drop her off in front of the ice cream place. "Do you have a Ventra card?"

"What? No. No credit cards."

The girl explained Louise needed this card to get around on public transportation. She pulled her wallet out of her back pocket and plucked out a blue card. "It looks like this. You can't use cash on the bus or train anymore."

This was too much for Louise. "But I only have cash." Her voice wavered. Angel picked up on it and started crying again. Louise jostled her and rocked back and forth. "I—I don't know what to do."

The girl looked at her card, then at Louise, then at the baby, and placed the card on the desk between them.

"Here. You can borrow mine and then give me the cost of your rides. If you're going there and coming back that'll be four-fifty. Okay?"

Louise put Angel back in the stroller and gave the girl five dollars.

The bus ride turned out to be easier than Louise worried about while waiting in the enclosed bus shelter. The driver was patient and held the bus door open as she wrangled the stroller to its collapsed size, all while trying to keep Angel trapped between her legs so she couldn't wander off. He even grabbed the stroller from her as she climbed aboard with Angel on her hip. He seemed to ken she couldn't manage the two steps into the bus unless she used the handrail. An unwelcome reminder of how much her weight was a literal burden.

Louise settled into a seat at the front near the driver and let Angel stand on the seat next to her. She wrapped her arm around the little girl's waist for protection. Angel grabbed the metal pole next to her seat and seemed mesmerized by the oncoming vehicles appearing and disappearing through the front window. The earlier snow had stopped.

Louise felt the familiar creep of paranoia. Trying to appear nonchalant, she scanned the interior of the bus. Two teenagers sat at the very back, both intent on their cell phones and paying no attention to her. One elderly woman dozed, her head against the window, a few seats in front of the teens. Across from Louise a man with gnarled hands held a newspaper up, obscuring his face. The bus was otherwise empty. She took a deep breath. No one seemed a threat.

She turned her attention back to Angel. The little girl was gnawing and slobbering all over the pole she still gripped. Should she pull her away ? It was probably filthy. Louise reconsidered. Angel was trying to soothe her gums, and Louise didn't want to antagonize her. If they caused a scene in this enclosed space, people would remember her. The ice cream would help the little one. Then Louise would have to find something more portable to give her for teething. And she would. That was her job now.

When the bus arrived at the fast-food place, the driver again was almost chivalrous toward Louise. He put the bus in park, carried the stroller down the two steps and opened it so she only had to step out and place Angel in it.

"Cute little fella. What's his name?"

Louise straightened up, alert. "Oh. He, uh, he's called Mel. For Melvin. But I like Mel better." She reached down to rearrange the scarf around the little girl's face.

"Mel? Okay, Mel. You and your mommy have a good rest of your day. Stay safe." He patted the baby's head and climbed into the bus. The door whooshed shut and he pulled away.

Louise stood still for a long moment watching the retreating bus. She raised her hand in a late farewell to the driver. Her heart had lifted when he referred to her as mommy. And he fell for the disguise, buying Angel as a little boy. A tinge of hope settled on her. Maybe this would all work out. A little more practice taking the baby out in public before returning home to Gerry and starting their new life as parents, as a family.

But right now, ice cream! Angel started fussing again. To avoid attention from passersby she plucked the baby out of the stroller and soothed her a bit before entering the store.

23

LOUISE

4:00 p.m.

T he trip back to the hotel was murder. The bus was standing room only, full of rowdy drunk men who boarded from some hockey game. Late afternoon shoppers crowded the aisle with their packages, making it impossible to navigate, and reminded her Christmas was next week.

No one gave her a seat and she stood, Angel on her hip, the stroller left at the bus stop because the driver wouldn't help her bring it on board. Her feet were frozen because she had no boots, her shoes soaked from the heavy snow that started up again while waiting for the bus back. She gripped the bag holding two large chocolate milk shakes, those more important than the abandoned stroller anyway.

Dried evidence of the ice cream Angel had devoured remained on her face. Louise didn't have any of those wipes she knew most mothers carried. Another thing to buy. She didn't bother to clean up the little girl because it would interfere with the soothing effect of the ice cream. Angel always pulled away when Louise tried to wipe her face.

At the hotel, Louise entered the lobby but saw no one at the front desk. Angel was fussing again and Louise hurried toward the elevators. She would have to return the bus card later.

Inside their room, Louise deposited Angel in the crib and stowed the milkshakes in the mini fridge. Angel started crying and chewing on the railing of her rectangular prison. Louise scouted around the room for something to give the baby to chew on. Nothing. She wet a washcloth and approached Angel to wipe down the little girl's face. Angel grabbed at the washcloth and sucked on it, giving Louise an idea.

She left Angel in the crib and exited the room. At the ice machine she filled a bucket with ice and hurried back to the room. Angel's crying morphed into screaming. Louise quickly packed the washcloth with ice, wrapped a rubber band around it, and handed it to the little girl.

The ice pack was magic. No more screaming. The baby lay down and held the soothing pack against her open mouth. Louise sighed. This was what it meant to be a mother.

24

DANA

12/22 8:00 a.m.

As I whisked egg whites and assembled some veggies for an omelet, the radio announced showers throughout the day and a high of forty-five degrees, downright balmy for December in Chicago. A short while later, I sat at my desk and tucked into another successful meal on my PP food plan. Yesterday, the dessert table at Saint Nick's holiday party didn't upend my plan, either. Funny thing about that. Eating one brownie or one cookie never stopped there for me, something took over and I was on my merry way to eating a dozen sweets. It seemed the same with booze. One drink started a chain reaction and ended with me drunk.

Washing the dishes and actually drying them and putting them away gave me an odd sense of satisfaction. I paused at my fridge. Mickey's tree picture, secured there with tape, reminded me of Father Mik's words about suffering not happening in vain when people helped other people. Especially children. Imagining Mickey's new family and my small part in his emancipation gave me a boost. I wanted more of this kind of feeling instead of the hurt and anger I harbored against Nuts at his clear rejection. Sort of like wanting more cookies, except healthier.

It would be easy enough to let go of any involvement in the Margot Stuckless murder investigation, but what about the baby? Louise Conway's depression at not being able to have a child, after all she and her husband went through to conceive, could easily spur her to more desperate measures like kidnapping. Whether that drove her to murder I couldn't say for certain without more evidence.

My anger at Nuts melted into annoyance as I worried about the missing baby. I wasn't ready to give up if it meant finding her. The info from Gerry Conway, in addition to Bear's video—which Nuts had to watch in order to understand Louise's frame of mind—were key to pursuing Louise Conway. I was sure of it.

Since Nuts deleted the video and in no uncertain terms told me to butt out, it seemed the only way to reach him would be in person. Clint Rokick's party—kind of an open house, drop-by-if-you-want deal, from 1-8 p.m.—would be perfect. If nothing else, I could literally shove the video in Nuts's face and make him watch. I was sure Louise Conway made the case herself when she reached for the baby and Margot Stuckless freaked out.

But as I settled in to read the paper, drink coffee, and smoke cigarettes on this dreary, rainy day, my resistance to attending the party escalated. The lousy weather, slated to continue all day, was one factor. Hunkering down in my cozy studio to laze and keep the world limited to the news or something on TV seemed much more inviting than facing the other cops from the squad. I hadn't seen since most of them since my suspension.

God only knows what kind of gossip already circulated about me. I didn't need to be subjected to pity, curiosity, or dumb cop jokes. But Nuts would be there, I was sure, now that he and *Clint* were such buddies. I would stay only as long as it took to talk to Nuts.

My mission was established: Lead this particular horse to water and dunk his head in it.

25

LOUISE

8:45 a.m.

Louise slept later than usual. Angel routinely woke her up at six, crying from a wet diaper or hunger, and sometimes screaming when both were true. Now, the clock said almost nine. She hefted her sluggish body from the bed and stretched, then approached the crib.

The perfect little girl, still asleep, sported the griminess of an imperfect little boy. Dried chocolate ice cream still crusted her cheeks and chin, and her choppy hair stuck out in uneven patches. The teething washcloth lay deflated next to Angel's head, a large wet spot spreading underneath.

Angel heaved a noisy sigh, her breathing loud and ragged. This was new. The baby's cheeks were a bit flushed with pink, prompting Louise to reach out and touch them. Angel was warm but not overly so and rolled toward her emanating a farting noise.

A powerful stink arose and Louise quickly retrieved a fresh diaper. When she flipped Angel onto her back the little girl woke up but didn't challenge the diaper change, just watched Louise in a half-lidded stare.

Louise ripped open the tabs of the soiled diaper and lowered the front, but the overpowering smell—as bad as a rotting animal—forced her to back off from the crib. She hurried over to the window and raised it further, taking a minute to breathe in fresh air.

Louise returned to Angel. She held her breath and quickly swapped out the soiled diaper, which revealed the source of the stink, a hideous green diarrhea. She neglected to clean the baby's bottom, having no latex gloves to protect her hands, and let the fresh diaper cover over the remaining mess.

It never occurred to her the baby might get sick. She had no way to take Angel's temperature. The small arsenal of baby paraphernalia she'd assembled in haste held nothing helpful.

Margot the Monster always presented Angel as healthy, clean, and dressed with care. Perfect. And really, the baby was all Louise wanted. When she'd gone to the Monster's house and found the sliding door to the bedroom unlocked, she took it as a sign she could enter. Freeing Angel from the crib was easy.

But the Monster interfered. She came into the baby's room, her phone clutched in her hand, and started yelling at Louise. She ordered Louise to let go of the baby, like she had cooties or something, so of course she had to shove the woman away. Was it her fault the Monster fell over and hit her head? Angel was hers, in her arms, sleepy from her morning nap, snuggling her head into Louise's chest, which felt natural, right, and complete.

Until that godawful woman came to and began to scream and scratch at Louise's legs. Louise wasn't about to let go of the baby, *her* baby, so with her arms full she did the only thing she could think of. She collapsed her full weight onto the Monster's head, sitting on her, pushing her screaming face into oblivion, not letting her breathe one more second on this earth.

It didn't take long. The Monster struggled some trying to push her off, but Louise had more than enough weight to grind her backside into the nose and mouth beneath her, cutting off any possible air supply until the thrashing stopped.

The baby started fussing then. Louise stood and thrust her back in the crib. She circled the body on the floor, dipping her hand into her jacket pocket to retrieve bite-sized Butterfingers, ripping open the candy and ceremoniously dropping the wrappers on the Monster while she downed the sweet relief of chocolate and peanut butter, so ingeniously married in the portable morsels.

That was the first time the baby had extended her arms, crying *mama, mama,* just for her. Just for her.

But now Angel was again dead to the world except for the noisy rough breathing. Louise would let her sleep, which would help if the baby was sick, wouldn't it?

Remembering the Butterfinger candy triggered her craving for chocolate. She opened the mini fridge and pulled out the chocolate milkshake from yesterday's jaunt, preparing to drink it down instead of using a straw. Uncapping it revealed a melted sludge with an oily residue floating on top. Ruined. Why couldn't it stay nice, like liquid ice cream? Another small thing adding to her stress.

At the bathroom sink she made to pour the ruined milkshake down the drain but stopped. She closed her eyes and guzzled it, not stopping to taste it, savoring the sugar hit on her empty stomach.

While Angel slept, Louise could take a quick shower. She shut the window because rain was blowing in. Rain in December? But even though it was warm enough to not be snow, the air was still chilly. She wondered if, in trying to rid the room of the garbage and dirty diaper stink, the cold air caused Angel's ragged breathing.

As Louise stepped into the shower, someone knocked on the door and a woman's voice announced she was from housekeeping. Louise ignored the summons, but the woman repeated her presence and stated she was unlocking the door. Louise donned a robe and hurried to head off the intrusion, but she was too late. A young Latina in a blue uniform stood at the open door, her face scrunched at the room's stench.

Louise lunged at the woman. "Get out! Get out!"

The housekeeper backed up a step and gestured at the six garbage bags lined up along the wall. "For the garbage, yes? I will take. Okay?"

"No! Go away!" Louise grabbed her diaper bag and swung it at the woman, catching her squarely in the chest. She doubled over with a grunt. Louise advanced and shoved her into the hall, then slammed the door shut and threw the deadbolt.

26

DANA

1:00 p.m.

I had to park four blocks from the 'L' stop closest to my studio in order to catch the train to Rokick's condo downtown. It was cheaper to take the train than pay for sky-high parking in the South Loop, and the 'L' stopped half a block from his place. The rain continued throughout the train trip and when I exited and made it down to street level, the wind blew decidedly colder.

Rokick's condo was one of the newer ones sprouting all over the South Loop for young professionals not yet married, or those without kids, who rejected owning a car and could walk or Uber it to work. Inside the lobby, a real marble floor greeted me. Near the elevator, a fountain hosted twin dolphins spewing water at each other, and a security guard stood stationed behind a podium.

There were no buttons for the elevator. The guard asked me who I was visiting. Still searching for buttons, I stuttered Rokick's name and then hoped the guard didn't think I was a weirdo. He did something on a tablet and the elevator doors opened. I was going to ask him how

I would get back down later on but reconsidered. Rokick would probably wow us all with a similar gizmo. No buttons inside, either.

The elevator whooshed me up to the top floor and opened onto a hall with more pinkish marble flooring. The wall to my right was solid glass facing east and revealed a brief portion of downtown and Lake Michigan beyond, although the intense cloud cover and non-stop rain made it difficult to appreciate the view. I turned to my left and began walking down the hall when a door opened at the far end and Rokick stepped out and waved.

"Down here!"

I returned his wave and hurried toward him. On the train ride I began to get nervous about who would be at the party, how much I would tell the other cops about my suspension, and most of all, what I should drink. In IOP, Marvin made us draw up specific plans for when we were in such situations. At the time I thought it was pretty lame. I usually drank at home. Alone.

But here were all kinds of reasons to have a plan. A tonic water with lime could pass for a mixed drink and might keep questions at bay, although anyone who really knows me knows I'm a beer and wine drinker. Hard liquor screws with my head. A mock vodka tonic would work and I wouldn't look like a loser around the others, most of them typical booze hounds who considered teetotalers suspect.

"Dana! Great to see you. Glad you could make it." Rokick reached for my jacket as I unloaded it. He stepped inside and let me pass in front of him. I caught a whiff of his cologne, a heady mix of woodsy and dead animal. He closed the door, and we stood in front of the closet in the foyer where he hung up my jacket. Deep voices hummed in the next room along with the clink of glasses and the aroma of something warm and cheesy.

"How're you doing, Rokick? I almost didn't come because of the lousy weather. Still raining out there."

"Yeah? It's almost Christmas, for chrissakes. Bring on the snow." I followed him to the entrance of a large living room. The entire north end was capped in floor-to-ceiling glass, which wrapped around a bit on the east side, sure to reveal a glorious view of the sunrise over the lake. I stopped and admired the architecture.

"This place must've set you back," I said. Having grown up in a working-class neighborhood in a small bungalow on the South Side, I didn't have many opportunities to observe how the other half lived. Being a cop only reinforced the experience.

Rokick scrubbed his hand over his face, leaving his cheeks and forehead pink. "Truth? My father bought me this place when I graduated from college."

My father bought me a bouquet of flowers when I graduated from the police academy. "Oh?"

"Yeah. It was a reward he set up. He wanted me to stay in school, but I thought that was for suckers and eggheads. He didn't want me to be a cop."

"But it looks like you got your way. And scored a prime place to live." I couldn't help the envy creeping into my voice. A happy couple now occupied my former home, the one where Jimmy and I once shared a life. Tonight, I would return to my dingy, one-room studio.

Rokick gave me a funny look. "Yeah, well." He waved his arms at the room full of cops, most from our squad. "There's lots of food over there," he pointed at a large banquet table loaded with catering trays and a dessert table farther on. "Drinks are there." He gestured at a bar fashioned from what looked like cedar wood, a mirror spanning the wall behind it. "You'll have to help yourself. The guy I wanted to bartend called in sick at the last minute."

I wanted to ask Rokick if he got Bear's video I sent, if he'd watched it, what he and Nuts thought about Louise Conway as a prime suspect. I hesitated. He walked me over to the buffet table, but before I could ask about the video he started to regale me with the story of how he caught Mac Stuckless.

I interrupted. "So, you didn't watch the video?"

"Oh, I did, I did. It doesn't add up to me, you know? The vic's husband's got so much more reason to kill her. I mean, a woman like in that video? Just 'cause she tried to hold the baby doesn't prove anything."

"You get what I sent you about Gerry Conway? He's got a lot to say about his wife's mental problems."

Rokick shoved both his hands in his pockets and turned away. "Look. Demeter. I watched the video, like you asked. It didn't change my mind. Why would I waste my time talking to her husband?"

I was unsurprised Rokick didn't follow up with Gerry Conway. But I was surprised—and annoyed—Nuts didn't bother telling Rokick about Louise's baby hunger casting her as a viable suspect. "Where are you on the Amber Alert?"

Here Rokick appeared stricken. "Nowhere." He picked up a plate of canapés from the table and offered it to me. I waved him off. He pinched a cheese and cracker combo from the array, stuffed the whole thing in his mouth and placed the plate back on the table. While he crunched he held up an index finger, chewed some more, and then swallowed.

"Hey. You're a woman. Lemme get your take on it," he said. A few cracker crumbs spewed from his mouth and landed on his navy sweater.

His theory echoed what Nuts already told me, but I let him ramble. "I mean, she said it herself. Stuckless hated his wife, wanted to see her dead. Wouldn't take much for Chen to push him into acting on it, them both needing dough and all. I got her on house arrest for harboring and being an accessory. She's stalling for immunity but that ain't gonna happen."

I nodded. "Okay. But what about the baby? Where is she?"

Rokick stuffed another combo in his mouth, again holding up an index finger, and chewed. He reminded me of a cow grinding away.

"Stuckless is putting on a good show of being upset his daughter is missing," he put quotes around the last word, "but I got him. Together, both life insurance policies point two million fingers at him."

I shrugged, trying for non-committal. Rokick wasn't buying it.

"Aww, don't be jealous I caught him." He actually patted me on the head. Asshole. "Your theory with the wacko woman stealing the baby doesn't work. Mine makes a lot more sense—dollars and *cents*—get it, Demeter?" He laughed.

I had to admit there was *that.*

"Here's another idea," I said. I didn't want to agree with his theory. Mostly I wanted to screw with his mind and make him squirm. "The girlfriend convinces Stuckless to kill his wife for the money, yes. But," I held up my index finger to mimic him, "her real reason is that she wants the *baby.* So he kills his wife and gives the baby to the girl-friend, and she hides the baby somewhere. I mean, otherwise, why clam up and demand immunity?"

"Hey! That was *my* idea!"

"What're you talking—"

Rokick chuckled. "But I threw it away. Didn't make any sense. I mean, when I nailed Stuckless sneaking back to his girlfriend at two o'clock in the morning, he woulda had the kid with him, right? I mean, the guy's parents are dead, her parents are in New York, so there was no time and no place to stash the kid."

A third cracker with cheese arrived in Rokick's mouth, and he furi-ously chewed while looking at the floor. "No. That baby's dead, Demeter. I'm sure of it. Abandonato, too."

My evil side decided to goad him and I leaned in. "If the two of you are so convinced the baby's *dead*, why keep the Amber Alert?"

Rokick crossed his arms and nodded as if seriously considering my question. "Yeah. Yeah, I wanted to cancel it but my partner," he stopped and gave me fake embarrassment, "Abandonato told me I should keep it active. For a while, anyway."

Don't react to his bait about Nuts, I told myself. A tiny part of me wanted to mention Mac Stuckless's allergy to chocolate. The Butterfinger wrappers—to me—indicated someone other than Mac, and Louise Conway was foremost in my thinking. Rokick couldn't agree with my theory because he wasn't operating with complete information. Then again, he didn't dig as deep as I did and settled for an obvious suspect.

I waved my hand dismissively and stuffed my anger. "So that's my womanly take on it, Rokick. Just my two cents." I held back saying anything more. I doubted if he had other theories to toss around about how Stuckless killed his daughter and hid the body. Clearly Rokick was satisfied with his big catch, satisfied with money as the explanation for both murders, and with the exception of the Amber Alert, not actively searching for baby Melanie.

One of the caterers cut in on our conversation with a problem needing Rokick's attention, so I sauntered over to the bar where Jack O'Malley, a longtime detective and a friendly face, seemed to be standing in for the missing bartender.

"Hey, Demeter. Rokick told me you might make an appearance tonight. Enjoying your time off?"

"Jack, Jack. Yeah, almost didn't come but then I knew I might see your ugly mug and decided it was worth slogging here in the rain. And you know, I was right. You're a sight for sore eyes. Or is it the sight of you makes my eyes sore?" I posed in mock consideration.

He groaned at the old jibe. "You haven't lost your lousy sense of humor, I'm afraid. Let me make you something. What'll you have?" He gestured at the double row of liquor bottles glowing in the reflected light from the fireplace.

I waited a beat, my formulated plan for just this question suddenly a big blank.

"Or you could try the punch. With or without vodka." His voice leaned on the second option. Two large bowls of deep-red punch sat on the end of the dessert table. I wondered if Jack had the inside scoop on my failing the Breathalyzer test Koz administered prior to putting me on suspension. Or maybe Jack was trying to find out if the rumors were true.

"You know, that looks really good," I said. Jack walked with me, and while I filled a large plastic cup, he caught me up on his wife and kids. He also took in my choice of the virgin punch. I listened to more jabbering about his home life, scanning the room for my absent partner. I berated myself for not checking with Rokick about Nuts attending the party, and wished I hadn't left my warm, cozy place and come all the way down here. In the rain, no less.

A few of the cops from the squad stopped by for a quick hello while Jack and I talked, but most of them remained in their small cliques arranged around the living room and in the kitchen. I refilled my cup with punch, the sugar in it a real treat since I wasn't eating or drinking anything else not in my food plan.

After about half an hour of strained socializing, I decided if Nuts didn't show in the next thirty minutes, I'd book. He was the only reason for my attendance. Since Rokick figured he had the Stuckless case sewn up, I needed to convince my former partner why this was wrong.

During the next half hour, Rokick flitted around acting the courteous host, and twice refilled Jack's drink and my punch cup. I loosened the fashion scarf around my neck because the room was heating up as more people arrived.

Koz was one of those people. I debated approaching him. We hadn't seen each other since his sharp command to me to attend to my *issues*. Rokick brought me another cup of punch, which I downed quickly because I was overly warm now, and the stuffy air in the room made it hard to breathe. I went to the bathroom and splashed cold water on my face. My flushed reflection in the mirror appeared fuzzy. My inner debate subsided, giving me the courage to talk with Koz. Besides, the other cops here would note I avoided him and only add to the gossip about me.

I returned to the punch bowl to get a refill. I didn't seem able to slake my thirst or cool off. At the end of the dessert table only one bowl remained, the tag for the non-alcoholic drink next to it. I filled my cup, drank it down, and refilled it. Where was Koz?

I spied him at the entrance of the living room talking with Rokick, who was handing Koz his coat. His appearance was a short one, and he was preparing to leave. I gulped my punch and clutched my empty cup as I made my way over to talk to my boss.

He spoke first. "Demeter."

"Hi, Koz. Isn't this a great party?" I turned to Rokick. "A hearty party," I said, saluting him with my cup and chuckling at the silly rhyme. Koz eyed me.

"I'm doing what you said, Koz. Working on those *issues*." It came out sounding harsher than I intended. "You know, what we talked about. In the parking lot." I struggled to make sense. Neither Rokick or Koz said anything. Rokick offered to get me another drink and I handed him my empty cup.

"He's a great guy," I said to Koz, nodding at Rokick's retreating figure. "Really. Nuts is lucky to have him. Hell, the whole squad is. Better than with me, right? He doesn't have *issues*."

Rokick returned with two small glass punch cups instead of my large plastic one. I drank the first one down. "Do you, Clint?"

"Huh?"

"Have *issues.* That's what I have. That's what makes me so hard to work with, right Koz?" I toasted Rokick with the second cup, closed my eyes, and chugged it. When I opened them up to see why Koz wasn't responding, he had disappeared and the front door in the foyer was closing. Suddenly Nuts appeared and pulled on my arm.

"There you are! I've been looking for you." My voice, a happy singsong; his face, a serious mask. "What's wrong? Come on! Smile, partner!"

"Let's go. You're going home."

"No, no, no! This party's just getting started. Right, Clint? Your hearty party?" I laughed again at the silly rhyme.

Nuts pulled hard on my arm, and I stumbled to my knees. The living room chatter went dead, everyone staring at us. I struggled to my feet, still holding the two glass punch cups.

"Hey!" I waved both hands at the group, toasting them with the cups. I laughed but only got a silent stare in return.

"Fuck all 'a you!" I aimed the first cup at a group sitting on the couch but it didn't get far and dropped harmlessly on the snow-white carpet. Rokick hurried over to pick it up, remnants of the deep red juice dripping from the cup and leaving a stain.

The opulence of his condo and his ease in acquiring it surfaced in a bolt of envy. Why was this guy, this guy who didn't even need to work because Daddy had plenty of money, why was *this* guy my replacement?

No one spoke. Rokick was on his knees using his handkerchief to soak up the red blotch, to little effect. He glanced back at me. "Guess the rumors about you are true, Demeter."

I squinted at him and launched the second cup. "Fuck you, Rokick!" The cup bounced off his arm. Nuts got behind me, pushing me into the foyer. He found my jacket and thrust it at me.

"Come on. I'm driving you home." He yanked me out the front door.

"Okay, okay. Christ! Quit pulling on me."

By the time the elevator reached the lobby I managed to get my jacket on, although the zipper was impossible. Nuts wouldn't talk to me. He handed his ticket stub to an attendant summoned by the security guy —guess *partners* get the perks—and a few minutes later his Prius glided up out front.

The security guy gestured at the glass-fronted entrance. "You take 'er real easy out there, ma'am. It's all ice."

27

LOUISE

1:00 p.m.

Angel was too heavy. Louise stopped walking, shifted the baby from her left to right hip, and then continued trudging to the Walgreens three blocks from the hotel. The balmy weather still held and the rain continued. She had no umbrella. And anyway, she needed both hands to carry the baby.

The raised hood on Louise's coat kept the rain off but was getting soggy. Angel's little Cubs cap didn't help much, so Louise draped her scarf over the baby's head. The heat from Angel's head where it nestled on Louise's neck proved oddly comforting.

The heavy sleep worried Louise. The little girl didn't wake up even with the jostling when Louise transferred her to the other hip. More worrying was Angel not eating anything today and the gross diarrhea.

Louise considered a hospital ER but quickly dismissed the idea. And it wasn't as if she could drop the baby off and leave, could she? No hospitals. Too risky.

The store was fairly empty. Then Louise remembered Christmas was in a few days, so of course, most people would be quickly buying those last-minute gifts or traveling to be with their families. She pushed away thoughts of her husband, Gerry, in their quiet condo, but part of her yearned for the clean, orderly home she'd made there, where she wanted to bring Angel.

Louise walked up to the pharmacy section at the back of the store and stood at the window marked for prescription drop-off. One lone pharmacist worked behind the counter filling a bottle with some kind of white pills. Louise waited for him to notice her. When he didn't, she sat down in one of the three chairs lining the wall. She needed a break, her feet killing her. Angel stirred a slight bit but didn't wake, and Louise sat for a short while, letting the little girl's body drape across her own.

Another customer arrived at the pharmacy and when the pharmacist ignored her, too, the woman rapped on the counter to get his attention. He hurried over to her.

The woman gestured at Louise. "She was here before me."

Louise was startled at the attention. She pulled Angel's cap lower around her head and shifted the baby to hide her face. "Oh. That's okay. You go ahead."

The woman finished quickly. The pharmacist turned his attention to Louise and asked for the name of the person whose medication she was picking up.

Louise stayed seated, not wanting to lift Angel again for a while or to expose the baby's face to the man behind the counter.

"No, no medication. I, uh, my son has diarrhea and doesn't seem well. Can you suggest something for me to give him?"

The pharmacist frowned. "Have you called your pediatrician?"

Louise shook her head. "We're from out of town. Visiting family. I don't think it's very serious."

"You can still call your doctor, can't you? Or Zoom with them? There's always someone on call with urgent care centers, even on holidays." He said this with a smile and Louise could tell he was trying to be kind. She didn't have any more lies he would believe, and she started to panic.

"Okay. Here's the truth. I don't have insurance. I don't have a doctor. Can't you just help me?"

The pharmacist walked around the side of the counter and came to sit next to Louise. "Let me see." He touched the baby's shoulder. Louise pulled away.

"No! Don't touch him." She hugged Angel closer and hid the baby's face from the pharmacist.

"What are his symptoms?"

Louise described the diarrhea and not eating.

"Okay, I think you would do well to give him some Pedialyte right now, to make sure he doesn't get dehydrated from the diarrhea. Other than that, all I can suggest is you take him to the ER, let a doctor look him over. I can't make any diagnosis or anything, see? I'm not a doctor."

Louise did see. The pharmacist showed her where the Pedialyte sat on a shelf and then returned to his work. Louise recoiled at the price. Seven dollars for a quart of water? She opted for Gatorade instead, at a third of the cost. Angel might like the cherry taste better than water. She went back to the chair to sit with the baby for a bit longer before the three-block trek back to the hotel.

28

DANA

6:00 p.m.

When I got outside, I saw what the security guy meant. The condo sidewalk had a liberal covering of salt, but as soon as I stepped onto the street to enter the Prius my foot went out from under me, and I hit the curb hip first. I lay there, my body draped half-on and half-off the sidewalk, panting at the pain.

"Fuck!" I wanted Nuts to help me up but he didn't, just let me recline in agony. From my low vantage point I took in the leafless trees lining the sidewalk on either side of me. The ice-coated branches sparkled under the light of the street lamps. The street glistened with a crusted covering of more ice. Where were the plows with the salt?

I struggled to stand, winded from hitting the ground and hard put to get my feet under me. I kept slipping and banging my hip. Through it all I could feel Nuts glaring at me. I finally got enough purchase with my hands on the passenger seat to pull myself into the car. I shut the door against the frigid wind.

Spotty traffic in the street moved at glacial speed, but spinouts occurred anyway, cars resting at crazy angles. The earlier balmy, rainy weather had turned treacherous. The temperature must have dropped so quickly there was no time for the water to dissipate, leaving the city wearing an icy jacket.

"Get your belt on."

"Why're you so mad? Seems like I should be pissed at you. Rokick seems to know all about my drinking and it's a good guess you're the source."

"You're drunk. You shit all over everybody in the squad, insulted Koz. Is that what you're learning in treatment?"

I only heard the first two words clearly. He was right. I was drunk. "But I drank the red stuff. Without the booze." Didn't I? But I recognized the weirded-out effect of hard liquor. It creeps up on me as I drink it, not feeling anything at all for the first few drinks, then whammo—I'm wasted.

"I insulted Koz? No. Can't be. I saw him leave. He left." I sounded more certain than I felt. I knew for sure Koz hadn't witnessed me throwing the cups. And all he saw me drink was punch.

Nuts said nothing. His first attempt to pull into traffic ended with him spinning his wheels. The second time he took it very slow and headed north on Michigan Avenue. Nuts was freezing me out, treating me like someone he didn't like. I had to make him understand. I didn't drink. Not on purpose.

"I—I *am* drunk. But I drank the punch without the booze, so I don't —" Rokick refilling my cup. Me refilling my cup. The tags mixed up? "I've been dry since last month." I was too drunk to remember or count how many days I'd strung together. "Really. You can check with my counselor if you don't believe me."

My voice shook. I was afraid he wouldn't believe me. Even more afraid he'd narc on me to Koz, tell him I was drunk. That would be the end of me, of us.

We headed toward Lake Shore Drive. Downtown was pretty deserted and the few people who were out weren't walking as much as hanging onto each other, slaloming, sliding, and falling. I lit a Kool, earning another glare from Nuts, so I lowered my window halfway and stuck my cigarette hand outside.

A text from Bear lit the car's interior. He wanted confirmation I'd be at the next PP meeting to interpret for him. I sent back a thumbs-up emoji. It took my scrambled brain a minute to arrive at the next thought. Bear's video! I tried to turn sideways in my seat to face Nuts but only managed to inflame my already stinging left hip. I took a drag and exhaled out the window.

Nuts stared straight ahead. I held up my phone. "Listen. You're the whole reason I went to Rokick's fucking party, to get you to watch this video." I shook my cell at him. "You've got to. Please! I know this woman's involved."

Nuts skidded to a lopsided stop at a red light. He groaned and spat out, "Christ! Again? What is it with you harping on this baby?"

"What is it with you ignoring my work? You never questioned my gut before *Clint.*"

That shut him up for a minute and I tried to calm down. I couldn't get him to watch the video if he was so pissed.

The light changed and Nuts gingerly touched the gas but the tires spun in place. Two guys standing at the curb slid over to us and lined up at the back bumper. Their hands clamping onto the Prius's rear pushed the car down a bit and one guy yelled for Nuts to take it slow while they pushed. We gained enough traction to pull away. Nuts beeped his thanks with a staccato horn.

"Look. I don't have proof she killed Margot Stuckless. I *do* know she was primed to kidnap that baby. Rokick told me you both think the baby's dead. I'm telling you she's not. This woman has her." I managed to get this out in a reasonable tone of voice, hoping he would listen.

His response was to pull the Prius over to the curb in front of the Art Institute. He flicked on the dome light. "I think I get it, now."

I was so happy I almost hugged him.

Then he continued. "You don't even see it, do you? You lost your baby. So you gotta save this one."

His surmise was so off base I stared at him in stunned silence.

"Get out," he said.

"What? Why? Can't you at least—"

"You never quit, do you? It's not enough I tell you to butt out. No. It's not enough Clint feels sorry for you and invites you to his party, even though he didn't mean it. No. It's not even enough Koz sees you at a party when you're supposed to be toeing the line, doing everything you should to earn back his respect and your place as my partner. All because you think you know best. I'm done."

I flicked my cigarette onto the sidewalk, and it slid away in the dark. I raised the window and opened my door. Nuts sat in profile. I pulled up Bear's video and tapped the start button. "Look at this."

"GET OUT!"

We'd disagreed many times in the three years as partners, but he never once raised his voice to me. Now twice in as many days. The full force of his words hit me. Did Koz know I was drunk? He wasn't there at the end, that much I could remember. I paused the video and sent it to Nuts's cell again, then shoved my phone into my backpack.

I gingerly stepped onto the sidewalk, grateful to find salt liberally applied. I gripped the door frame of the Prius and leaned a bit inside. "You've got the video. Watch it."

Before I could let go of the door Nuts accelerated away, the force of the forward movement swinging it closed. Luckily, I stayed upright. The Adams Street entrance to the 'L' was about two blocks away. Not seeing any taxis, I'd have to hoof it. The frigid wind helped a bit with my wooziness, but my balance was shit on the icy sidewalks. I hit the ground twice before getting to the long staircase up to the tracks.

The 'L' platforms—for trains heading north and south—were crowded with people, many carrying shopping bags. I dimly recalled Christmas was next week and I needed to get my parents something. Twenty minutes later a train heading north arrived, and I was glad to get inside even though the car was poorly heated.

As the train inched toward my studio, putting in at every stop along the way, I sat with my partner's last two words screaming in my ear, my mind spinning. Someone had spiked my punch. There was a blank spot about what happened after Koz left. I could only remember Nuts dragging me out of the condo. The city night slid by my window. This was the end for me, for Nuts and me, for my future as a cop. It all hinged on whether Koz saw me drunk. Or worse, Nuts telling him so.

The sign for the Irving Park stop appeared in my window and I exited along with a large group of people. A CTA worker was busy dusting the platform with sand. The wind, which had been blowing steadily downtown, now howled. I shuddered. My studio was four blocks to the north, but my car was parked south of the station. My choice was to walk the four blocks home or head south to my car and drive drunk. After the party fiasco, no way would I chance being pulled over with booze in my system. I could pick up my car in the morning. Maybe by then the icy sidewalks would be in better shape.

With the wind directly out of the north, I tucked my head down and began the slow navigation on slick ice. During the first block I managed not to fall and settled into a kind of sliding shuffle, my warm studio and hot chocolate as distant rewards pushing me forward. I put everything else out of my mind. The booze left me worn out. There was little traffic, and the neighborhood was silent except for the eerie crackling of ice-coated tree branches.

The second block was harder to manage. I fell twice, landing on the same hip I'd bruised getting into the Prius. Instead of trying to stand again, I scooted on my ass all the way to the curb at the end of the block. Salt was scattered in the crosswalk, giving me purchase to walk across to the third block. Mercifully, small patches of dead grass fronted apartment buildings, allowing me enough traction to crunch my way along. My pants were soaked and began freezing on my skin.

At last, I arrived at the front walkway up to my building, my hip burning, my head aching, my lower body freezing. Sandor, the manager, had not salted the walk. Then I remembered he and his wife were in Hungary visiting family. I began my shuffle slide again and promptly hit the ground, this time banging both knees.

"Shit!" My eyes smarted with tears. Suddenly there was a man behind me, a large man, helping me stand, holding me up. He put his arm around me to steady my wobble. My head fit neatly under his armpit. I was so happy to have his help I started blubbering my thanks, but he shushed me. I could smell booze but wasn't sure if it was him or me. We got to the door of the foyer. I turned to him.

"You are a lifesaver." He opened the door and indicated I should go in. The foyer wasn't heated but at least we were out of the biting wind. I turned to thank him again.

He took a step back and landed a roundhouse punch to the side of my head. I fell to the floor. He was on me so fast, ripping the front of my pants with a knife, I couldn't begin to fight back. I tried to push him off. He let loose with another crack across my temple, and I passed out.

When I came to, he was gone.

29

LOUISE

6:00 p.m.

After buying the Gatorade at Walgreens, Louise had trudged a block farther in the rain to a McDonald's in order to get something cheap to eat and treat herself to some SoftServe ice cream with hot fudge. She was soaking wet but it was worth the effort.

While she waited for the rain to let up she held Angel in her lap and finally got her to wake up a bit, enough to take a few sips of the cherry drink. Louise tried to push a french fry into the little mouth but it only led to the baby crying, so she stopped immediately, not wanting to draw anyone's attention.

She laid Angel down on the bench and while the baby slept, Louise ordered another sundae and two chocolate shakes. She consumed it all. She would need her strength to go the *four* blocks back to the hotel.

The rain stopped around three. Louise wanted to get back to the hotel before dark. She stuffed the Gatorade bottle in her coat pocket, hefted the sleeping baby and struggled to stand. The four blocks to her destination seemed a mountain to climb, her wet coat a stone burden, but she had to get Angel to bed.

During the long slog back Louise battled a rising wind as the temperature seemed to drop minute by minute. The surface of her wet coat began to crust over with ice in a few places, adding to its weight. She had to stop several times each block to shift the baby in her arms and take a break.

At last, Louise had arrived at the hotel and entered the lobby out of breath, Angel draped over her shoulder like a large bag of rice. She stopped to rest on an overstuffed couch by the electric fireplace across from the empty registration desk. Angel continued on in her deep sleep. Louise laid her on the couch and rubbed her own arms, numb and tingling from carrying the baby.

Louise shrugged out of her heavy coat, welcoming the flow of heat from the fireplace. The couch was so comfortable Louise let Angel sleep on, while she enjoyed the fireplace warmth and watched the sky morph from day to night through the hotel's front window.

After a while Louise could smell the stink of Angel's dirty diaper, so she gathered the little girl to take her to their room. She would change her, clean her up, and administer more Gatorade. Then Angel's diarrhea would go away and everything would be fine.

The limp baby was so much heavier in sleep but Louise managed to get upstairs to their floor, then exit the elevator and head down the hall. At the far end, Louise could see the area outside their room was piled high with junk. As she got closer, she could make out clothes, plastic bags, and an opened box of cookies. Arriving at the door of their room, she realized all the stuff piled high in the hallway was *hers*. Panic.

She laid Angel—still asleep—on the carpeted floor, took out her key card, and swiped the lock. A click sounded but a red light blinked behind the door handle. She tried to open it. Nothing. She swiped again and again. No green light.

Louise knelt in front of Angel, asleep on the carpet of the hotel hallway, and undid her diaper. More of the messy green poop. She cleaned her up as best she could with some paper napkins from McDonald's and slipped on a fresh diaper. She then rooted through her belongings and packed only what she could fit into the diaper bag. She abandoned the Gatorade as it was too heavy, took up too much room, and she couldn't get Angel to drink more because the little girl continued her heavy sleep. She stuffed cookies in both of her coat pockets and ate the six that remained.

Louise wanted to go downstairs and yell at the hotel manager about locking her out of her room and make him open the door. That meant she had to either carry Angel down there or leave her here. The thought of carrying the baby only added to her exhaustion. She sat on the floor next to Angel and leaned her back against the wall, closing her eyes.

30

DANA

9:30 p.m.

I don't know how long I was knocked out lying on the cold tile floor in the unheated foyer. My thighs were freezing. My pants were ripped open, ragged from the waist to the crotch and bunched at my calves. Worse, my underpants had been yanked to my knees. As I hurriedly pulled at them to cover up, they slid over wet slime on my inner thigh. Fuck.

I only wanted to get to my studio and out of this frozen hell. My torn pants made crawling difficult, but I managed to get to the locked foyer door leading to the inside stairway. I rested for a moment on my sore knees only to realize my backpack was gone. I had no keys, no cell phone.

My head throbbed from my attacker's punches and drunken dizziness continued to dog me so much I stayed on the icy tile floor and crawled back to the trio of mailboxes for our three-flat. Sandor and his wife were gone, so ringing their first-floor buzzer was pointless. I hit the doorbell of the college guys who lived below me, hoping against hope they hadn't gone home for Christmas break.

Nothing.

I had to get inside. Get warm. Get safe. I sat on the foyer floor with my back against the wall, knees up, and rested my sore head on my arms. I don't know how long I dozed but I awoke feeling like some of the booze from Rokick's party had dissipated, leaving me a bit more with it. I clutched my pants so they closed at the waist and stood, imagining how an old person must feel because I now walked like one, and made my way out of the foyer.

At the back of my apartment building the external wooden staircase provided access to each floor, and the individual landings held our trash cans dutifully emptied by Sandor every three days. Hand over hand, I hung onto the banister and managed to drag my beaten body up three flights of ice-coated stairs. Somewhere in my somewhat functioning brain I thought I could break the small glass window in the back door of my studio, reach in and flip the lock, and gain entrance that way.

Once at my door, I realized too late the lock operated with a key on the inside, too; a key I didn't have. It was a fire code violation I warned Sandor about when I moved in a couple of months ago. He promised to change it but hadn't yet.

I sat on top of one of my metal garbage cans. Good thing my ass was already numb from the cold. Crossing my arms to contain my body's heat, I closed my eyes and leaned my head back a bit to relieve my sore neck. Nearby, a church's bell tower chimed. When I opened my eyes a few minutes later I took in the back door to my studio apartment leading to the kitchenette.

Above the door was an old-fashioned transom as wide as the door frame and somewhere between one and two feet high. If I got up there and broke the glass in the transom, I could jimmy the inside latch to open it wide enough and then squeeze through the space, home at last.

The boots I wore to Rokick's party were decorative, not functional; three-inch wood heels with metal taps I favored for the sound. They were another reason I kept slipping and falling on the long walk back. I pulled both boots off, moved one of the garbage cans in front of the door, and after clamping one boot under each arm, slowly clambered onto the can.

A wave of dizziness and nausea hit me as I straightened up. I steadied my hand on the brick wall, waiting for it to pass. I vomited instead—fast and hot—half of it landing on my jacket.

The good news? The nausea ceased. The bad news? The smell.

But standing on the can brought me chest-high level with the transom, making it easy to follow through with my half-assed plan. I grabbed my boot by the toe and pointed the heel at the part of the glass closest to the transom's inside latch. All I needed was to make a hole big enough to get my hand through. I closed my eyes and tapped the glass.

Nothing.

I tapped again but the glass didn't yield. Okay, no more girly taps. I hauled back with my full arm and swung the boot heel into the glass, shattering it with a satisfying clangor. The glass crashed inward and outward, onto the metal garbage can, a crescendo loud in the quiet night. Warm air spilled through the transom and ruffled my hair.

I was going in!

I reached through the shattered window to work the latch and drop the wooden frame of the transom to the open position inside my studio. I tossed both boots inside and put my hands on the ledge where the bottom of the transom met the top of the door frame and heaved my body halfway into the small space. My acrobatics pushed the metal garbage can over with a loud crash.

If the breaking glass didn't wake someone, then the clanging garbage can did the trick. But I couldn't worry about that right now because I had another problem. I was stuck. Like Pooh Bear in the fucking Hunny Tree. Shit. My winter jacket had me wedged tight and even though my hands were free inside the studio, they weren't much help moving me forward. Could I push myself back out, and then take off my jacket and try again?

Hanging half-in and half-out high above my back door, my ripped pants practically falling off in my struggle to move, I heard the blare of a police siren not far away and getting closer. And closer still. In the alley below me the siren whooped once more. Red and white lights strobed through the metal bars on my kitchen window and onto the wall of my kitchenette. Car doors slammed, one after the other.

"Hold it right there! Don't move! I have a gun! I'll use it if you try to move!"

Sounds of feet on the back stairs and some slipping and swearing. Two cops coming to arrest me for breaking and entering. Well, entering halfway.

An abrupt chorus of laughter and muffled discussion ensued when the cops finally arrived on my landing. Frankly, I was glad I couldn't decipher what they were saying, with my ass barely covered and exposed to the world. As a cop, I knew I'd be reacting exactly the same way if I came up on a scene like this. It was mortifying to be on the receiving end.

A short while later, I heard a key being inserted in the back door below me and the lock snicking open. Someone swung open the door inward and entered, training a mag flashlight at my eyes, rendering me stunned.

"I'd tell her to hold it right there, but it looks like she can't do anything else," a male cop said, and then barked a laugh.

The second cop, also male, laughed. "Yeah. Or how about 'put your hands up?' Oh, wait. They *are* up. *Way* up." More laughter. Then, "Okay, Mr. Sandor. Come on up."

Sandor? "Hey, asshole, ditch the mag light, huh? I'm a cop." I reeled off my name and number for them to check. Suddenly my kitchenette was flooded with light and my predicament was laid bare, somewhat literally. I moved my arms to try to push my body through the transom, but the bald cop below trained his gun on me and bellowed to hold still.

"Take it easy, take it easy. I live here." He didn't lower the gun, but he did shut off the flashlight. Two middle-aged cops stood in my kitchenette with another younger guy who definitely was not Sandor, my building manager. Shit. I closed my eyes and screamed as loud as I could.

"Demeter! Demeter!" I heard Baldy calling my name while screaming myself out. "Shut the fuck up! We got you ID'd."

"Who the fuck is that guy?" I waved my arms at the man standing by the light switch. "I've never seen him before. He sure as hell isn't Sandor!" Even though I can't remember anything about the face of the guy who raped me, I'm freaked out it's somehow this guy.

The young guy had the nerve to smile at me but said nothing.

Baldy hooked his thumb in the guy's direction. "This here's Mr. Sandor who called in your B and E."

"Listen to me, you jerk! That is *not* Sandor! He's a lot older! And he's on vacation!" I struggled to push my body through the transom but was stuck fast. I upped the volume in my voice to command pitch. "Get him in cuffs and hold him. Trust me. I'll tell you why in a minute. Get me down first!"

The two cops looked at each other and shrugged, but they managed to cuff the guy—who hadn't moved and showed no resistance—and sat him down. After an embarrassing show of pushing and pulling me, the two cops made a concerted effort to take off my jacket, which finally allowed me to clamber through the transom and drop to the floor like a clumsy gymnast.

When I straightened up all three men visibly recoiled from me. At first, I thought it was my appearance, face banged up, pants torn and flapping open down my legs, no boots; then I realized it was my smell. It made me recoil, too.

I pointed a shaky finger at the guy sitting a few feet from me. "That fucker raped me earlier tonight. In the entry downstairs." I clutched at my torn pants to keep them together in front of these men.

The guy on the chair jumped up at my accusation. "The hell I did!"

"Keep him right there," I said, and Baldy pushed the guy back onto the chair. "Listen," I peered at both cops' name tags, "Lees and Duncan. I need to change my clothes real quick, okay?" Unsurprisingly, they both nodded, Lees with enthusiasm.

I escaped to my dresser and snagged some clean sweats, then did a quick wash-up in the bathroom while avoiding my face in the mirror, adding a quick spritz of vanilla cologne Jimmy loved. I kicked the soiled clothes under the sink to take care of later.

Back in the kitchen Lees and Duncan scrolled on their phones and ignored the guy in the chair.

I stood in front of the guy. "Okay. Who the hell are you? Let's see some ID."

He motioned with his cuffed hands. Lees helped him up. The guy towered over all of us. He turned around, his back pocket obviously stuffed with a wallet. "In there."

Lees unearthed the guy's license. "DL says here, Detective, he's one Botund Sandor, address on Clark Street near Wrigley. Not too far from here." Lees handed me the guy's license.

The guy spoke again. "People call me Bo. I'm a firefighter at Engine 78's house. Lakeview."

I studied the DL, doing my best to hide my chagrin if what he said was true. He was six-four, 250, blond and blue. Born the same year as me.

"My parents live here and manage this building. I'm filling in while they're in Hungary." His voice was mild. "What time is it?"

Lees checked his phone. "Just after 10:30. Why?"

"Call my father. Hungary is seven hours ahead of us. He's up early. He'll vouch for me."

I handed Lees the DL. "Check the Lakeview Station, too."

While Lees phoned Sandor senior and then verified Bo was indeed a firefighter, I grabbed a cigarette from my desk and, after lighting it, took several deep drags to calm down. Again, all three men visibly recoiled. Christ, I should award this bunch a medal for Most Sensitive Sniffers.

I chain-smoked at my desk. Once Bo was identified and uncuffed, he left. Lees and Duncan canceled the initial break-in call. Duncan checked with me about reporting the rape and going to the hospital for an exam. I waved him off, but he persisted.

"You should oughta look at it, ya know, Detective. They can do the SAEK. Even if you don't report the, you know, the attack."

I stepped closer to him to give him the full benefit of my bad breath, got right in his face, and spoke to him at dimwit speed. "I. Am. Well. Aware. I. Can. Submit. To. A. Sexual. Assault. Evidence. Kit. Collection."

He gave me a look but backed off.

Here's the truth. I was so defeated from the attack I could not stand the idea of people interrogating me, much less submitting to an internal exam. I was drunk and got raped. My own fault. Happened to women all the time. Now me. Drunk me.

I followed the cops to my back door. Lees held out the key Bo gave him to open it.

"Here. Use this next time. Lot easier than the way you came in." He laughed and waited a long beat, as if wanting me to join his clever banter.

I tilted my head to one side and stared at him. "You think this is funny? Some fucking asshole *raped me* and stole my backpack, which has my keys. *Including* the one for this back door." I swiped the key from him. "Get the hell outta here."

The two mopes headed down to the squad car waiting in the alley, their departure marked by the siren blasting out one final whoop. I locked the kitchen door and pocketed the key, now the only way I could enter my place until I got some new keys made. Then I noticed the front door to my studio ajar and I hurried over to shut it. Bo stood on the landing outside.

He gestured at my back door. "It's pretty cold. Let me rig up something to cover the transom right now until I can fix it."

He was right. Cold air flowed in through the transom's broken glass, but right now I couldn't stand any more dealings with anyone. I just wanted to be alone. I pushed my body against the edge of the front door and spoke to him through the thin slice still open. "No. It's okay. Maybe tomorrow."

To his credit, he didn't argue or try to change my mind. He started down the steps, his one glance back radiating nothing but pity.

31

LOUISE

9:30 p.m.

The next thing Louise knew someone was shaking her shoulder and in a loud voice telling her to wake up. The manager!

"You can't stay here. Get your things and leave. Otherwise, I'll call the cops." The man had bad breath. He bent over her, his face inches from hers, spewing his greasy smell. She sat straighter and with both hands shoved the man's chest. He stumbled backwards and hit the floor with a thump.

"That's it! I'm calling the cops." He struggled to stand and then hurried down the hall to the elevator, jabbing at the down button.

She screamed after him. "I paid for this room! I still have five more days! You can't kick me out!"

"You live like garbage! You attack my staff—and me! Get out!" He stopped leaning on the elevator button and headed for the stairs.

Louise glanced at Angel, still asleep. She had to get her baby up and away from this man. And the police. She stood. He called her garbage. Well, his hotel was garbage, and she would show him.

She picked up Angel's folded dirty diaper and opened it, slapped the poop side on the wall and smooshed it around trailing the green, smelly contents. Then she threw the diaper on the carpet, used side down, and stomped on it.

She opened the Gatorade and poured the whole quart bottle on the beige carpet, the red stain leaching outward in a spidery shape, and threw the empty bottle down the hall. She slung the diaper bag over her shoulder, leaving everything else she owned in a heap, gathered Angel in her arms, and headed for the elevator.

She had to get somewhere safe.

32

DANA

11:00 p.m.

I latched both locks on the door, suddenly paranoid the bastard who raped me was somehow in the building. I stuffed my stinking, torn clothes in the garbage. In the shower I washed my body in a frantic way I couldn't control and then donned another pair of fresh sweats. I still felt high from the booze, but it didn't help the pain from the huge lump forming on the side of my head where I'd been clubbed. I palmed four ibuprofen and downed them with a large glass of water. What I really wanted was a lot more booze to blot out all my pain, and not only the physical kind.

But first I had to talk to Nuts, tell him what happened. I started to search for my phone and then remembered it was in my stolen backpack. I called him from my computer. The call went directly to voicemail.

"You're a fucking coward, Abandonato. Can't even answer your fucking phone when you see it's me." The truth of my statement dropped on me like the clout from my attacker and I started sobbing. "I just got raped! It's your fucking fault for throwing me out on the street. And this asshole is out there somewhere. He knocked me out. I didn't even get a good look at him." I sobbed harder at not being able to defend myself, at the physical pain coursing through my body.

My anger took over and I grabbed one last chance to shake him up, to force him to admit I was right about the baby's kidnapping, to reclaim my place as his partner. "Watch the goddam video. You'll see." I reiterated Louise Conway's mental problems, described her penchant for chocolate, and revealed my shiny fact about Mac Stuckless's allergy to it.

"One more thing. Rokick set me up, spiked my drink. It wasn't me." The desperate denial was the only way I could explain my drunkenness. I cut our connection.

A noise sounded from the rear landing outside, and then a knock. I pushed aside the curtain covering the small window in the back door. Bo stood there in shirtsleeves holding a step stool in one hand, a piece of plywood clamped under his arm and a drill in the other hand.

I unlocked the door and stuffed the key back in my pocket, reminding myself to attach it to a larger keychain so I wouldn't lose it.

I swung the door open. Bo apologized. He propped the step stool against his leg. "Look. I realize you said tomorrow. But my father called and insisted I close it." He pointed up at the transom, gave a small laugh, and shrugged. "My father's cheap. He wants me to repair it now because the heating bill will go up if it's left open."

Reminded me of Evie and her refusal to lock her back door because she wanted easy access in and out when she worked in the garden. She wouldn't budge when I bawled her out about safety. Then she got conked on the head by an intruder. Time to take my own advice about safety.

"Parents," I said, as I opened the door wider and let him in. I gestured at the broken transom, cold, cold air pouring in and down on us. "Not sure what I was thinking. I would've frozen with it like this if I'd waited until morning."

Bo nodded. "Give yourself a break. Hard to think straight after what you said happened." He peered down at me, a slight squint to his eyes as if he wore glasses but forgot to put them on.

"Yeah."

He made quick work of screwing in the piece of wood over the transom. We agreed there was a need to change out the back door lock for one up to code, and get a locksmith in to rekey the other locks.

"I'll get an up-to-date back door lock and replace it tomorrow." He glanced at the clock on my microwave and smiled. "Well, soon to be today. Afternoon good for you?"

"Sure. I have to be somewhere at six, so maybe 4:30?"

He hesitated. "Tell you what, I need to do something in the afternoon. Let me text you when I finish and then I can come up if that works." We exchanged numbers and I told him my cell was in my stolen backpack, but he could reach me on my Mac.

"Okay. Or I can come up and knock on your door. You know, the way the old people do it." He waited a beat for my reaction, but I had nothing. Joking and laughing seemed like a distant island I might never visit again.

Bo swept up the broken glass I'd left littered on the floor, folded the step stool, and wrapped the drill's cord in a tidy way, then started for the front door.

"Hey. Why'd you come up the outside stairs? I mean, why not inside?"

"Well, I wanted to spread some salt. Stairs are pretty bad, slippery. I figured two birds with one stone since I had to come up here." He made a self-mocking gesture, tapping his temple with an index finger. I couldn't even smile at his lame attempt at humor.

I pointed at the transom. "Thanks for this. Maybe see you later?"

"Yep."

After he left, I considered calling Jimmy but hesitated—he would be all over me about the drinking, he had some kind of sixth sense about it—and then called anyway because I was so enraged at what happened. I needed to talk to someone who cared about me. At the very least he could calm me down, help me figure out what to do.

I wrapped up in my full-length robe because I couldn't get warm and then sat on my futon trying to arrange my body in a comfortable position. Impossible.

"Call Jimmy Gennaro," I ordered the computer. The line rang a couple of times and then a recorded message played telling me the number was disconnected. That had to be wrong. The digital assistant had misunderstood my command. I pulled up Jimmy's name in my contacts and clicked the call icon. The same thing happened again. Disconnected.

There couldn't be a worse time to find out my ex-husband changed his phone number and kept it a secret from me. I lay down and pulled the futon's comforter over my sore body. When Jimmy and I made love here—only three weeks ago—staying together seemed like a hope that would blossom. This time I wept at the reminder of how swiftly I lost him.

I was exhausted but wide awake, sleep out of the question. I kept replaying the moment I turned to thank the hulk who attacked me and got slammed in the head. No face came to mind, just a blank wall.

33

LOUISE

11:00 p.m.

The elevator doors opened slowly at the second floor. Louise checked up and down the empty hallway before exiting. She shifted Angel's dead weight to her other shoulder and hurried toward the red exit sign above the stairs.

At the first floor landing she opened the door to the lobby a small crack, just enough to observe a different young woman at the desk than the one who loaned her the Ventra card. The manager was not in sight.

Louise entered the lobby. She ignored the desk clerk and headed straight for the front door. Just as she pushed it open the clerk called to her.

"It's pretty bad out there. Be careful."

Louise half-turned at the warning but exited the hotel anyway. Her feet crunched on salt spread at the hotel's entrance. The sidewalk beyond glistened in the streetlights, a coating of ice as far as she could see. She couldn't go back and she couldn't go on.

Angel moaned in her arms. Louise had to get somewhere safe before the police arrived. If they found her she would lose her baby. She stood there for a minute, rocking Angel, wishing she could call Gerry.

Gerry! She returned to the lobby and hurried to the desk. "I don't have a phone. I need to call Gerry to come get me! Please!"

"Of course." The clerk moved the desk phone closer to Louise. "Be sure to press nine first to get an outside line," she said.

Louise shifted Angel so the baby was propped up on the desk and called Gerry. A recorded voice told her the line was disconnected. She dropped the receiver on the desk and burst out crying.

"What am I going to do?" She hugged Angel's inert body to her, rocking back and forth.

"What's wrong? Can I help you with anything?" The clerk reached out and ran her hand up and down Louise's arm.

Just then the manager appeared from a back office and came to the desk clerk's side.

Louise grabbed Angel and stepped back. She eyed the manager but spoke to the clerk. "He—he's kicking me out! I can't stay here. My husband's phone is broken. I don't know what to do!" She sobbed, burying her face in Angel's jacket.

Louise heard the front door open and what sounded like some static and a voice coming from a radio.

"It's about time," the manager said.

Louise turned toward the noise. Police.

34

FELICE

Before heading to his health club for a treadmill five-miler—the ice from last night still cloaked the city and made running treacherous—Felice put his phone on speaker and played a message from early this morning. Dana. Crying. Screaming at him she'd been raped. His fault. Then more about that goddam video. He played the message again and again, shock reigniting with each repetition. He had no idea what to do. Too early to call her.

He ran the five miles, grabbed a quick shower, and texted Rokick before heading downtown. As he got closer to Rokick's condo, he passed the mayor's office on LaSalle Street, irked the Task Force was on hiatus the entire week because of Christmas.

Felice chose a parking lot between his two destinations downtown. He covered the distance to Clint's condo in a slow methodical way, his mind on Dana at the party. Koz had already left and hadn't seen the worst of her performance—her drunk performance—cursing out the squad and throwing the punch cups. Koz wouldn't be clued in, necessarily, Dana was actually drinking booze.

Felice did know, though. Could he keep the damning info to himself? And what of her charge Clint set her up, gave her spiked punch?

Last night, his own anger at Dana had soared past its limits. He'd relinquished hope she would ever take her suspension seriously. She'd disobeyed Koz's orders—to get sober and lose the weight—too many times. Even if he didn't tell Koz about Dana's behavior at the party, it seemed clear there was no way she could or would return as his partner.

Felice stopped at a Starbucks on the way and picked up a venti green tea. As he approached the condo his cell buzzed against his chest. He retrieved the phone from his jacket's inner pocket. Rokick.

"Abandonato."

"What's so important you gotta come to my condo?"

"I'm here, actually. Okay if I come up?"

"Sure, yeah."

The condo foyer appeared quite ordinary in daylight compared to last night; the marble floors needed sweeping, the twin dolphins in the fountain near the elevators looked garish in the red and green spotlights, the guard harbored a half-eaten doughnut on the podium.

The elevator doors stood open. Felice entered and the guard set the computer-guided ride in motion up to the floor where Rokick stood at the door of his condo.

"What couldn't wait?" Rokick said, admitting Felice and shutting the door. They entered the living room, the recent sunrise flooding it with light through the eastern facing windows. Felice squinted at the view. The shallow edge of the lake was frozen, a white crusty layer riding the top. Farther out, the sun's sharp reflection on the open water forced him to turn away.

Felice sat at one end of the couch and motioned for Rokick to sit. "I want to talk to you about last night."

"Last night?" Rokick perched on the edge of the couch. "Demeter was smashed." He held up his cell phone and gave it a little wave. "Everybody's talking about it." He pointed at the white carpet. "I'm having a hell of a time getting those stains out. Demeter's gonna have to pay for that."

How to respond? Especially after Dana's call. She was dealing with being raped and Rokick was whining about a carpet stain.

Felice took a sip of tea and burned his tongue. He pointed at Rokick's cell. "Don't gossip, Rokick. There's nothing you gain by doing it. And it'll come back to bite you in the ass."

"Sure, sure." Rokick ducked his head as he said this, a disarming move not fooling Felice one bit. Extensive discussions with Dana about body language taught him this particular move, especially when accompanied by verbal agreement, usually meant the exact opposite.

"Speaking of Koz, I wanted to run something by you," Rokick said.

"Were we?"

"What?"

"Speaking of Koz."

"Oh. No, I guess not. But I mean, I don't want to bother him with this if you have some ideas?"

Felice realized Rokick didn't want to appear weak to Koz, like he was unsure or stupid. The recognition came from his own wanting to please Koz, to have his Lieutenant consider him capable and smart. Koz's words when assigning him to the Task Force—*you're the best we've got*—had stayed with him.

He glanced at his phone. "What've you got?"

"This Amber Alert thing isn't bringing in anything. No sightings, nothing. The husband clammed up after the polygraph said he's telling the truth about the baby. He don't answer about the wife. He's still the best we got for her, so holding him's no problem. So, what's next? We keepin' the Amber Alert on the kid? What do I do about the kid? You think she's dead, right?"

Felice considered the question. It made little sense Mac Stuckless would murder his wife but have nothing to do with his daughter's disappearance, regardless of what the polygraph showed. And the insurance money Stuckless would receive from each death made him highly suspect.

So far there was little else, with the exception of Kristi Chen, who was on home detention but refused to talk unless they offered her full immunity from prosecution. That couldn't be promised until the State's Attorney agreed.

"I do. Stuckless killed his wife and daughter for the money. But keep the Alert on for now until we're sure. I haven't dealt directly with kidnappings or abductions, if that's what this is. The feds can be called in if the baby's taken to another state or overseas. In this case we don't know. Any word about Chen's immunity?"

Rokick shook his head.

Felice scrolled through his contacts list, found the one person he'd worked with in the FBI, and sent the info to Rokick. "Check with him, find out what he says about working with the feds. Otherwise, keep in touch with ISP and the state's attorney. Chen rolling over on Stuckless is our best bet."

"Good, great. Thanks." Rokick tapped something into his phone, then glanced at Felice before settling on the view of the lake's expanse through the floor-to-ceiling windows. "Back to Chen. Suppose, just suppose, that baby ain't dead like we think. I mean, she talked a good story about not wanting kids, but what if she's lying? She *wanted* the baby. She got Stuckless to kill his wife and take the kid. Means Chen's got her stashed somewhere."

Felice tapped on his cell in a show of looking up something to grab a minute to think about what Rokick presented. While the rookie detective had shown a slight ability for logical thinking, his imagination was sorely lacking. So why was Rokick revisiting his original theory about Kristi Chen wanting a baby?

A clip from the party last night surfaced, Dana and Rokick in extended conversation. Rokick's theory actually had Dana written all over it if he substituted the Louise Conway woman as the one responsible for the murder and kidnapping.

Dana was messing with Rokick.

"Listen. Kristi Chen will deliver on Stuckless. Eventually. He killed his wife and daughter for the money. Believe it. And the forensics will back this up when we get it."

He put his cell phone back in his jacket and stood. "The Task Force is on break this week. I'm taking lead back on Stuckless."

"Koz do that? Am I still on it? Or is Demeter back?" Rokick's questions rushed out in one breath.

"You're still listed as lead but I'm calling the shots."

"Sure. Good. Okay." Rokick stood and paced back and forth in front of the sofa. "I thought she'd be canned now, I mean, with Koz here last night and seeing her soused and everything."

He couldn't leave it alone, could he? "Look, it's not my call about Demeter."

Rokick held up his hands in a gesture of surrender. "Hey, understood. Except it does affect me. And us. If she's out, then we're partners. Which is great. Just what I want."

"I already told you. *Koz* already told you. What happens with Dana is up to him. Got it?"

Rokick faced him full on, his voice hard-edged. "Yeah, I *got* it. One thing I don't get is you. Why're you always defending her? She's a fucking lush. Think you'd want to be shut of her and her problems."

The sun streamed through the glass and hit Felice squarely in the eyes. He squinted and took a step back from Rokick. He flashed on his wedding three years ago, standing at the altar, waiting for his fiancee who never arrived. His then-new partner Dana and her husband rescued him from the front of the church. He went home with them, staying for the week of his aborted honeymoon, thus cementing their friendship and strong partnership.

Felice shook his head. "Just leave it. She's still my partner."

Rokick sat down and fidgeted with his phone. "Yeah, sure. There is one thing. I wasn't going to tell you this 'cause I didn't think it was all that important. But I want you to trust me, like a partner, so I'm telling you. You decide." He shifted in his seat and leaned forward. "Shit. I almost feel like a snitch."

Rokick's inability to cut to the chase irritated Felice and he motioned *hurry up* with his hand.

"Okay, okay. When I talked to Janey Foreman about how to call the deaf-mute guy—she had no clue, by the way—she said Demeter had been there, interviewed her about the case. I mean, you told Demeter to back off, but looks like she didn't."

Felice felt his face heat up in a combination of anger and embarrassment—anger at Dana all over again for ignoring what he'd told her about butting out, and embarrassed Rokick thought Dana dissed him. Then he realized Rokick wasn't going to let the partner thing go and was trying to impress him by making Dana look as bad as possible. As if Felice couldn't appraise her behavior for himself and needed more evidence.

Last night in his car Dana denied drinking booze not once, but twice. He'd dismissed these as more of her lies. But now he revisited the real possibility she mistook the spiked punch for the virgin one. Or was unknowingly served the booze by someone else. He'd seen Rokick refresh her drink more than once. In the message Dana left him, she charged Rokick set her up, spiked her drink. A third denial.

It rang true. Rokick's eagerness to reiterate his wish to be partners, in addition to his mealy tattling about Dana interviewing Janey Foreman against Felice's express wishes, revealed his obvious ploy.

He stepped next to Rokick, bent down, and lowered his voice to maximum threat. "I know what you did last night with the punch. You won't get away with it. And you will never, ever, replace Demeter."

35

LOUISE

7:30 a.m.

L ouise woke up in a homeless shelter. At seven, each person was given a to-go breakfast of a muffin and a banana. Then they all had to leave, because the shelter was only open for overnights. If she wanted coffee, she had to go somewhere else and buy it. She only had a little money left in her change purse, but she had to have caffeine. Hot chocolate would be nice, too.

A little later, Louise sat in a McDonald's. Angel was asleep in the used stroller she was able to score from the shelter to transport the baby. It helped so much not having to carry her now. She hoarded a cup of hot chocolate, mixing bits of it with each free coffee refill and savoring the mocha.

Last night, the police must have seen how scared she was of them. They had been kind to her and never once asked to look at Angel. They mostly talked to the manager about why he called. The manager screamed at the police about what she did to the hallway, but when the woman cop went up to look around and then came back down, she said it only needed to be cleaned. Nothing was actually damaged.

Louise tried to tell them the manager owed her money, a refund, for the week she just paid him. But they were firm and said no, the manager could keep the money to clean the hallway. When Louise tried to argue, the woman cop shushed her. "You don't want to go to jail, do you? We would have to take your baby."

The cops even gave Louise a ride to the shelter. The place had been warm, though, too warm. Awake a good part of the night, she lay on the cot without using the blanket, the baby tucked in next to her. She couldn't tell if Angel was hot from the room or if she had a fever.

She set down her coffee laced with hot chocolate and placed her hand on the baby's forehead, then she touched each cheek. Definitely hot.

36

FELICE

1:00 p.m.

Kristi Chen appeared pale. Sleepless nights bagged under her eyes, makeup forgotten, as she clutched her arms around her waist and sank back into her couch. Her waist-length hair trailed over each shoulder and down the front of her body, its black starkness a sharp contrast to her white sweater.

Felice waved his phone at her and she nodded, giving him permission to record their conversation.

"Let's start with your understanding that you agreed to this interview without any promise of immunity from prosecution in the death of Margot Stuckless."

Kristi Chen nodded and then caught herself. "Yes, I understand I'm talking to you even though my lawyer said it would not be good for me. I admit I lied to you about Mac staying here. My lawyer said that's the minor felony compared to the other charge I got."

"That's right. In addition to harboring a fugitive, you're an accessory to the murder of Margot Stuckless."

Kristi Chen shook her head at him. "No! I had nothing to do with that."

Felice held up both hands, palms out, in an appeasing motion. "All right. Why don't you tell me about Herman Mac Stuckless and your relationship with him. How did it lead to murder?"

"I can't stand it anymore. I've had this thing on seems like forever." She gestured at her right leg. "It's driving me batshit crazy." She leaned over and hiked up her blue jean pant leg. Her fingers lightly touched the skin around the dark gray monitor strapped above her ankle. "Look at that. It scratched the hell out of my calf and now it's infected."

Felice took in what looked like a minor rash and nodded but said nothing.

"And I can't go anywhere except stupid places I'd never go, like *church*. Or work. Except, oh yeah, I don't have a job anymore because of that asshole. I even have to get my groceries delivered."

Felice didn't interrupt her tirade. The angrier she got the more she'd spill everything about Mac Stuckless.

"I'm a smart person, right? Went to all the right schools, top of my class in high school and college. My parents wanted nothing less." She lowered her pant leg and tugged it over the monitor. "But then came the pressure to produce grandchildren."

Kristi Chen stopped. When it seemed she wouldn't continue, Felice picked up the narrative. "The last time we talked you seemed adamant about not having children."

A slight smile touched her lips. "So I did fool you? You believed my story?"

Felice nodded. "I did. Something along the line of not being interested in the 'little ones,' if I remember correctly—your own or anyone else's."

Tears welled up and spilled down Kristi Chen's cheeks but her voice didn't waver. "I got married right out of college to a guy I didn't even like but my parents adored. Asian, of course. I found out I couldn't conceive, would never have my own children. We divorced after three years."

Felice didn't like listening to the emotional details of Kristi Chen's life, but discipline rooted him, and he reminded himself to at least be tolerant in order to hear her out.

"I moved away from my parents, came to Chicago for a new start. Mac and I worked together as day traders. We hooked up a couple of times at work and it became a regular thing. You've seen him, right?"

"That's how you both got fired."

She nodded. "So, he brought his little girl over to my place one time and I just fell for this kid—Mac knew it. When I told him my story, he started in with how we could get rid of Margot and have Melly as ours."

"We?"

Kristi Chen swiped her hand at him in a dismissive motion. "Him. I didn't think he'd ever go through with it because Mac's pretty much a talker, not a doer. And he only said it a couple of times, like it was wishful thinking. That's all."

Felice never understood people talking matter-of-factly about murder. He'd seen the worst evidence of the depravity people inflicted on each other and remained horrified and repulsed by the behavior. Many cops in homicide seemed inured to it. Not him.

"I think that's the main reason I wanted to break it off with him. I'm an achiever. But the sex was A-plus. My mistake was thinking that great sex meant everything else with him would be great, too. Guys aren't the only ones blinded by their libidos." She pulled a tissue from her pocket and blew her nose.

"But then his ex turned up dead and he freaked out." She grasped a few strands of hair and began twisting them around her index finger.

Felice said nothing. He tilted his head.

"Like I told you last time, he hated his wife. He was thrilled she was dead. Couldn't believe his good luck someone else did it. He was all about the insurance money he'd get. I had to convince him to get the hell out of town because you all would be hunting *him* down."

"What did he say about the baby?"

Kristi Chen let go of the hair wrapped around her finger and took her time gathering the long mass into her hands and braiding it. She slipped an elastic band from her wrist and wound it several times around the end of the braid.

"Here's why I'm talking to you. I thought about this a lot since, you know." She touched her leg, an electronic monitor strapped at the ankle.

"When Mac first told me how much money he'd get from the insurance on his wife, I admit I was excited. I mean, we were out of work and here came a million bucks we'd share, right? And have the baby, too? Because he swore to me he didn't kill his ex, and like an idiot I believed him."

"So he left town?"

"Yeah. And I didn't want to know where he went so I could deny it. But he didn't have the baby. At first he wanted to go to you guys and tell you how worried he was about Melly, but I convinced him not to do that. Obvious reasons, right? So he just left."

"But he came back."

She nodded. "And he got nailed. Like I told him would happen. And then I got nailed because of him." She hunched forward and flipped her long braid over her shoulder.

Felice leaned forward. "Kristi. What about the baby? What happened to her?"

She locked eyes with him and shook her head. "I don't know. I've been over and over it since being stuck here. What makes the most sense to me is Mac killed both of them, and he was coming back to get rid of me because I could narc on him."

He took in her story, and it made sense. Stuckless could have done exactly what she said. He could even understand how Kristi Chen's baby hunger might have been become Stuckless's primary motivation for murdering his wife, a wife he hated. Felice never doubted Stuckless as the culprit. But the irony wasn't lost on him Chen had validated Rokick's early theory about why it happened. One Felice had chosen to dismiss.

But another bit of information from Dana's frantic phone message pricked at him. "Does Mac Stuckless have any food allergies?"

"Uh, yeah. Peanuts, peanut butter, anything peanut. And chocolate. Especially chocolate. Had to take him to the ER once because of it."

37

LOUISE

2:00 p.m.

L ouise sat at a computer in the small neighborhood library. Angel slept in the stroller next to her chair.

Louise was cold and exhausted. In addition to not sleeping most of last night, after sitting in McDonald's most of the morning, she made a slow pilgrimage back to Walgreens to get some baby aspirin for Angel's fever. When Louise saw the price for even a small bottle, she recoiled and placed it back on the shelf.

She did buy a large bottle of water and trekked to the library, where she could stay until closing at nine. The little one woke up for a short while and drank almost a whole baby-bottle's worth of water. Then she was out again.

Louise wanted Angel to be in perfect shape for when she brought her home to Gerry. She thought the fever could be due to the baby's teething and not illness. She hoped the diarrhea would stop soon though, so she could return to the condo. Just in time for Christmas!

So, she had today and tomorrow to get the baby presentable, and then home to Gerry on Wednesday.

She felt a bit of peace as she sat at the computer for the next three hours looking at things on the internet.

Then she saw a photo of baby Melanie Stuckless on her first birthday, side-by-side with a photo of Margot the Monster, and a photo of a man identified as the Monster's husband. The headline read *Baby missing, Father Held.*

She read the short article. Her body settled in the chair as she realized she was free! The Monster's husband was being held on suspicion of murdering her. The police couldn't find the baby but surmised the husband may have killed her too, and hid the body, because he would get insurance money. One million dollars for Angel! But they would not be looking for her anymore. Louise was safe. Angel was safe. She could take the baby back to Gerry and they would be a family. He wouldn't leave her now because he would have a baby to support.

Angel moaned in her sleep, startling Louise. She picked up the little girl and cradled her in her arms, shushing her. The librarian at the reference desk nearby met Louise's gaze and smiled. Louise gave a slight shrug and hugged Angel to her chest, still afraid the baby might be recognized even though she kept her little coat on and the hood tied tight around her head.

Louise could feel the heat emanating from the small body, which ratcheted up her alarm. Angel wasn't getting better. She untied and lowered the hood, hoping it would cool the baby. The little girl's choppy brown hair was matted to her head with sweat.

Louise didn't know what to do. She was hungry and she could smell Angel had a dirty diaper. Again! She grabbed the diaper bag, stood with Angel draped over her shoulder, and made her way to the bathroom.

Inside, the library had installed one of those changing tables she could open up from the wall. She laid the sleeping baby on it, unsnapped all the snaps on the inside legs of the boy pants Angel wore, and exposed the heavy diaper. This time the inside was filled mostly with pee and a smattering of the green poop.

Just as Louise folded up the dirty diaper to place it in the trash, the bathroom door opened and the same librarian who smiled at her entered. Louise quickly disposed of the diaper and returned to Angel, but the librarian stood at the changing table looking at the little girl. Louise rushed up and bumped the woman with her hip.

"Don't touch him!" She grabbed one flap of the unsnapped pants and lowered it over Angel's legs.

"Oh! No, I wasn't going to touch—him?"

Louise flapped her hand at the librarian to shoo her away. To her relief, the woman entered on of the stalls, ending the conversation.

Louise dispensed with cleaning the baby's bottom. She hurriedly slipped on a fresh diaper, snapped up the pant legs and left the bathroom without washing her hands. She raised the hood on Angel's coat and tied it tight, then laid her daughter in the stroller and headed for the exit.

38

DANA

2:00 p.m.

After the transom incident I spent the morning in bed dozing with the TV on for company. I considered calling in sick for IOP tonight, because I doubted I would feel any better. The attack could certainly justify my absence.

Three warring ideas fought for primacy: I didn't want to show at IOP, deeply ashamed of being unable to defend myself because I was drunk. I did want to show at IOP because I was scared: I'd run out of excused absences and would be kicked out. Then there was the threat of a surprise urine drop.

Being scared won. I would attend IOP tonight and Rosie was here to help me.

I had called her at 1:30 this morning when I couldn't get to sleep after the attack, and she wanted to come over right then. I nixed the idea, and asked her to stay on the phone with me while I recounted what had happened, which she did.

Now she administered ibuprofen, lots of coffee, and orange juice. I was too nauseated to eat anything. Having a hangover was one aspect of drinking hard to tolerate. The memory of it never stopped me from drinking the next day, though.

Rosie helped me get dressed, a decidedly slow process. My knees sported large black and blue marks from hitting the sidewalk on my slip-and-slide way home; my left hip, similarly marked, screamed when I stood or moved. Since my keys were in my stolen backpack, Rosie would drive me to IOP tonight and then help me with getting another car key made.

Rosie showed me how to apply makeup to help hide my hideous bruises, and her skill with the concealer and thick foundation was mostly successful. In addition to a large purple lump on one side of my head, I had a black eye and several bruises on my chin and throat. After knocking me out, my attacker must have slugged me several times and then tried to strangle me. Shit. Bad enough he raped me, but the fucker tried to kill me.

Just as Rosie approached me with what I assumed was *her* curling iron, since I've never used or owned one in my entire life, my doorbell buzzed. Rosie headed for the intercom.

"Wait, Rosie." Some sixth sense told me who might be outside my apartment. A peek out my window to see who stood at the outer door below validated my hunch.

Nuts leaned on the doorbell again. Rosie looked at me with a questioning face and I waved her off. "Nobody I want to see. Ignore it."

Nuts persisted a few more times. He probably guessed I was home—where else would I be after the beating I took—and didn't like my silent refusal.

Too. Fucking. Bad.

A short while later a knock sounded at the door. Rosie motioned for me to stay seated and went to answer it, opening it only as far as the safety chain allowed. I recognized the visitor's voice.

"Hi. I'm Bo. From downstairs. Is Miss Dana home?"

Miss Dana? "It's okay, Rosie. Let him in."

Bo entered, all six-four of him, and stopped right inside the door. He held up my backpack. "This yours?"

I held out my arms and motioned with my hands for him to come over to me. "Yes! Yes! Where did you find it?"

He handed it to me along with a small towel draped over his shoulder. "It's pretty wet. Found it behind the bushes next to the building, shoved in a snow drift."

I laid the towel on my lap and set my backpack on it. My wallet was intact, money, credit cards, license, car keys, all there. The side pocket yielded my cell phone.

"Son of a bitch took it to scare me." I stood slowly and started to return Bo's towel but then pulled back. "Let me wash this for you." I emptied the backpack and put it in my laundry basket along with Bo's towel.

Just as I started to introduce Rosie to Bo, the Amber Alert for the Stuckless baby played on the TV. I pointed to the little girl's picture. She and her mother wore matching outfits.

"I'm working that case." I gave them both a quick rundown of what I'd discovered so far. Bo's attention to and seeming interest in what I said reinforced my certainty about Louise Conway kidnapping the baby.

"I hope you find her. Both of them," he said. He gestured at the back door. "The lock'll have to wait until tomorrow. Had to order it. But Amazon promises delivery by five." He smiled.

"Not a problem. Thanks again for my backpack."

Rosie opened the door for Bo.

"Rosie, Bo. Bo, Rosie," I said. They both chuckled, shook hands, and Bo left.

Rosie closed the door. "That's good news," she said, nodding at the heap of stuff dumped out of my backpack.

"Yeah." I eyed my keys next to my cell. "You don't have to drive me now." I winced at the prospect of walking four blocks to my car. As if reading my mind, Rosie asked me where I was parked. I told her.

"Then I will drive you to your car." She smiled and waved the curling iron at me. "This is cold now. I will heat it up again and show you what to do. You will be so pretty no one will notice, you know," she said, using her palm to make a large circling motion at her face.

"Okay, Mom."

MARVIN FOLLOWED me into his office and closed the door. I gingerly sat in a chair next to his desk. He retrieved a manila folder on top of the file cabinet and handed it to me as he sat in his desk chair, leaned back, and hefted one leg across the other.

"Results from the urine drop earlier tonight. Want to guess what it says?"

I didn't need to guess.

Marvin continued. "Now, these instant tests are pretty accurate but not one hundred percent. I could send it out for further testing but let's be real. All that'll do is give me a more defined number."

I said nothing and tossed the file on his desk.

"Last time we met I mentioned what would happen if you drank again, I think I even said something about you would need a higher level of treatment."

I folded my hands and rested my gaze on them.

"Right? Inpatient treatment." He picked up the folder and gave it a little shake. "This confirms you had alcohol in your system sometime during the last forty-eight hours."

How could I explain this to him? That I didn't purposely drink booze and I actively avoided the spiked punch but got ambushed. Would he even believe it? He probably already knew every story from every alcoholic about how it wasn't their fault.

Marvin tossed the file on his desk and scrutinized me, his arms folded across his chest. He gestured at his own face and then at mine. "Were you drinking when it happened?"

I touched my temple lightly, registering pain. My attempt at covering up the bruises from the attack didn't fool Marvin.

"And don't be telling me nothin' about you walked into a door, or fell down the stairs, or tripped on somethin' or other. I've seen this before. Too many times."

"I don't know."

Confusion on his face. He rolled his chair closer, our knees almost touching, and peered at my face. His voice softened. "Where else?"

I sighed and rolled down the high collar of the turtleneck sweater I wore, knowing it was no use trying to hide further evidence of the attack. I plucked several tissues from the box on his desk and gingerly wiped my face, removing the foundation Rosie so lovingly taught me to apply.

Marvin reacted immediately to what surfaced underneath.

"Who did this to you? I want a name. Give me a name."

A name? Not familiar with the asshole by name. Just a random prick on the move looking to attack someone and finding success with a drunk woman who couldn't defend herself. A brief question about my backpack niggled at me but I lost the thread before I could consider what bothered me about it. The clout on my head plus a serious hangover joined forces to muddle my thinking.

"I wish I could tell you." Before I could continue Marvin pushed back his chair and stood over me.

"I'm a mandated reporter and I know *you* know what that means. I want a name." Hands on his hips, he stared down at me through squinted eyes. "Was it your ex?"

Men. Testosterone takes over and they're ready to duke it out at a moment's notice. And there are times I appreciate that lightning reaction—even depend on it—just not right now.

I looked up at him. "Have a seat, Marvin. I'll tell you what happened." And I did. All of it. Including Rokick's subterfuge. "So, what happens now?"

Marvin ran his hand over his face several times. I almost felt sorry for him. From his point of view, I'm sure I was a difficult client. To say the least.

Once before, when I discovered Mickey in the closet, Marvin let me skate on the rules. I pleaded with him to let me skip IOP so I could stay with Mickey and his sibs until protective services showed up. To his credit, he capitulated. But he issued a stern warning it was my last chance; any more infractions and I would be kicked out of IOP, the end of my job as a cop.

Now it seemed like the end was here. I shifted in my chair but there was no getting comfortable. The ibuprofen I took earlier had worn off. My entire body raged at me and the urge to get drunk tapped me on the shoulder.

Marvin pushed the folder aside. "I can't make this decision. Have to talk to my supervisor, see what she says about your situation."

"Thanks, Marvin. Really." I swiped at my tears of relief with the makeup-mussed tissues. "That means a lot to me."

"Not promising anything, okay?"

"Got it. Sure."

"For what it's worth, you get lots of bonus points from me personally for showing up to IOP tonight." He held up his hand for a high five.

I allowed myself a private smile. "I understand from a friend of mine that nobody does that anymore." But I gave his hand a light tap, not wanting to jolt my body too much. As I stood to leave, a peculiar insight popped up, causing me to abruptly sit again.

Marvin gestured at me. "You okay?"

"Uh, yeah. In an extremely weird way this whole thing suddenly makes Step One, I don't know, understandable?" I pointed to a large poster of AA's 12 Steps on the wall above his desk. *We admitted we were powerless over alcohol—that our lives had become unmanageable.*

"Powerless over alcohol. Yes. Even though I wasn't consciously picking up a drink, once I got going there was no stopping. Anybody else, well, anybody who's not an alcoholic, would've tasted it and put it down, right?"

Marvin nodded. "There's a physiological reaction. The brain springs awake with delight and wants more, more, more." He sang this last part and chuckled.

"Yeah, gotta have more. There's not any thinking, just wanting. And god, unmanageable life? I mean, I can point to all the stuff that's happened to me so far, but I never believed it was because of my drinking. But shit, Marvin, last night I was so drunk I tried to get into my apartment by breaking through a transom window and ended up stuck."

I shook my head, trying to clear the memory of hanging half-in and half-out, seeing my kitchenette from aloft inside and feeling the freezing air on my bare legs as they kicked uselessly outside, and cops shouting at me to *hold it right there.*

"Seemed like a good idea at the time."

D<small>RIVING</small> <small>HOME</small> I neared Louie's Liquor Palace, slowing down and finally pulling over to the curb. I lit another Kool from the butt of the one I was smoking, flicking the spent cigarette into the street. Regardless of my Step One insight, I wanted to drink.

The earlier urge to get drunk now spread through my entire thought process, demanding oblivion, offering a break from my physical pain, and promising to soften the harsh truth: my future depended on Marvin and his supervisor. All excellent reasons to get wrecked.

My cell phone buzzed in the back pocket of my jeans. I extricated it and stared at the screen as Siri announced my ex-partner, his name lighting up the dark interior of my car, Springsteen's *Born to Run* his calling card. There was no way I could talk to him, no way I could listen to anything Nuts wanted to say, especially after what happened last night. He probably wanted to chew me out with some caustic comeback to my hysterical phone message.

Today my anger at him continued unabated, though at a simmer, and now it welled up and erupted like a ripe blister. I debated whether to answer and blast him again without letting him say a word. But...no. He wouldn't even get that from me. I turned off the ignition, stuck my phone back in my pocket without answering, and headed into Louie's for some relief.

Back at my building, as I passed the unit on the second floor on the way up to my studio, loud music blared from behind the closed door and spilled onto the landing. Where were they last night when I needed them? Right now I had no desire to confront drunk college boys about turning down the noise. I'd leave it to Sandor's son, Bo.

Inside my place I laid two six-packs and a bottle of wine on my kitchenette counter. The glass in the transom above my back door good as
new, Bo replacing it while I was at IOP. My studio felt decidedly
warmer. I took a long, hot shower to soothe my aching body, put on
sweats and my long fleece robe, and then settled down to drink and
watch a movie. With any luck I might pass out.

My cell phone dinged an incoming text.

> Did you get my msg? pls listen to it. I was
> wrong.

I lit a cigarette and re-read the text several times. Nuts rarely admitted
being wrong. Of course, he rarely *was* wrong. My curiosity about his
message overrode my anger. As I tapped the message icon my
stomach growled. I hadn't eaten at all today, trying to assuage my
nagging nausea. I stopped his message from playing and got up,
scrambled three eggs and buttered *two* pieces of toast—take that, PP
—and made quick work of the whole thing.

And then I listened. Nuts apologized. For not believing me about the
punch, for not driving me home, for putting me out on the icy street.
"Don't worry about Koz. He doesn't know. I'll take care of Rokick and
what he did to you."

What *Rokick* did to me? That was junior high stuff. Nuts was the one
who put me out of his car, which precipitated the attack. Graduate
level, pal.

He ended sounding sheepish about the Louise Conway video—he'd
deleted it again—and asked me to re-send it to him.

I wasn't mollified by Nuts's message, except to appreciate he did call
me, did affirm what I told him about Rokick. But so what if he
believed me now? What difference did it make? Louise was still out
there with the baby. At least I hoped so. And Mac Stuckless sat in jail
charged with two counts of murder.

Even though Nuts assured me about Koz not knowing I was drunk, I couldn't assume everyone else at the party would also stay mum, especially Rokick, if what I suspected about him was right. Anyway, now the decision rested with Marvin's supervisor.

As for me re-sending Nuts the video of Louise Conway? Good friggin' luck. Three strikes and all that. Rokick had watched the video, discounted it, and charged Stuckless with his wife's murder.

No. Louise was mine and I was going to find her, I was going to find that baby, and I was going to present it all to Nuts and Rokick, proving I was a hell of a lot better detective than either of them.

Koz would see, too. Even if Nuts had decided part of my motivation for pursuing Louise was to impress our boss, I didn't harbor any delusions my work would persuade Koz to drop my suspension. We were way past that. But my pride wanted him to be aware it was me.

I played Nuts's message once more. He said nothing about the attack, which infuriated me all over again. One tiny silver lining I identified in therapy earlier tonight was that the rapist walloped me unconscious. I wasn't awake during the actual act, meaning I wouldn't have to re-live that specific horror. Truthfully, getting beaten up in the attack was frightening enough, and the physical pain remained a continuous reminder of last night.

I scrolled my messages, found Nuts's text, and replied: *STOP.* Like he was nothing but annoying spam.

I flipped on the TV, pulled a can of beer from the six-pack, and set it on the floor next to the futon. The same Amber Alert for baby Melanie Stuckless appeared on the screen. I stopped what I was doing and gazed at the little girl's photo, then grabbed my phone and took a pic.

A beautiful child, beautiful in the way only babies can be; perfect skin, clear eyes, nothing of the horrible world reflected on a face smiling and open to all possibilities.

While I was pregnant, I imagined just such a baby waiting inside of me to be born, certain it would be a girl. My daughter. Our daughter, Jimmy's and mine. But my miscarriage ended all that and I drank. Then my drinking ended my marriage.

With anger on my side, I now had a double-duty reason to find Louise Conway: I would rescue baby Melanie, which in turn would help keep at bay reminders of the recent attack.

A text on my phone registered with a ding. Rosie was downstairs and wanted to come up for a second to check on how I was doing. I buzzed her in, then saw the rest of the booze sitting on the counter. I quickly stowed it in the fridge and hid the single can of beer under the pillow on my futon.

"Hola!" She always trilled this song-like version of her greeting, and it always made me smile. I knew *poquito* Spanish, but I hola'd back and we hugged. Her hug was intentionally light, a nod to my injuries. Inside, I fixed us both some herbal tea. While Rosie was in the bathroom, I heard her exclaim something in Spanish and then call out to me asking if I had a tampon she could borrow.

"You can have it, Rosie. No borrowing." I was trying to make a joke about her returning a used tampon, but it fell flat. No corresponding laugh. "They're under the sink. Should be a box of them."

Rosie emerged from the bathroom. "Thanks, mija. My little friend arrived two days early. You only had three left. Let me buy a box and bring them over."

I held up my hand. "No need. I'll get some tomorrow." The mention of her period arriving two days early gave me pause. I don't track my period on a calendar or app with any precision the way some women do because my body always gives me a lower back pain warning followed by some nausea. Invariably, my period arrives the next day. But right now, my total body pain from the attack masked any other normal pain, so I couldn't rely on my regular forecaster.

I retrieved two cups of chamomile tea from the kitchenette, and we sat on the couch.

"Mmm, so good," Rosie said. "Warms me up. It's pretty cold out there."

"Really glad the salt trucks got most of the streets in shape after Saturday night."

We chatted a short while about what the weather would bring for Christmas, Rosie in favor of a white one, me, only a dusting. That way I could drive JJ and Evie to Saint Nick's for midnight mass without having too much trouble on the roads.

Rosie scrutinized my face. "Are you feeling any better since yesterday? How did your program go?"

I recounted what happened with Marvin. Rosie, being the good friend, was properly shocked. "But that wasn't you drinking on purpose! Your counselor must understand this, yes?"

"I know, I know. Marvin's a good guy, really. He is. He's let me slide before. I have to wait and see what they decide." I surprised myself at sounding so patient about a decision that could possibly mean the end of my job as a cop.

Rosie deposited her tea bag on a small plate on the side table, then held the plate out to me so I could do the same. We sipped in silence for a minute.

"What is it? You are frowning. Are you in pain?" Rosie put her cup down and scooted closer to me. "Can I get some pills for you?"

I smiled at my friend. "You are such a good person, Rosie. Always taking care of me. No. I already took some ibuprofen and it sort of helps." Not to mention the two six-packs and bottle of wine that would *really* help. I touched the side of my head and then recoiled from my own hand. The lump would sure smart for a while.

I frowned again. "No. I was trying to remember when my period was last time." Before I could continue, she cut in.

"I can get the Plan B pill at the store. I can go right now." She stood.

I slammed my cup down on the side table. "Jesus, Rosie! I don't even want to think about that! Bad enough he raped me—don't make it worse."

She retrieved a sponge from the kitchen sink and wiped up the spilled tea from my outburst.

I gestured for her to sit. "I—I'm sorry I yelled at you. I wasn't trying to remember my last period because I'm scared I might get pregnant. That's not why. I mean, there's more to it."

Rosie jumped in again. "But those pills only work if you take them quickly after, after the, you know, *rape*."

I smiled at her rolling *rrrr*, making rape sound musical, almost friendly. "I don't want to take the Plan B pills because I'm not sure if the bastard came inside me."

I pointed to the lump on my head. "He knocked me out, so I don't know what really happened. When I came to, his slime was on my legs, so it seems like maybe he didn't go all the way inside? I just don't know."

"Oh." Rosie took my free hand in both of hers and held it in her lap, a simple expression of consolation and support.

After a minute I stood and went to the fridge. Mickey's tree picture—his little beacon of hope—seemed to throb in the overhead light. I unearthed the two six-packs and bottle of wine and repacked them in the plastic bag from Louie's. I hauled the bag over to my friend and handed it to her.

"Here, Rosie. I was going to get totally wasted tonight. But you interrupted me and I'm glad you did. Take it. Do whatever with it." The noise from downstairs had toned down a bit but it sounded like the party was still a thing. "Maybe give it to those guys on two on your way out."

Rosie accepted the bag with a solemn nod but no words and left soon after.

I was tired, sore, and exhausted from every minute of the the last forty-eight hours. I wanted the sweet release of sleep. Wearing my sweats to bed was a no-brainer and I lay down on my futon. My head hit the pillow and something hard: the can of beer I initially hid from Rosie.

I grabbed the can and went to the back door. The latch on Bo's new up-to-code lock, now in place, was easy to twist open. Outside, I stood near the railing and cracked open the beer, poured it over the side until it ran out, then pitched the can clinking down the alley as it skittered away. Now I could sleep.

39

DANA

12/24 7:00 a.m.

At breakfast the next morning I rededicated myself to following my food plan in order to drop the weight and eventually get back to my real work. I had to pretend—hope was too hard—I wouldn't be fired.

The PP program wasn't complicated, but I was surprised at how much food—actually, make that how little food—I was supposed to eat, especially compared to the amount I normally ate. Three meals and two snacks a day. A snack in PP parlance meant a piece of fruit or some cut-up vegetables dipped in fat-free dressing. A snack to me? A bag of Cheetos. A large bag.

Three meals hasn't been a reality since becoming a cop ten years ago. I always ate something in the morning, but lately it depended on how I felt. When I battled a hangover in the morning the only thing my stomach would tolerate was a popsicle and a cold, cold Pepsi. Both helped my headache and furry mouth.

The squad room always had junk available; almond crescent rolls from a nearby Italian bakery, foil pans of Sara Lee brownies, or a sack of McMuffins if someone felt motivated to buy something "healthier." But then came long periods of going without, working homicide cases for eighteen or twenty-four hours straight, most often cadging cups of coffee on the run and little else. The work came first, personal needs last.

I stared at my instant oatmeal interrupted by a few raisins and drowned in fat-free milk, willing myself to enjoy it. I couldn't. The taste made me gag, so I held my nose as I shoveled it in, the gooey texture annoying but tolerable. At least it dulled my hunger. I dutifully recorded it on my app and immediately began thinking about lunch.

As I cleaned up, my cell rang. Marvin. My stomach clenched. I considered letting it go to voicemail. But I couldn't wait: was I in or out?

"Demeter."

"Morning, Dana. It's Marvin. How're you doing?"

"Hey, Marvin. Still pretty sore but on the mend." This last part was a lie, but I didn't want to dwell on my injuries. "What's up?"

"I had that talk with my supervisor about your situation, what happened."

As soon as I heard his apologetic tone of voice, I knew what was coming. I jumped in.

"And I'm kicked out, right? No more IOP?" I sat at my desk, flipped a cigarette out of my pack of Kools and lit it. Deep drag. Sharp exhale.

"Kicked out? No. Not how I'd call it. Transferred. My supervisor thinks you'd do better with the inpatient program. She—"

"I don't have time for that, Marvin. Locked up for a month? Come on." The smell of unwashed bodies and urine stink from Rameeka's inpatient unit came back full force. Thirty days of that?

"Look. There's some silver lining here, you know. Right now, there's no bed open, won't be until about the first of the year. Or maybe a little after."

I pictured drinking during that time—from now until then—the idea both appealing and appalling. Marvin kept talking.

"Unless one opens up before. But listen. I put in a while back to transfer to our inpatient unit, to be a counselor there, and it was finally approved. I'll start about the same time a bed should open up for you. My supe said I could continue as your one-on-one."

There was a smile in his voice I couldn't help responding to. Marvin liked me.

"I wanted to let you know first, before any of this is written up and sent to the EAP at your job."

My job. Crap. "You think I'll be fired because I failed IOP?"

"Not up to me, of course. But my boss will go over it with your EAP and they take it from there with your boss."

Koz. Koz at Rokick's party. Rokick refilling my cup with spiked punch. Nuts pushing me from his car onto an ice-slicked sidewalk. Sliding, falling, a stranger helping me into the foyer and wham—the whole night rushed in at me.

"I'm tired, Marvin. Do I have to give you an answer right now about inpatient?" I tapped a long ash from my cigarette onto the floor.

"No, no. It won't be me, see? Your boss—" I heard paper shuffling in the background.

"Lieutenant Kozlowski."

The paper shuffling stopped. "Right. He'll be the one to talk to you about your job. This'll take some time, maybe about a week or a little more, for everything. Think about what you want, Dana. What do you want?"

Marvin went on for a bit about some other details, but I stopped listening. What I *want* didn't fit into any of my recent experiences. Nuts and I were on the outs, he'd get a different partner if Rokick didn't succeed, and my entire body continued to shriek from the attack.

I stood and doused my cigarette in the dishwater, then smushed the grey ash on the floor with my sock-covered foot. Marvin ended the call with the news I wasn't required to attend IOP anymore but strongly encouraged it until the inpatient bed opened up. You know, just to have something to do. His not-so-subtle message? Something to do instead of drinking.

The nausea from yesterday still persisted, although now I couldn't tell if it originated from the lousy oatmeal, Marvin's bad news, or something more worrying. I checked out Rosie's idea of Plan B, not really knowing much about it.

The online information startled me: it was only effective three to five days after the attack, best if taken within the first 72 hours. I counted backwards to Sunday night, which came to about 34 hours. Then I read women weighing 150 or more—meaning me at 180—wouldn't benefit as much.

I checked in online with my health plan's urgent care center. The physician's assistant asked me a series of questions and I said Jimmy and I had sex a few weeks ago. I didn't mention the rape because I was unwilling to be quizzed about why I didn't report it, but also for the same reason I told Rosie: I didn't know if the bastard finished inside me.

Then came the kicker about the date of my last period.

"I'm not sure. That's the problem. If I had to guess I'd say it's been four weeks."

"At your age, being late can happen. It's even normal, in fact. Especially if you've been experiencing undue stress."

Uh, yeah. Miscarriage. Job suspension. Divorce. On the outs with my former partner. Physical assault and rape. Now failing IOP and having to join the other sickos for a month of inpatient.

"That must be it. There has been a lot of stress." I'm amazed at how calm I sound.

"Make an appointment with your gyne, get a full workup. Or you could get an OTC pregnancy test if that's your concern. Also, abortion is legal in Illinois, so that doesn't have to worry you."

The irony wasn't lost on me. After eight months of grief over my miscarriage of a wanted and cherished baby, I was now looking for a way to terminate a possible pregnancy.

I clicked off. The stress idea really did appeal to me, explained a lot. I'll give it another week, about the same length of reprieve Marvin gave me to think about what I want, and if my "little friend" doesn't show then I'll go to Walgreens.

40

DANA

8:30 a.m.

After Marvin's bad news, I had about an hour before reporting to PP to interpret for Bear. I'll admit I acted out a bit, angry about the very real possibility Koz would can me after the EAP gave him the news I failed IOP.

The acting out? I rationalized I didn't need to lose forty pounds as part of my agreement to keep my job. In the event I might be pregnant I wouldn't have to follow those regs. So, I took myself out to breakfast at The Elite restaurant where Nuts and I had a permanent table for the past three years discussing our cases over excellent Greek omelets. The weight loss would become an issue once I decided whether or not to go through with the pregnancy. For now, I wanted some comfort food and a friendly atmosphere.

Prior to heading out I assessed my bruises—still frightening enough to draw stares from people—and decided to pack on the makeup Rosie gave me. It took several layers, but I finally managed to hide most of it. My turtleneck sweater covered the attacker's stranglehold marks.

I slid into one of the red leather booths on the far side of the restaurant, purposely sitting with my back to the well-stocked bar near the bathroom. A thought slithered in: I had a week or more before reporting to the inpatient program, a week where it didn't matter to Koz, or Nuts, or even Jimmy, whether or not I drank. That was assuming I would acquiesce to the thirty-day program.

I held onto the slim notion Koz would wait and see if I could succeed there and reward me with reinstatement to my job and partnership with Nuts. But our original agreement applied to successfully completing the *outpatient* program which, clearly, I did not. So.

In a nod to possibly being pregnant I opted out of drinking coffee, which lately tastes metallic to me, and ordered hot chocolate. My oatmeal this morning a distant memory, I ordered a gyros omelet, complete with hash browns, pancakes, and a side of fruit. I ate every last bite.

Chris Sepsakos, the owner, met me at the register.

"Good to see you, Detective. It has been a while." He took my cash and made change.

I agreed it had been. "I've been doing some undercover work." Not the truth but not a complete lie, either. I stuffed the change in my jacket pocket.

Chris peered at me, an intense once-over of my face. Maybe he didn't believe my lie. Or maybe he was studying my incongruous, inch-thick makeup. "Your partner has been in several times." He frowned and gestured at the table next to the register. "With some other man."

I nodded. "Yes. Well." I wasn't going to discuss my errant partner or the scum temp. "Good to see you, Chris. *Kala Cristouyenna.*" Merry Christmas.

He smiled. "*Hronia Polla.*" Happy New Year.

Since that was the extent of my speaking and understanding Greek, I flashed a thumbs-up and headed out to interpret for Bear.

AFTER INTERPRETING AT PP, I pulled Bear aside and told him this would be my last meeting. Since I didn't need to lose weight right now, I wouldn't be bartering my services in exchange for membership anymore. He looked crestfallen.

"I need you for interpreter. Can't understand what they say—too fast." He waved his arm indicating the women exiting the meeting.

"I know. I'll talk to J-F." I fingerspelled Janey Foreman's initials near my mouth—our invented sign name for the leader—and braced for an uncomfortable conversation. *"Come with me."*

We made our way up to the podium in front of the meeting room where Janey Foreman stood reading something on her phone. Before we reached her, I stopped and quickly told Bear I was going to tell her a little bit about the law requiring interpreters. Since it's impossible to sign in ASL—Bear's preferred language—while speaking in English, he'd have to trust me on this. I also told him when she responded to me, I'd hold her info until our conversation was done, then give it all to him in ASL. He agreed, and wanted me to interpret something to Janey afterwards. I nodded.

"Hi, Janey. Got a minute? I have a bit of news and then Bear wants to say something."

"Of course. How was your weigh-in?" Since she was looking at Bear, I went ahead and interpreted this to him. He shrugged and mimed a see-sawing of his hand. I voiced "so-so," even though I knew he gained weight again this week, because that was up to him to spill.

"And how about you?" Janey asked me.

"Well, that's part of what I wanted to talk to you about." I signed this to Bear also, and then told him I was going to use my voice now and not sign. He nodded.

When I told Janey Foreman I was dropping out of PP she exclaimed, "Oh! I hope it isn't anything I've done."

I wasn't sure how she came to this conclusion, so I ignored it and told her it was for health reasons. "Since I won't be here, Bear is going to need an interpreter for these meetings." I summarized the law—the American with Disabilities Act—about providing access for people with disabilities and reiterated in Bear's case this meant interpreters. I gave her a couple of names of agencies where she could hire someone.

She pointed at Bear. "So, do I send him the bill then? For these interpreters?"

Internally, I swore; externally, I smiled. "Afraid not. That's the whole point of the ADA. Places that provide services to the general public," I gestured at the room, "like PP, need to provide equal access to those services for everyone. So, you've seen outside this building are steps leading inside, but next to the steps is a ramp for someone who might be in a wheelchair. That's physical access."

"Oh, sure! I get it."

"Whoever built this building *paid* for the ramp to be included. Same goes for our PP meetings. But in this case the access Bear needs is information in a language he can understand."

The light came on for her. "Oh! So, *PP* has to pay for the interpreter."

I nodded. "You and I bartered for my services up until now and that's another form of payment. You might be able to do that with another interpreter. Or they may ask to be paid."

Janey Foreman face showed she didn't follow.

"Paid with cash. Money."

Long pause before the light went on. Then, "How about I just give him some written materials he can read?"

I was getting aggravated at having to explain this stuff, especially considering the ADA became law in 1990. Why the hell weren't people aware of it by now?

"Look, Janey. I have someplace to be and don't have time to go through all this with you. Here's my suggestion. For next week's meeting call one of the agencies and hire an interpreter. In the meantime, call your corporate office and talk to someone in, and write this down, risk management."

She looked worried. Guess she knew it meant lawyer. She jotted this in her phone.

"It's a lot cheaper to hire interpreters than it is to be sued. Trust me." I turned to Bear and explained what had transpired, assuring him he would have an interpreter next week, and if not, text me. *"Your turn."*

"I like your meeting and need interpreter to understand everything. Please get interpreter for me." He gave Janey a big grin and patted her shoulder.

Fingers crossed, this would suffice.

41

LOUISE

9:00 a.m.

Louise returned to Walgreens on Christmas Eve pushing the stroller with Angel asleep in it.

The first night at the shelter was bad, but last night was worse. The heat! Louise was awake all night, little Angel snoring next to her on the cot, waves of fever rolling off the baby like a furnace stuck on high. When it came time to leave this morning, Louise felt feverish, too. She couldn't shake it off even outside in the cold winter wind.

She was convinced the germs in the shelter made Angel sick. They were not going back there tonight. The only good thing the shelter provided was a Christmas bag for each person containing enough food for the whole day.

Walgreens was almost empty except for the pharmacy and one cashier. Louise went to the pain reliever aisle, picked out two different large bottles of baby aspirin, and pretended to compare them.

Holding both bottles in one hand, she bent low over the stroller, feigned adjusting the baby's coat, and dropped the bottle she wanted onto the stroller seat next to the baby and quickly pulled Angel's blanket over it.

She fake-shopped for a short while and then bought a small bottle of Gatorade and exited the store. The cold air was a relief to her feverish body and she left her coat unzipped, waving the sides open and closed a few times to hurry the cooling.

The cherry Gatorade was refreshing and Louise guzzled almost the entire bottle, only to remember she needed to give some to Angel. She unearthed the stolen baby aspirin from the stroller and tapped one out for her baby. It was hard to get it down Angel's throat because the baby kept turning her head away, so Louise stuck her finger in the little one's mouth and pushed the tiny pill back, back, back, until Angel swallowed.

Success! Louise was able to get Angel to take a few sips of the cherry drink, though most of it dribbled down her little jacket, the droplets freezing there. Sleep. That's all the baby needed now. Louise laid her back in the stroller and tucked the blanket around her.

She needed someplace to go so she and the baby could recover enough to go home tomorrow and be with Gerry. His Christmas present. She ran through the places she had been but discarded them all, still not wanting to risk being found.

In the distance, she heard the rattle of a train running on the tracks.

42

DANA

11:00 p.m.

E vie and JJ always attended midnight mass at Saint Nick's on Christmas Eve, and this year was no different. When Jimmy and I were married we would go with them, as often as not, unless we were working a case. The family tradition back when I was a kid was to go to midnight mass with my parents, twin brother David, and younger sister Daphne.

After that, home to bed. No Christmas tree decorated our living room, even at that late date; no presents, nothing to indicate it was special and not simply another night.

And then? Christmas morning the three of us would jump out of bed before daylight and run downstairs to the living room where a fully decorated tree waited for us, lights twinkling and presents stacked underneath. Santa had done it again.

Years later—*after* I stopped believing in the big guy in the red suit—I quizzed JJ about why he and Evie waited until the night before to do up the tree. He responded with one sign, rubbing his thumb back and forth over his fingertips, the universal gesture for money. A city lot selling trees near Saint Nick's stayed open all night on Christmas Eve and the remaining inventory went really cheap. JJ would drop us off at home after mass, and while Evie put us to bed he returned to the lot and secured a tree.

"Sometimes the tree was free!" JJ admitted he played the deaf card, so the guy pitied him. Most of what we considered the good gifts under the tree were from our grandparents, who played along with the charade and let us think the gifts came directly from the North Pole. My parents supplied the mundane stuff—underwear, socks, and school supplies.

Tonight, as my parents and I entered Saint Nick's, Evie stopped to chat with a friend, and JJ and I continued ahead to sit in a pew near the front. He shed his winter jacket and gestured at mine as if to help me take it off. I shook my head and told him a lie.

"I'm cold." The truth was I wore my shoulder holster and carried my Glock now, something I never used to do outside of work. Since the attack, I swore I wouldn't get caught again without being able to protect myself. I still blamed myself for the ease with which that bastard overpowered me. Also, I doubted JJ would approve my carrying while in church. I was pretty sure Father Mik would frown on it, too.

After we admired the altar replete with large poinsettia plants alternating in red and white, JJ teased me. *"Want to come home with us and wait for Santa?"* He used the older ASL sign for Santa Claus, a curved hand on each side of his mouth and puffing outward and down twice, as if outlining Santa's beard.

I gave his knee a light slap and grinned. *"You fooled me a long time! I still believed in Santa 'til I was thirteen."* I used the newer sign for Santa Claus I'd seen deaf kids use, touching my chin first with the letter *s* and then opening up to the letter *c*.

My father's huge smile dimmed, and he looked down at his hands resting on his knees. I laid my left hand over his right and he raised his eyes.

I signed with one hand. *"Making Christmas morning magic for us, letting us believe Santa came overnight and set it all up, that was the best thing about Christmas. You did that."* I squeezed his hand. He let go and patted my knee, nodding his head, his expression still melancholic.

"What?" I gestured, infusing the one sign with the idea I was responding to his facial expression, his seeming sadness, with my own mirrored expression.

JJ dismissed my question with a small wave of his hand. I pressed him again, unused to seeing him like this.

"OK. A short minute I thought about your baby," and then he used the sign for *gone*, as in disappeared, instead of the actual sign for *dead*, which would be crude or shocking in this case. The sign he used also carried the meaning for dead—more like the euphemism *passed away* in the hearing world—but was softer and considerate of the other person's feelings, something my father always demonstrated.

I put my arm around his shoulders and hugged him to me. In my self-absorbed grief about my miscarriage, I never considered how it affected my parents. They would have been grandparents for the first time. And now our little joke about JJ's Christmas charade laid out his hidden feelings and made me realize he looked forward to continuing the tradition with the next generation. He never said. Until now.

Evie bustled into the pew, breaking the moment. She sat next to JJ, full of news from the deaf grapevine, and informed me they wouldn't need a ride back home after mass.

"Eggnog at Sarah's," my mother announced. JJ's surprised expression —raised eyebrows and widened eyes—conveyed his normal reaction to Evie's last-minute social date; she plans, he follows. Only lately has JJ struck out on his own, bowling with guy friends—no women

allowed—or hoisting an occasional beer while playing darts at the local bar. Even though it was past my parents' normal bedtime, I knew JJ wouldn't resist this invite. Sarah Gilbert was a long-time friend of his.

After mass my parents joined the crowd heading out. I trailed behind. Father Mik stood at the back of the church wishing the parishioners a signed *Merry Christmas,* or sometimes using the abbreviated finger-spelled *M-C.* He thanked people for coming out on such a cold night and hoped they would attend St. Nick's later on this morning to celebrate Christmas mass with him.

"Dana, hello!" Father Mik signed and spoke his greeting, always sensitive to any deaf people around, even though the majority had already cleared out. I followed his lead and wished him a signed *Merry Christmas.*

"Doubtful I'll be back tomorrow, though," I said and signed. I winked at him. Father Mik was well aware of my resistance to most things Catholic since I stopped attending church with my parents when I was sixteen.

"No pressure. You know that. Although I could try to entice you. There will be plenty of Christmas hymns tomorrow before and during mass." He used only his voice. We now were the only two people—hearing or deaf—left in the church. Even the deaf altar boy had hurriedly snuffed the candles after mass and rushed out to meet his parents.

"Hmm." I pretended to give his offer some consideration. "As much as I like the Christmas music, sleeping in has more attraction for me these days." And my sore body reminded me in no uncertain terms I needed more pain relievers, the earlier dose now depleted.

Father Mik had the good grace to chuckle at my confession but then turned serious. "Do you have a few minutes? I would like to talk with you about your email."

I agreed, my promise at the Saint Nick's holiday party to follow up with him all but forgotten. I detoured upstairs for some water and ibuprofen while he locked up the front doors of the church.

We met in the sacristy on the first floor of the parish hall. I stood at the door and peered into the office.The only light emanated from a gooseneck lamp on Father Mik's small desk, where he sat perusing a printout of what I assumed was my email about Fabrizio's $45,000.

"Maybe I can explain more—" I said as I started to enter the room, but he cut me off with a raised hand.

"No need. I cannot accept this money. I understand your impulse to help Mickey and his foster family and yes, this money would be an immense help. But the money's origin is suspect. And the danger attached is frankly frightening." He laid the printout on the desk and folded his hands, not looking at me.

"I...I'm sorry for putting you in that position." I stayed standing, not even sure if I should sit. What could I say? I thought the money would be welcomed regardless of Fabrizio's possible retaliation. The familiar bump of the Glock under my arm reinforced my personal understanding of the priest's fear.

Father Mik was quiet for a long moment. He beckoned me to sit across from him, which I did. I picked up the email and studied it, too embarrassed to look directly at him.

"You have the heart of concern, and thinking of Mickey's family is a most admirable trait. Please do not let my rejection of this money stop your generosity toward others."

I shook my head no. In my mind I was already trying out other schemes to part Fabrizio from his dirty money. More consideration of who should get the money would take a while.

I looked up from the email. Father Mik was staring intently at me. He gestured at his own face with an open palm. "What on earth happened?"

I touched the still-sore welt where my attacker's blows knocked me out. Too late, I realized Father Mik could see my black eye and the purple stain still spreading down my cheek, which ended in a hideous mix of green and yellow. While I was upstairs getting some water, I'd moistened a paper towel and scrubbed off Rosie's thick, itchy foundation, forgetting what lay beneath.

I forced a fake chuckle. "I don't suppose you'd believe I walked into a door?" I said, harkening back to Marvin's line. I could tell from Father Mik's expression he wasn't having any of it. He didn't need to say a word.

"I was attacked. And pretty beat up." I hooked an index finger over the top of my turtleneck sweater and lowered it to reveal the bruising from being choked.

Father Mik gasped. I didn't intend to relay the whole story but once the slide show started in my mind I launched into the entire sordid episode about the night of Rokick's party and the aftermath.

"And I might be pregnant." This spewed from me like a blast of water from a broken pipe. "I don't know what to do. I'm not going to carry that bastard's baby." I said nothing about the possibility it could be Jimmy's.

When I finished, Father Mik stayed silent for a moment. Then, "I understand your reluctance in that regard."

I knew Father Mik well enough to realize he had a lot more to say but was holding back. "*More, please,*" I signed. I wanted his counsel but didn't trust I could keep my tongue from spitting out the sarcastic reply: Oh, you *understand*, do you?

Father Mik placed his hands on the desk, palms down, and tilted his head to the side, his thought pose. Then, "First, the Catholic Church considers abortion a mortal sin. Murder."

I started to object but he held up his hands. "So, I cannot suggest abortion as a means of solving this, you see. I cannot." He shrugged.

I nodded. Of course he couldn't. Probably the Vatican Police would show up and arrest him.

"We often cannot know God's plan until later, when we look back, and then it is revealed."

Okay. More pablum. I leaned forward across the small desk to chew him out about this particular crap. "God's plan was for me to be *raped*?"

Father Mik recoiled—I was really in his face—and shook his head. "Forgive me, Dana, I am a bit tired and not at my best. Here is what I am trying to say. Think of the pregnancy this way. The baby is not to blame for what happened. He or she just *is*. You have to ask yourself if you can accept this gift from God without criticizing the origin."

"Oh? So don't look a gift horse in the mouth?" I said, slinging as much sarcasm as I could muster.

Father Mik winced and cracked a small smile, his voice dry. "I am not in the habit of thinking of God as a horse, but yes, I think you get my drift."

"No. No way I can do that. Not any more than you can take the money I'm trying to donate because its origin is suspect." I drew quotes around this last phrase.

I briefly considered if having a baby would lift my sadness about the miscarriage, then argued with myself I wanted Jimmy's baby, not just any baby. Yet following hard on that thought came the face of Mickey's little sister, Emma, who I loved and would gladly adopt as my own.

I didn't voice the rest of my worries: What do I do if I *am* pregnant with Jimmy's baby? How do I tell him? *Do* I tell him? If it is his, how do I live with the utter irony of it now we're divorced? There's a lot more to consider if this is Jimmy's baby, and I'm not even sure if I am pregnant or not.

I left Father Mik at his desk and walked out in a huff. This was not the kind of *gift* I was expecting on Christmas.

43

DANA

12/25 6:30 a.m.

I got home from Saint Nick's at 1:30 Christmas morning and piled on more pain relievers before crawling into my futon. The streetlights' orangish rays strayed through the windows above my futon. Gotta get those curtains. I pulled my comforter over my head. A short five hours later Evie called me on videophone, frantic.

"Your father didn't come home!" Apparently, their friend Sarah's eggnog invite included a bunch of other deaf people and the party went late, my parents got a ride home, and Evie admitted to *sleep fast, too much booze.*

When she woke up JJ wasn't in his customary place next to her in bed or anywhere in the house. I tried to calm her down with a few ideas about where my father could be this early on Christmas morning, but truly I didn't believe any of them myself.

"Call hospitals, cops, ambulance place! Find him!" Evie's orders set me on edge, but I had to admit they also worried me. I had no idea where to start with so little to go on. I assured her I would make

some phone calls and then get back to her. In the meantime, I told her to call their mutual friends and check if JJ was with any of them.

No sooner did we finish on VP than my cell rang.

"Demeter."

"Is this Dana Demeter? Detective Dana Demeter?"

"Yes. Who's this?"

"I'm Sergeant Roscoe with CPD. Is your father John Joseph Demeter?"

I started crying, thinking the worst. "Yes, yes. What happened? Is he okay?"

The sergeant told me JJ was arrested early this morning for breaking and entering into a house on the north side. He was also drunk and disorderly and they had to tase him in order to get the cuffs on. JJ? My mild-mannered father?

The sergeant gave me the address of the station, not far from Jimmy's and my former house, and asked if I would be willing to come interpret for JJ because they couldn't get an interpreter this early, especially on Christmas.

"And the interpreting agency is wanting to charge us double time and a half once they do find somebody. We got no money in the budget for that, so if you can help us out..."

I wasn't about to launch into what the 1990 law required even though I wanted to ream this guy for so blatantly skirting the ADA. I told him I'd be there within the hour and disconnected. I texted Evie a short message telling her I found JJ, he was okay, and I'd bring him home in a while.

During the previous five hours while I was asleep a snow squall hit the city and dumped a fresh four inches over the slush and dirty snow lining the curbs. I had to get some coffee in me before facing this truly puzzling situation.

My father has never gone afoul of the law, not even so much as a parking ticket. He praised Jimmy and me countless times over the years about our jobs as cops, keeping the peace, throwing bad guys in jail; he was a model citizen, for sure. I downed only about half the cup of coffee from Starbucks, the funny metallic taste still dogging me, then smoked a cigarette and made my way to the station.

When I arrived, JJ sat in an interrogation room, his hands in his lap, a bottle of water on the table. I rushed to him and started peppering him with a million questions. In response, he held up his cuffed hands.

"Get those off him," I ordered the sergeant. "How do you expect him to talk?"

"Talk? He's deaf and dumb, isn't he?"

I almost slugged the guy. "He's *deaf*. He talks with his *hands*. Ever hear of American Sign Language? Isn't that why you called me to come interpret? What did you think I was going to do, write him *notes*?" By the end of my tirade my voice had hit the squeaky outrage register. I sounded like Mickey Mouse on a rampage.

I motioned again at JJ's hands in cuffs. At least the sergeant blushed and looked sheepish when he unlocked the manacles. While JJ and I waited for the detective on duty to come question him, I got the full story. It was my fault. All of it.

JJ admitted to having too much to drink at Sarah's party. It didn't take much to affect him, since he rarely drank more than one beer with a meal. He was feeling pretty happy when a friend drove him and Evie home.

"Your mother conked out. Drunk." He laughed and I had to smile because she, too, rarely drank and probably didn't even finish one cup of eggnog. JJ felt wide awake and couldn't sleep because he had a

great idea: after reminiscing with me at Saint Nick's about how he set up the tree overnight when we were kids, he decided he would surprise me by doing it again. So, he left Evie in bed and went out to the local corner lot and got a cheap tree.

"Not free this time. The man didn't care about deaf." He shook his head at this change.

He tied the tree to the top of his car, drove north to Jimmy's and my former home, and proceeded to use his key to enter the house thinking he would set up the tree and surprise me in the morning.

"The furniture was different. I thought you got new." In the midst of JJ hauling the tree onto the porch and inside, the new owners, the Johnsons, heard him downstairs and called the cops. They came and carted him away. He had no idea why different people were in my house.

All my fault. I didn't tell my parents about selling the house because that would lead to having to tell them Jimmy and I divorced. I completely forgot my father carried keys to our former place, and apparently the Johnsons hadn't yet changed the locks.

I explained the situation to the detective on duty, he in turn called the Johnsons and relayed the story, they declined to press charges and asked only that I come and take the tree off their front porch. I agreed. The detective waived the drunk and disorderly charge as a professional courtesy.

I hustled JJ into my car. We swung by my former home. The large blue plastic tarp covering the addition being built on the second floor was gone and the siding was finished. The Johnsons had managed to get the nursery—my nursery—completed in the few weeks since moving in. The house was whole.

I walked up to the porch with JJ and helped him with strapping the tree on the top of my car. A very pregnant Mrs. Johnson waved at me from the front window. All I could manage was a shrug of the shoulders and a sheepish smile. She winked, waved again, and let the curtain drop.

JJ and I didn't talk on the way back to my parents' home. I think my father was so embarrassed by his behavior he never asked me about the bruises on my bare face or about selling the house. I wouldn't be as lucky with Evie.

44

LOUISE

7:00 a.m.

After riding the 'L' all day yesterday and overnight, back and forth between Howard Street and 95th on the Red Line, Louise needed caffeine and a bathroom, in that order, in the worst way. At Howard Street, where they made her get off yet again, she left the station instead of crossing over and heading back south.

At a DD next door she was surprised there was no line. But of course there wouldn't be, it was Christmas.

"You will buy something first, then I give you key," said the Asian woman behind the counter.

"Yes, yes. I know." Louise ordered the largest coffee, four crullers, an orange juice for Angel, and maybe one of those donuts with sprinkles if the baby woke up. It took the last of her money. She wasn't worried. The hotel clerk's Ventra card would let her ride the train again today and by then, surely, she and Angel would be well enough to meet Gerry tonight.

Louise changed the baby's diaper. No more green poop, but there were streaks of red in her pee. She shoved more aspirin down Angel's throat and dribbled in an orange juice chaser. Her own fever seemed worse and she had a headache tightening around her forehead, so she dumped a handful of baby aspirin into her palm and tossed them in her mouth. Instead of swallowing, she let the sugary orange pills linger on her tongue in a slow dissolve.

The donut shop didn't stay open late today, only 'til one, so Louise rested there until it closed and then made her way back to the train to ride during the afternoon. Her plan was to surprise Gerry at the condo this evening. She and Angel would be waiting for him, he would come home from work, and their little family would be united.

At the station she tapped the Ventra card on the turnstile but no green light flashed to let her through.

She tapped again and again. Nothing.

45

DANA

Noon

Near my parents' home JJ and I stopped at a city park and pitched the offending fir into the Christmas tree recycling bin. By the time we arrived at their house it was almost time for lunch, and Evie had a spread out as if welcoming the troops home from war. She was full of questions. And not only about JJ. I got a wide-eyed stare at my beat-up face, but my father got the inquisition. It was all I could do to bite my tongue and restrain my hands from telling her to knock it off and leave JJ alone. Poor man was embarrassed enough without having to relive the entire event.

Instead of submitting to Evie's grilling, JJ invited me to stay and eat with them and I gladly agreed. My mother may be a busybody but she's also a great cook and I was ravenous. Normally we go out to dinner on Christmas, so I figured I would have lunch, then hang out and watch an afternoon Bulls game with JJ until our traditional mealtime.

"Gotta use the bathroom but go ahead and start. Be right back."

I lied about the *be right back* part. I spent a good ten minutes in the john trying to figure out what to tell Evie about the house. I had nothing. Maybe this time the truth would have to suffice.

On my return to the kitchen I passed through the living room. Seems my parents downsized Christmas this year; a table-top miniature Christmas tree sat on the coffee table, its decorations cheap things that probably came with the fake tree. Not displayed were any of Evie's myriad ornaments collected over the years. Maybe another reason JJ wanted to surprise me with a life-sized real tree.

I entered the kitchen. My parents sat across from each other at the round table. I pulled up a chair so we formed a triangle and could see each other comfortably while we signed.

"I'm so hungry!" I said this for my mother's benefit because it always made her glad to see her company eat. True to form, she beamed and pushed a plate of sliced roast beef my way, then watched while I stacked a sandwich with tomatoes, lettuce, and sweet pickles, slathering the whole wheat bread with mayo and layering on some meat.

"Potato salad, please. And chips. And..." I took in the spread before me, trying to decide what else I could stuff on my plate, my PP plan now defunct. I spied an apple pie waiting in the wings. I pointed to it. *"That. Later with coffee."*

JJ enthusiastically endorsed my pie idea, his face crinkling in a broad smile. Sliding his Y-shaped hand back and forth between the two of us, he used one sign, *"same,"* and in one economical move gave Evie all the information she needed.

Evie nodded at both of us but didn't take her eyes off me. Even though I knew why, it was frankly beginning to weird me out. I bit into my sandwich hoping my nausea would diminish, although my headache from earlier still throbbed. I put down the sandwich and locked into Evie's stare.

"What? You look look look at me." I signed *look* in a repetitive motion, the two fingers of my hand aimed at my own face and rotating in a tight circle, a mime of her eyes on me. *"Why? Beautiful me?"* I laughed to try to elicit a smile from her with my joke, but she only responded with adding a slight squint to her gaze. I knew what was coming.

This morning I left my studio without wearing any concealer or foundation, more intent on breaking JJ out of the slammer than considering how my parents would view my injuries. And they were still quite the sight, morphing from deep blue and purple to a sickly green and yellow, as if a kindergartner plastered my face with watercolor paint while I slept.

Evie sat back in her chair and crossed her arms for a moment, then flung them open with gusto. *"Your face! What happened?"*

I heaved a big sigh, relieved to finally have it out in the open. Typical for JJ, he'd said nothing about my appearance from the time I met him at the station through sitting down for lunch. He was a polite and modest man. Evie, on the other hand, couldn't contain herself.

I ate some chips, took a leisure bite of my sandwich, and then pointed to my face. *"This? A fight with a bad guy."* For maximum effect I added, *"I shot him."*

I kept my eyes lowered at my plate with this last lie, hoping my parents would accept it. As a cop I had sustained injuries from time to time. Not unheard of. JJ sat up straight and gave me the *congratulations* cheer, his hands clasped together and shaken slightly at the left shoulder and then again at the right. But then he got serious.

"Dead?"

Crap. Now I had to elaborate because he wanted details he could visualize. *"No, no. Only in foot. After that he stopped hitting me. Finish."* How I wish this part was true. Only it wouldn't be in the foot—I would kill the fucker. I changed the subject and asked about their miniature tree but realized my mistake as soon as the signs left my hands. My father's face turned bright red, and I immediately apologized to him.

Of course, Evie was in the dark about all of it, so I decided I might as well come clean about the house and Jimmy. Everything else, my DUI, my suspension, failure at outpatient treatment, and the rest of the unknown about my job, would remain under wraps. I needed to salvage some modicum of my pride. The thought crossed my mind that if I was required to attend inpatient in order to keep my job, explaining the thirty-day treatment to Evie and the reasons for it would be impossible for me to lie about.

I made short work of telling Evie why JJ was arrested. She expressed puzzlement about the house sale but did understand JJ's intent of wanting to surprise me Christmas morning. If she was going to chide him it would probably happen after I left. Her dreaded next question arrived.

"You and Jimmy buy new house when he comes back?"

I hesitated. My mother put all of the responsibility for the success of my marriage on my shoulders. In the past she criticized me for being fat, for drinking too much, and even for my miscarriage; all reasons, in her mind, for her perfect son-in-law not wanting to return to me from L.A. As a result, I never told her Jimmy decided to stay in California and we divorced, our house the last vestige of our ten-year marriage until we sold it a few weeks ago.

"No. No new house. Jimmy's staying in California." And in case that wasn't clear enough, I used both hands to strongly repeat *stay* where I placed the sign for California. I said nothing about the divorce. If Evie wanted to know, she had to ask directly.

I could tell JJ sensed my discomfort with this discussion because he pushed the apple pie across the table toward Evie. He then directed me to make coffee while he cleared the dishes and suggested we have our dessert in the living room. I took his cue and asked Evie to cut me a big slice, which JJ again echoed as his wish. I escaped to the bathroom and sat on the closed-lid john, trying to time my hiding with JJ's clearing the table, intent on avoiding time with Evie.

Over dessert we chatted about what my siblings were doing in their lives—apparently too busy to return home for Christmas—and I expressed my frequent wish they would visit more often. I finished my pie and took a sip of coffee, which again left a strong metallic taste on my tongue. I made a face and put the cup down.

"Coffee taste okay to you? Like metal. Maybe I made it wrong," I signed. I pushed the cup away. Evie and JJ both attested to the coffee's normal taste.

I went to the bathroom again—this time for real—before the game. When I returned to the living room, JJ was in the kitchen washing dishes and Evie stood near the front door closet. As I passed her, she stopped me with a tap on my arm.

She plastered me with one of her patented, full-body gazes I became familiar with as a teenager when she checked me over before, and especially after, my dates.

I struck a pose.*"Like my outfit?"* Again, trying to jostle her with a little humor. This rarely works with my mother when she's got something on her mind. Usually something I don't want to know.

"Are you pregnant?"

I thrust my face forward at her and opened my eyes wide, raising my eyebrows and blinking hard a few times to let my surprised expression carry the entire message without using any signs. When she didn't blink or back down, I signed with maximum passion, *"No! Impossible!"*

With cold efficiency Evie ticked off numbers on her left hand and signed with her right. *"One. Coffee tastes funny. Two. Your breasts are bigger. Three. You go to bathroom a lot."* Here she formed the letter 'T' on her right hand and shook it once, twice, three times, each iteration more exaggerated than the last.

She stepped closer and peered up at my face. *"Pimples, too. All can mean P-R-E-G-N-A-N-T."* Even though there were various signs for this last word, she chose to fingerspell it—slowly and clearly—to impress me with her certainty.

I opened the coat closet and grabbed my jacket, then hurried to the kitchen, startling JJ with a quick goodbye. I rushed past Evie without so much as a thank-you-for-lunch and slammed the door behind me as I left.

On the way home I stopped at Walgreens and bought a pregnancy test. The double line blistered me with the result.

Evie—damn her—was right.

46

LOUISE

7:00 p.m.

At last. Their condo. Louise entered the six-unit building, rode the elevator up to the third floor and worked hard to push the stroller across the shag carpet in the hallway.

She had used up every last ounce of her strength and energy to get here. And she almost didn't make it. The Ventra card had run out of money. She stood at the turnstile, rocking the stroller back and forth, too feverish to even figure out what to do.

Several people passed by her without a glance, clicking through the entrance to the train with ease as if mocking her. She finally sat on a bench near the empty teller cage and closed her eyes to block out her failure.

When it got dark at 4:30, a man carrying a clipboard and dressed in a dayglo green vest layered over his winter jacket approached her.

"Everything okay, ma'am?" He gestured at the baby.

"What? Oh." Louise glanced at Angel, still snoring away in the stroller. "Yes. She's not feeling well." She shrugged. "Neither am I."

"Maybe good to get the baby inside a warm place. It's cold. They don't heat these stations, you know."

Louise wished the man would go away. The cold station felt good to her and she was sure it did to the baby, too. They were both so hot. She still held the Ventra card in her hand and waved it at the man.

"It doesn't work. I can't get home." Then the tears came. Reality loomed large. She would not reunite with Gerry, couldn't bring Angel to him, they couldn't be a family. She threw the card on the cement floor and sobbed, covering her face with her hands.

The man bent, picked up the card, and walked over to a vending machine across from where Louise sat. A minute later he returned and handed her the card.

"It should work now. Merry Christmas."

Now Louise stood at the door to their condo, keys in hand. She had to discard her wish to present a perfect Angel to Gerry. But it would only be momentary. Once she was in her peaceful, clean home, she would shower and then bathe the baby in the tub, dress her in clean, clean clothes, and Christmas would be perfect.

Louise inserted the key in the lock and tried to turn it, but it seemed stuck. She felt so sick and weak, maybe she didn't have the strength left to unlock the door. She knocked several times but Gerry didn't answer.

Bonnie's condo was across the hall. She would certainly be able to help. But when Louise knocked on the manager's door there was only silence.

The baby slept on. Louise sat on the shag carpet next to their condo door and ate Angel's donut with the sprinkles. She'd never liked the carpet, so full of dust and germs. How could it not be? Impossible to keep something like that clean.

Her eyelids fluttered and closed. She tilted over on the loopy rug, grateful for the soft, mushy comfort it provided for her worn-out body.

47

DANA

12/26 8:00 a.m.

The day after Christmas I sat in Koz's office, nauseous as hell from morning sickness, waiting for his assistant Veda to bring coffee for Koz and a diet Coke for me. At least now I knew the reason for the metallic taste I experienced with coffee.

Koz asked me how my Christmas was, and I debated whether to tell the story of JJ and the Christmas tree as a humorous anecdote but discarded the idea, worried my boss would think deaf people were stupid.

"Nice," I lied. "My mom knows how to put on a spread. Did you spend time with your daughter?"

As I said this I cringed a bit inside. Caitlyn might be a sensitive topic for Koz. I was responsible for exposing her crooked fiancé, Alberto Carrera. I brought evidence against him for the subsequent charges of extortion and letting a murder suspect go free. Caitlyn called off her engagement to Carrera prior to his conviction this past week. Didn't want to hold her wedding in prison, I guess.

Koz nodded in response to my question but said nothing, small talk uncomfortable for both of us. Veda bustled in with our drinks and smirked at me. I assumed she knew why I was meeting with Koz. Not much got by her. Koz dismissed her with the order to hold all calls and interruptions.

I cracked open my pop and took a long drink, the fizz settling my stomach a bit, grateful for the caffeine. Koz opened a file on his desk and extracted two pieces of paper, handing one to me and placing the other in front of him. I set my pop on his desk and glanced at the paper, an email with my name in the subject line.

"You can read this at your leisure, Dana. It's basically a description of your intensive outpatient attendance and the reasons you're being recommended for inpatient treatment. I understand your counselor," he glanced at his paper, "Mr. Marvin Williams, has already informed you of same. There will be a full report from the EAP probably some-time next week and you will get a copy."

I put the email on my lap and picked up my Diet Coke, taking another long drink. "Yes, Marvin called me. So, am I canned?" I couldn't look Koz in the eye with my bald question even though I knew the answer.

Koz waited so long to reply I was forced to make eye contact. He leaned forward, elbows propped on his desk, his hands clasped in a prayer pose.

"I want to ask you something, just me to you. Forget about this." He picked up his copy of the email and placed it aside. "It's not why I called you in today." He paused and leaned forward. "Forget about your job or that I'm your boss. Don't answer what I'm going to ask you the way you think I want to hear. Yes?"

I couldn't have been more surprised than if Koz had asked me to go out on a date. His intensity made me wary. But my curiosity about what he wanted to ask outweighed my hesitancy.

"Okay, I guess. Yes."

"What's the most important thing you need in order to have a life?" He leaned back in his chair.

I was stymied, unsure what he was asking me. Was this a general question with answers like: I needed to have a job, or a partner to share with, or be a contributing member of society, in order to have a life? Maybe he wanted to know if I had any religious leanings, as if he were Father Mik and wondered if I believed in God or not. Or was it even a weird inquiry into the specifics of my daily routine? To have a life I must eat healthy, shower regularly, be a friend to others. Before I could suss it out, he spoke again.

"Because for me," he pointed to his chest, "the most important thing I need to do on a daily basis is not pick up a drink." He squinted at me. "That's why I have a life today."

I sat with this for a long, silent minute. Was Koz telling me he was an alkie? Koz a drunk?! I tilted my head at him. "You're—"

He nodded and cut me off. "Yes. I'm an alcoholic. Sober twenty-eight years, but the length of time doesn't matter. My point is my question to you. To me, the most important thing for me to have a life is to not pick up. Period. I do that with the help of AA. I'm asking if having a sober life is the most important thing to you now." His index finger tapped the email on his desk. "*Especially* now."

I didn't have an answer. I was still trying to process his disclosure.

"This email describes your repeated difficulties in the outpatient setting, and the recommendation for referral to inpatient. Per our agreement, failing IOP would result in your termination from the police force."

There it was. Finally. He was telling me I was through as a cop.

"Marvin told me he was recommending inpatient treatment," I said.

Koz started shaking his head at this.

"I thought that meant if I did the thirty days there I could come back to my job."

Koz locked eyes with me. "Jobs don't matter, Dana. Nothing will matter if you continue drinking. Because I can tell you from my own experience you will lose it all, maybe even your life, if you screw up enough. Driving drunk, killing someone, or killing yourself by wrecking your health or committing suicide."

He was throwing a lot at me. Mostly what I heard was my life as a homicide detective was over, though what he described was nothing short of hopelessness.

"What do you want?" Koz asked.

There was Marvin's question again. And I had lots of answers. I didn't want to be pregnant from being raped, I wanted my body to stop hurting from the attack, I wanted to quit smoking and lose forty pounds, I wanted Jimmy back and our lives together. But I wasn't going to go into it all with Koz. He wasn't interested.

What I saw in an instant was how all of my "answers" could be further explained by my drinking. My life was unmanageable, first noted in Marvin's office, and now slapping me in the face again. Unmanageable because I drink. Because I can't stop drinking, to be accurate. And honest. My nausea churned.

I downed the rest of my pop and tossed the can into the trash next to Koz's desk. "Does Abandonato know?"

"No. Not formally. I thought you would want to be the one to tell him you're officially terminated from being a detective."

I heard a parsing of language in Koz's statement, something about the way he said it. "But I'm still a cop? Knocked down to street level?" I had a hard time tamping down the hope in my voice.

"No. Nothing to do with active police work."

Any idea I might have had about carrying this pregnancy to term, having the baby and raising it on my own, was struck down with his words. Forget about losing the very job I'd loved for the past ten years, forget about losing my partnership with Nuts and the end of the work we accomplished together.

All I could foresee was being alone, trying to support myself with freelance interpreting. Raising a child was absurdly expensive. The money Jimmy gave me from the sale of our house would be eaten up by inpatient treatment. I would be broke. Working as an interpreter, the only other thing I knew how to do, was not what I wanted. At all.

"I'm pregnant, Koz." I blurted this out and covered my face with my hands, not because I was going to cry, but from sheer embarrassment.

"Dana."

I dropped my hands to my lap and looked at him. "I don't know why I told you that. It's—it's a long story."

I considered telling him about the attack and rape and showing him my still-flagrant bruises hidden under my makeup. His daughter Caitlyn and I were the same age. Would he make that connection and join me in my self-pity? My hoped-for reaction from Koz didn't materialize.

"Anyway, I get what you're saying. I'm done as a detective. I'll tell Nuts next time I see him." I picked up the packet and started to stand but Koz motioned with his hands for me to stay seated.

"Your inpatient treatment will be covered by CPD and your insurance will continue subsequently for ninety days. Your union rep can give you all the details."

"Okay." It wasn't okay, but at least better than my anxiety led me to believe. I held off telling him inpatient treatment was a no-go for me. I couldn't decide right now anyway. "'Thanks for telling me about your—your situation."

"I am breaking my anonymity only to you. Truly, I do not care who knows I'm an alcoholic, as long as I don't forget it." He leaned back in his chair and crossed his arms against his chest.

"There are a lot of people who would be surprised to find out I am, you know." A small smile. "Then there are a lot of people who would not. But it's an anonymous program for a reason, so let's keep it between us."

I nodded. On the wall in Marvin's office hung a framed motto: *Who you see here, what you hear here, when you leave here, let it stay here.* I assumed it applied to my individual counseling sessions, but it made even more sense when I thought about my recovering compadres in IOP—dirty laundry, and all that. "Sure. Of course."

"I don't know how many actual AA meetings you attended. There is an unwritten, well, not rule, AA has no rules. But there's the idea that it's up to the person to call himself or herself an alcoholic. We don't reveal someone else's status. That is their own business, and they get to decide who to tell. Or *not* tell."

Koz said nothing else but gave me more of the squinted eye treatment as if he could read what I was thinking by holding my gaze long enough. Then he signaled my dismissal with a nod and I headed for the door.

48

DANA

8:45 a.m.

The break room for the squad yielded a small box I could use to pack my stuff, and I headed to the front of the room near the elevators to clear out my desk. It didn't take long. Rokick had moved in and taken over the top two of the four desk drawers, throwing my stuff in the bottom two.

The surface of my desk was a sloppy mess, which was the way I normally operated, but I recognized nothing in the mess as belonging to me. All Rokick.

Nuts's desk was next to mine, so neat you'd think no one worked there. I sat in his seat, the packed box at my feet. On the wall in front of our desks hung a child-sized whiteboard I'd crudely nailed there in what started out as a simple way to keep track of our cases. Visual prompts helped me, probably stemming from growing up in a deaf household. Over time, Nuts referred to and then came to rely on my board and added his own notations. It became a focal point for the two of us when we sat at our desks trying to tease out elusive aspects of a particular case.

I stared at the board and considered taking it down because I didn't want to share it with Rokick, didn't want Rokick sharing it with Nuts. Only one case was listed there.

Nuts's neat block printing started a timeline with the name Margot Stuckless, 'v' for victim and 'f' for female in parentheses, then the word 'baby' and (v/f). Below this line came a list of people interviewed, among them Janey Foreman, Kristi Chen, and Mac Stuckless, the last two names circled and the word *charged* scrawled in loopy handwriting.

No other info, no need to continue the timeline. Rokick was convinced Mac Stuckless murdered his wife and daughter.

Even though I owned the board I would leave it for Nuts, a subtle cipher marking our former partnership.

As if I'd conjured him up, the exit door next to the elevators opened, and Nuts stepped into the room. I stood as he approached, aware I sat at his desk, and lifted the box holding my work stuff.

"You're here," he said. His voice gave away nothing.

The last time I had any contact with him in person was the night of Rokick's party, the night I was raped, when he again refused to watch the video of Louise.

I shifted the box onto my left hip. "I could say the same for you." My stomach turned over at forcing my voice to stay neutral when I wanted to ream him out. "No task force?"

He shrugged. "They move at a glacial pace. Koz said it would be 24/7, but it's more like nine to four—with an hour and a half off for lunch —five days a week. Oh, and we break early on Fridays. We're off this entire *week* because of Christmas."

"Sounds like a vacation compared to here."

"Yeah. I hate vacations." Nuts came around our desks and sat in his chair. I placed my box on Rokick's messy desk and sat in my old chair.

"The task force is nothing but a screen for the mayor to make it look like something's being done, but the rest of the people on it have nothing to do with working homicide. Or investigations of any sort, really."

I nodded.

Nuts leaned back in his chair and propped his ankle casually on his knee. "You never responded to my message, my apology. Been bothering me ever since. I got the video from Rokick and—"

"What happened to *Clint*?" It felt good to chide him.

A slight smile. "He's wrong about Mac."

"And you're surprised?" I could barely contain my sarcasm. "What about you? Are you wrong, too?"

Nuts regarded me in silence for a long moment before nodding. He crossed his arms and looked out the large window near the elevators. "I got the video from Rokick. It's Louise."

A rare admission from my partner I relished, but only for a moment. I didn't want to be at odds with him. "What changed your mind?"

"That's the kicker here." He explained from the first interview with Kristi Chen he believed she broke up with Mac Stuckless because he got her fired.

"I completely bought it. Chen planted the idea Stuckless hated his wife, wanted to see her dead. And she was adamant about not wanting to have kids, her own or anyone else's. She convinced me."

I gaped at him and motioned with my hand to hurry up and tell me the rest.

"Yeah. So, Chen did conspire with Stuckless to kill his wife for the money. Although she swears he acted alone."

"Wait. You said Rokick was wrong about Mac."

Nuts nodded. "Chen initially believed Mac saying he didn't kill his wife. She told him to get out of town because we'd be after him, so he took off."

"But he came back and Rokick nailed him."

Nuts nodded. "Chen wanted the baby."

I slapped my hand on the desk and laughed.

"Yeah, I thought that was you. Winding him up again." Nuts actually winked at me. Not much gets by him, not even my bullshitting Rokick.

"You can stop laughing, because that part is actually true. Chen wanted the baby. She lied the first time. After questioning her again, more things came out. And then watching the video."

I pursed my lips and appraised him with squinted my eyes. "Finally. About fucking time."

Nuts held my gaze and raised his palms, patting the air between us. "Okay. *Finally.* When I saw Louise Conway, the idea she wanted a baby and would do anything to get one rang true. Transferring Clint's theory from Chen to her made me see it."

"How the hell did that happen? Why didn't you trust what *I* kept telling you. Over and over." I wanted to heap more scorn on Nuts for rejecting the video, clear evidence of mistrusting me. The gall. That he would credit *Clint* with finally opening his eyes.

He stood and stepped closer to me. "Look. What's important is Rokick's wrong. More to the point, you're right about Louise Conway."

"At least about the kidnapping."

"Right. But not only. Stuckless never turned the baby over to Chen. She had time in home detention to think about that and came to the conclusion Mac killed his wife and baby for the money and was returning to kill her."

My confusion must have shown on my face. Nuts held up his index finger.

"*You* told me Stuckless was allergic to chocolate and peanut butter, which Chen confirmed. Then we got the forensics back on the finger-prints on the Butterfinger wrappers."

"Louise."

"Yep. I got a search warrant for the Conway condo and found a hair-brush in the bathroom cabinet. I talked to Koz about pushing it to the head of the line and he got it done. Tests came back early this morn-ing. Positive."

I had a strong urge to light up a Kool in order to calm down. It was a lot to take in all at once. I was extremely pissed at Nuts's admitted perfidy regarding the kidnapping—and trusting Kristi Chen instead of me about Mac's allergy—but super excited to be proved right about what I'd been saying all along.

"Here's another thing." He motioned for me to move so he could sit at the computer on Rokick's desk. After a minute of searching he turned the monitor toward me. "Read this."

I leaned over his shoulder. It was the autopsy report from the ME's office. Margot Stuckless's cause of death was suffocation. Her nose was broken, the orbital ridge over her eye collapsed, and her lips were cut from extreme pressure against the teeth. Whatever was used to suffocate the victim had been heavy—even her windpipe was crushed—and yet very soft. I pictured an obese woman sitting on Margot Stuckless's face.

"So Louise got to Margot first."

Nuts tapped his index finger to the tip of his nose. We grinned at each other.

"I talked with Koz first thing," Nuts said. "I didn't go into it with him how I knew about Louise."

I stared at him. "Koz didn't say anything about it to me." But why would he? I was suspended from active duty and as of today no longer a detective.

Nuts glanced back at Koz's closed office door. "He took me off the task force, gave me back the lead on Stuckless. For now, I'm going to let Rokick's charge against Mac Stuckless hold."

I opened my eyes wide in surprise. "You're going to let the wrong person get charged with murder? Who are you and what have you done with by-the-book Abandonato?"

He waved his hand in a dismissive motion, not acknowledging my joke. "You and I are going to get Louise Conway and save that baby."

I had to admit I was caught up in Nuts's certainty and positive attitude about us, and wanted in the worst way to hop on the thrill ride that defined our partnership.

"Once we find Louise Conway, Stuckless and Chen will get reduced charges. And Rokick can suffer the consequences for the screw-up. Payback for what he pulled on you. Hopefully he'll be shunted back to rookie beat-cop. This was only probation for him, you know."

No, I didn't know. I hefted the packed box to my right hip. Nuts gestured at it, a quizzical look on his face.

"I'm done. Just got the word from Koz."

Nuts frowned. I knew he understood what I meant.

"I wanted to talk to you about that," he said.

I held up my open palm toward him. "Doesn't matter. I've had my chances. I blew it."

He motioned for me to sit but drawing this out would make it harder than it already was. "No. I gotta go. I can't do this anymore. And really? Rokick got what he wanted by setting me up. I'm finished and he's your partner."

Nuts shook his head at this.

"Well, for now anyway," I said. "Koz gave me a choice about more treatment, which I'm going to think about, but that's all. You have everything I know about Louise Conway. I'm done." I shifted the box to my other hip and nodded at the white board. "You can list it all there."

"No. I don't want to do this alone." He stood and tried to take the box from my arms, but I pulled away.

"You're not alone. You've got *Clint*."

Nuts had the good humor to grimace at my second dig about Rokick's name. "He's not you."

For a split second it was like we were back together, united in our likes and dislikes. I turned to head for the elevator. He touched my arm.

"I also talked with Koz about what happened at Rokick's party. Wanted him to understand you were sabotaged."

I slammed the box down on my desk—*Clint's* desk—and stepped close enough to get in his face. "Where were you when it mattered? Goddammit, Nuts. We were partners. That means having my back all the time, not just when it's convenient for you. Or when you think you're right and I'm wrong. *All* the time. I know I fucked up with drinking. But boy, you fucked up too." I grabbed the box and started for the elevator. My cell chimed.

I dug it out and answered. "Demeter."

A woman's voice came out in a hurried whisper. "Detective? She's here. Right now. Louise is here."

49

DANA

10:00 a.m.

I pitched my box onto the floor next to the elevator, screaming at Nuts to fucking *move*. "We got her!"

He darted to my side. We scrambled down the squad room stairs and outside, and jumped into an unmarked SUV. I rode shotgun and Nuts sped north, siren blasting, to Gerry and Louise's condo.

We hit Clark Street. It crawled. Our siren didn't matter. No place to go with traffic clogging both directions of the two-lane street. Drivers couldn't get out of the way even if they wanted to, hemmed in by cars parked at the curbs.

Nuts pounded the steering wheel.

"Call for backup. Maybe they'll get there before us," I said. He put in the call. Arriving at an intersection, we broke free and headed east to Lake Shore Drive. I texted a terse message to Bonnie about our plan, hoping she could keep Louise somehow occupied, or at least stop her from leaving.

"Cut the siren," I told Nuts, the split second he reached to shut off the alert. We grinned at each other. A block later he pulled up to the condo, double-parked with the cherry top still flashing, and we jumped out. We beat the back-ups.

The manager hurried out to meet us. "She was upstairs! My place!"

As we rushed up to Bonnie's condo, she yelled after us. "No! She's gone!"

FOR THE REST of the day until it got dark, Nuts and I scoured the area, hoping to spot a woman with a stroller. Two backup cops also assisted but so far, nothing.

Nuts and I circled back to get more info from the condo manager.

Bonnie had returned to the building this morning after two days away—for Christmas Eve and Christmas—and found Louise and baby Melanie asleep in the hallway.

"I brought them in to my place, made coffee for Louise, and let her use the bathroom. She wanted help getting into her condo, so I had to tell her Gerry changed the locks. That he was selling it."

"How'd she take it?" I asked.

She shrugged. "She seemed sorta foggy, you know? Like she was sick." The baby, according to Bonnie, was asleep and also looked sick.

While Louise waited in the manager's condo and we were stuck on Clark Street, the manager spent the time in her basement locker searching for some baby clothes she wanted to give Louise. "I thought she'd wait for me. The baby needed to be cleaned up and put in fresh clothes. Poor thing was a mess."

And Louise might have waited while Bonnie searched below. Except

Bonnie left her cell phone on the dining room table where Louise sat. Louise saw my text message and fled.

50

DANA

5:00 p.m.

After our fruitless search, Nuts dropped me back at the squad so I could retrieve my box and my Camry and then head home. I had no other leads for finding Louise and he was empty-handed as well. Nuts took a screen shot of Louise from the video and used it for an APB on her.

I suggested we get some sleep and head to Gary in the morning to check her mother's place, the only other thing I could come up with. We were both skeptical it would yield anything other than a waste of gas and time, but it was all we had.

In the foyer of my apartment building I grabbed the mail from my box—mostly ads and junk—and headed upstairs. Once inside, I drank some hot chocolate to warm up. I couldn't shake the body chill I picked up from the wind outside driving the temp down. My weather app clocked the wind chill at ten below.

Someone knocked on my door. I peeked through the peephole. Sandor stood on the other side.

I opened the door and grinned at the small man, replete with his Cubs cap on. "Hi, Sandor! Welcome back. Oh, and Merry Christmas. Late. Maybe I should start saying Happy New Year instead since we're almost there."

"Yes, miss, yes. The new year comes soon." He held out a medium-sized covered bowl, which had a small straw doll lying on top.

I took the bowl. "What's this?"

"Lentil soup my wife she makes. Eat on New Year's Day. You will be rich!"

I invited him in. "How do you mean? Rich?" I closed the front door. In the kitchenette I put the soup in the fridge and held onto the small doll. I wanted to get a closer look at it.

Sandor removed his cap, worrying it with both hands. "In my country, years and years children get idea from parents." He stuffed his hat under his arm and mimed a taller person handing something to a smaller person. "Then more years go and the children give same idea to their children." He continued his handing-down mime. "So always we have this! The soup lentils, they are round, like coins. You eat them, you will be rich."

"Oh, I see! It's a tradition in Hungary. Is that what you mean?"

"Yes, yes." He pulled out a small notepad from his back pocket and flipped to a page with several English words on it printed in block letters. He held it out to me. "Here. You write this word for Sandor. Tra...tra?"

I grinned at him and took the proffered pad, placing the small straw doll on the counter and grabbing a pen next to my toaster. "Tra-di-tion," I said, while mimicking the block printing on the pad as I jotted down the word. Sandor repeated my pronunciation and beamed when I handed back the pad. He read the word aloud several times.

I held up the small straw doll. "What's the tradition with the doll?"

"The tra-di-tion." He straightened up a bit and thrust out his chest, as if giving a lecture about the history of Hungary. "You throw in water," he mimed pitching the doll with an overhand thrust of his arm, "or put in ground, cover with dirt." He waved his hand. "Say bye-bye to old year."

"Thank you, Sandor. I didn't know these traditions." The soup one made some sense to me, but the doll? Kind of violent, especially if the doll was female. "How was your trip?"

"All fine. All fine. We visit our daughter Zizi. She is Botund's older sister."

The names intrigued me, and it must've shown on my face because Sandor gave me the lowdown.

"Yes, yes. Zizi is first child. This name is Hungarian, means follows God. Zizi."

We shared a smile at his obvious pride for his daughter. "And what does Bo's name mean? Botund?"

Sandor made an odd motion with his arm, as if swinging something around and around above his head. Made me picture a cowboy swinging a lasso. I had no idea what he was showing me.

He dropped his arm to his side. "Is for war, yes? To kill people." He tried to describe this weapon, at least I guessed it was a weapon, but even with my extensive experience with gestures used for description, not to mention weapons, I could not figure it out.

I waved him off. "That's okay, never mind. So, you and your wife have Zizi and Bo. No other kids?"

Sandor shook his head and then inspected the repaired transom. He tested the mechanism to make sure it opened and closed, and then secured the lock. Now I understood the real reason for his visit.

"Bo did a great job fixing it, didn't he?" I said.

"I see this, yes. My son helps me all the time. Tell me, miss. The police, they catch the man?"

I was confused for a moment, not sure what he meant, then realized Bo didn't tell him I was the perp breaking and entering through the transom, which spared me quite a bit of embarrassment, for sure. Bo also kept private what happened that night in case I didn't want Sandor to know I was raped. I didn't.

"Uh, I'm not sure, Sandor. Let me check, okay?" I wasn't sure what to tell him.

I couldn't shake the body chill after Sandor left, so I stripped down and took a long, hot shower. It felt good to get the thick, itchy makeup off my face. Afterward, I donned my sweats, wanting nothing more than to eat something and take it easy. I had no energy left after meeting with Koz and then the disappointing chase and search with Nuts.

I pulled out a pan and dumped Sandor's lentil soup in, then set it on a low flame. As it heated on the stove, I texted Bo.

> your dad just left. he approves of your
> transom work

Bo responded with a smiley emoji but nothing else. How to ask him the real question on my mind? The soup on the stove started to boil. I arranged some crackers and cheese on a plate and took it all to my small desk.

> he thinks a MAN broke into my apt. is that
> what you told him?

I waited a while, but Bo didn't respond as I ate the soup, which was delicious. I'd have to ask Sandor's wife for the recipe and check if it passed muster with the Pounds Police. Then I remembered it didn't matter anymore. I didn't have to lose weight because I was no longer a detective with regs to follow, didn't have to measure up to Koz's dictums to keep my job. My mind served up one more thing: *I didn't have to quit drinking.*

My cell pinged while I washed the dishes. Bo, responding.

> yes

Again, such brevity. I was beginning to think Bo didn't want to text with me. Then, he added:

> your privacy your business. u doing ok?

> so-so body still banged up and hurts also got
> fired today that hurts more

> understood free to meet for coffee at 8?

Having finally warmed up, I didn't relish the idea of heading back outside, but Bo suggested a coffee shop literally one block from my place. It suddenly became important to tell him his small kindnesses —fixing the transom, finding my backpack, keeping the attack private —meant a lot to me.

I changed into my heavy corduroy pants and a cotton turtleneck, opting to forego the makeup. Bo saw me at my worst the night of the transom fiasco, so I didn't need to hide anything. I smelled a lot better, too.

I strapped on my loaded Glock, the holster around my shoulder, and hid it under a loose sweater. I again cursed the bastard who took away my feeling safe even going out at night for a cup of coffee. As a cop, I knew shit could and did happen anywhere, there was no "safe" place in this world.

But my shame at not fighting off my attacker because I was drunk left me with no one to trust, not even myself.

51

DANA

7:45 p.m.

I made my way down from the third floor of my apartment building, feeling the tang of cold air increase as I got closer to the unheated foyer. I zipped up my jacket, wrapped my cashmere scarf around my neck and bottom half of my face several times, and pulled on my gloves; all Christmas gifts from Evie and JJ, who were familiar with my habit of losing these accessories. I stood in the foyer for a minute before venturing outside, not wanting to leave, and considered canceling with Bo.

It was dark out. Through the full-length glass in the front door I spied a car parked at the curb, exhaust from the tailpipe blooming in the cold air. Inside the dark interior the driver smoked a cigarette, its ember glowing brighter every few seconds, a winter firefly. For a moment I assumed the person in the car waited on someone, or maybe was listening to the radio while finishing a cigarette before exiting.

But when I left the building and headed down the sidewalk, I made the driver and his cherry red Jeep. I jogged over and banged on the driver's window, startling Fabrizio into dropping the cigarette in his lap. I jumped aside as the door whipped open and he stumbled out.

"What the hell, Demeter!" He turned toward the car and made a frantic search of the driver-side seat and then the floor, finally retrieving and holding up the still smoldering cigarette.

"Those things'll kill you, Fabrizio. Or in this case, maybe set you on fire and *then* kill you. Time to quit."

The dome light from the open car door lit up his glare at me. He flicked the butt onto the street, sending up a shower of sparks as it hit the cement. "Get in," he said, and started to climb into the driver's seat.

"Hold on. I'm on my way somewhere. What do you want?"

"You gave me a couple 'a things to find out, remember? Well, I did. Get in."

I was intrigued. After not hearing from Fabrizio since our last meeting a week ago, I really wasn't expecting him to follow through on what I wanted. I quickly texted Bo I was running fifteen minutes late and then went to the passenger side of the Jeep and got in.

I pulled the scarf down from around my mouth. "Make this quick," I said.

Fabrizio twisted his body toward me as he reached for the dome light switch. "Still the bossy bitch, Demeter." The light came on as he turned toward me. "Some things never—christ! What happened to you?"

The bruises from my attack still carried the power to frighten, their colors an amalgam of yellow and green, and the side of my head and cheek where the assailant clouted me still displayed a deep purple welt.

I pulled my scarf a bit higher around my ears, self-conscious about how I appeared, even to this lout. "Never mind. Just give me what you got."

He wagged his finger back and forth in my face. "You first. You change the name on them CDs?"

"No. They're still in my name. My only insurance keeping me alive."

"I ain't talking about that. It's the, you know, the benny—benny," he snapped his fingers.

"Repeat after me: benny-fishy-airy," I said, exaggerating the word in a slow drawl. Fabrizio's head bobbed in time with each syllable. He again tried to pronounce the word but mangled it and gave up.

"And to be clear here, the beneficiary is not the priest at Saint Nick's. I took his name off. By the way, I saw you at Saint Nick's on Christmas Eve. Unless you're shopping for a new church to attend, I don't want your ugly mug anywhere near there."

He started to object but I stopped him with a light shove to his shoulder. "Stop. The priest's not involved. And there's cameras posted all around the church. They'll tell me immediately if you try anything."

Fabrizio shut off the dome light. "Okay, okay." I let him sulk for a minute, then told him I recorded a new beneficiary on the CDs, a person who would remain anonymous for obvious reasons.

"The new person is my extra insurance for staying alive. So, my advice? Chill. Your CDs will come due early March and you'll get your money." I tried to say this as sincerely as I could to such a mope. I wanted Fabrizio to buy into my lie that he would eventually get his money back all nice and clean, laundered by yours truly. "But anything happens to me? You'll never see the money again and you'll never find out who has it."

Fabrizio grabbed my upper arm and squeezed. "Don't you fuck with my dough, Demeter, or all this talk we're havin' here is gone, erased, like it never happened. And I'll find a way to get it. You know I will."

I jerked my arm out of his vise grip. "Crap, Fabrizio! This is exactly the sort of shit I'm talking about. Threaten me or even touch me again and all bets are off." I rubbed my upper arm.

More sulking. Fabrizio lifted a fresh cigarette from a pack on the dashboard and lit up. "I still got that DUI report on you. One word to your Lieutenant and you're toast."

I laughed. And then laughed longer and harder.

"What the hell's wrong with you? I'm gonna end your career in homicide and you laugh like a crazy woman?"

I swiped at the tears from my laughter and cleared my throat. "Like I told you before. Go ahead and send it."

Fabrizio was silent and I could tell he was trying—and failing—to remember our previous conversation about the CDs.

"You gotta lay off the sauce, Fabrizio. It's screwing with your memory something awful. Really a bad sign."

He muttered something under his breath.

"Besides, Koz knows all about my drinking. I got fired today, so your little DUI blackmail leverage is worthless."

This brought him to attention. "No shit? What's Abandonato say about it?"

His question brought me up short. Chasing down the lead on Louise with Nuts earlier today was so satisfying. It reminded me of our three years as partners and how well we worked together. But we didn't have time to digest what my dismissal would mean between us. So I sure as hell wasn't going to gossip with Fabrizio about it like we were in junior high.

"You want to find out what Abandonato thinks, ask *him*. Christ! No indirect messages, okay? Isn't that what I've been saying this whole time?" I directed an exaggerated eye roll at him but doubted he could see it in the dark.

Fabrizio said nothing, but his breath came out in short bursts like he was trying—without success—to hide his seething.

"Chill, Fabrizio. Tell me about your conversation with Carrera."

Fabrizio harrumphed. "He ain't too happy with you, right? I visited him in the slammer, the one downtown. He's waiting to find out his sentence."

I smiled in the dark. This past week Carrera was convicted of extorting 200K from Charles Worthy, a murderer who killed not only a friend of my father's, but also a hooker friend of Rameeka's. The extortion allowed CW to escape arrest. CW then kidnapped Rameeka, intent on killing her, but we caught him in time. He'll soon be on trial for the two murders but flipped on Carrera in exchange for getting the kidnapping charges dropped. "I hope he goes away for a long time."

"You got it sorta right about the woman who attacked your ma. Manny set it up with one of his girls. I ain't seen him for a couple weeks now, but he ain't gonna tip who she is. Especially not to you."

"She's a hooker, right?"

"One of Manny's."

Okay. I'd have to deal with him directly. Me and Rameeka. "What about getting The Prick to leave my mother alone?"

"Yeah, about that. I told him what you said. You know, about us being pussies going after an old woman and all. He says he ain't gonna go after your ma anymore."

"Which tells me he admits it, he did set up the attack through Manny."

He drummed the steering wheel with his fingers. "He won't ever admit it to anyone else, Demeter, you gotta know that. You got what you wanted just knowin' he set it up."

Fabrizio was right. I could never prove Carrera orchestrated the attack, at least not in a way he could be charged with the assault. Instead, I had to find the woman who actually did the deed and then get Manny to roll over. It was going to take some time, and I was pretty sure with Rameeka's help I might succeed. But this was a start. "Okay. That's something, him backing off my mother."

Fabrizio took a long drag on his cigarette and exhaled a cloud of smoke into the small interior. His bad breath mingled with the smoke and forced me to open my window against the toxic assault. He cocked his head to one side. "But here's the thing. Seems he took you up on your offer."

I frowned. I hadn't talked to Carrera since our chance meeting in the lawyer's parking lot. And I sure as hell didn't *offer* him anything. "What're you yammering about?"

He snickered. "*You* know. You said if we wanted to send you a message, to send it directly to *you*."

"Well, yeah. I meant, leave my mother out of it. No indirect messages. Like attacking her to get at me."

"Carrera liked that. Said it'll be clear the message is from him." He switched on the dome light and leaned my way to flick his spent cigarette out my open window. As he leaned back, he swiped his index finger across my purple welt.

"Looks like he delivered."

52

DANA

8:15 p.m.

On the walk over to the coffee shop to meet Bo I mulled over what Fabrizio told me about Carrera. I'm not sure why I didn't put it together that the attack on me after Rokick's party was a direct message from The Prick. I assumed it was a random assault. I could only chalk it up to being so traumatized from the attack my thinking wasn't logical.

Now, with some time distancing me from the cold foyer disaster, Fabrizio's observation seemed obvious. I already knew Carrera didn't do his own work, he's at least smart enough for that. So, instead of going after Evie to scare me, he utilized the direct method to make good the threat. Somewhat my own fault, of course: I was dumb enough to tell them to come after me instead of Evie. I shouldn't be surprised they took me up on it.

I had sudden clarity about what bothered me about my backpack, too; it was intact, nothing missing. If it was a random attack and rape, the bastard would have stolen my wallet and cell. He took my backpack to scare me, and he succeeded, but I missed the message the attack was personal.

I hugged my arm to my loaded holster. Carrera was convicted and soon to be sentenced, so I'd have to be especially wary of what he might try. Fabrizio promised me he would keep tabs on what Carrera was planning—all in his own self-interest, of course—because if Carrera did kill me Fabrizio would never see his money again. Small comfort.

I pushed open the door to the Kozy Korner Koffee Shop—the obscenity of their KKK logo apparently lost on the owners—and tripped a small bell announcing my arrival. The place was virtually empty, not surprising on such a cold night. Bo sat in a far corner at a table for two, his hands wrapped around a white ceramic mug. He nodded at me. I bought a cup of decaf at the counter and went over to him.

"Sorry about the delay—couldn't be avoided," I said as I sat down.

He waved me off. "I'm a firefighter, remember? I get it." He leaned back in his chair and took a sip from the mug.

"Right." Cops and firefighters, along with doctors and ambulance drivers, had to be prepared for the call in the night, and then respond. But Bo's assumption I was late because of my job wasn't based in reality. I raised my mug. "Here's to getting fired." We clinked and drank. I almost spit it out but then swallowed and made a face. "Burnt." Not to mention the metallic taste in full force.

I put down my mug and shrugged out of my jacket. He noticed I was carrying, showing me a puzzled face as he gestured with a discreet motion at my holster bulge.

"A lot of cops carry when they're off duty," I said, "but not my habit. At least, not until now. I won't be caught again without protection."

He nodded, making a humming sound in assent. "Smart."

I didn't feel smart, only in survival mode.

Bo leaned forward, his forearms on the table. "So, tell me about what happened."

An hour later, my hot chocolate only dregs in a different ceramic mug, Bo and I stood to leave. The barista wished us a pleasant evening and I dropped a five on the table for her, Bo chipping in a couple more bucks. We walked back to my apartment building. I was surprised when Bo entered the foyer with me.

"I'm fine from here on," I said, unsure if he thought he was coming upstairs with me.

"Oh, I'm staying with my parents until New Year's Day. Kind of a Hungarian family tradition."

I smiled. "Your father brought me some lentil soup. I'm hoping the get-rich part of that tradition comes true."

Bo chuckled and held up both hands, his fingers crossed. "Personally, I'd stick with the want ads."

"Yeah, well. Thanks for meeting for coffee, as awful as it was."

"Meeting me? Or the coffee?" His mouth twitched at the corners.

"Good one," I said, smiling in spite of thinking it was pretty corny.

"And what about the hot chocolate?" He grinned.

"You know what? You're right. The hot chocolate was also a comfort."

"And it was free."

I nodded. When I complained to the barista about my burnt decaf, she supplied the free drink. "Are you always this relentlessly upbeat?"

Bo trained his gaze on his feet. "Practicing my social skills. I'm mostly relentlessly introverted."

"Oh. Probably why you're a good listener. I unloaded a lot of crap about my job—former job. Hope I didn't overload you." I unlocked the foyer door leading to the stairway inside and we entered.

"No, you didn't." He pointed to his parents' door and dropped his voice to a whisper. "How much do you bet my mother is on the other side of this door, right now, listening to our conversation?"

I laughed. "My mother would be doing the same only she's deaf, so she'd be looking at us through the peephole and trying her damnedest to lipread what we're saying."

Bo cocked his head. "That's interesting. She's deaf?"

"Yeah. Both my parents. And my twin brother and my younger sister. I'm the only hearie in the bunch."

Bo nodded in a slow, thoughtful way. "I'd like to hear more about that sometime."

I reached out and touched his forearm. "Sure. Me too. Goodnight."

He unlocked his door and we went our respective ways, Bo into the first-floor apartment, me to the third floor.

I got ready for sleep and slid under the comforter on my futon. Our conversation tonight at the coffeehouse centered mostly on my job with CPD, so Bo heard all about my suspension for drinking and my failure at IOP resulting in my dismissal today. I didn't sugarcoat my drinking or hide or lie about any of it. Since he saw me in all my hideous glory the night I tried to break in through the transom, there was nothing more to hide.

I even threw in a one-liner about my divorce from Jimmy. None of it seemed to faze him or cause obvious repugnance. He asked thoughtful questions and mostly listened, which reminded me of JJ, offering no judgement, only companionship.

His positive reaction to the fact my whole family was deaf surprised me. The topic usually seemed to make people uncomfortable and unsure of how to respond. A few people have even expressed shock at the fact and offered condolences, as if being deaf was a catastrophe. But Bo wanted to hear more about it. Like a friend.

53

LOUISE

12/27 7:30 a.m.

A light snow fell outside as Louise and Angel left the homeless shelter. Last night she had suffered through that hotbox one more time, having no choice because she was afraid the police were after her. Her old worries had rushed back. That internet story about the Monster's husband being held for murder, maybe it was fake and the police planted it to flush her out. At least the homeless shelter gave her protection, even if it was only for one more sleepless night.

That damn Bonnie! Texting the cops about her. But stupid Bonnie. Leaving a manila envelope right there on the dining room table, which showed Gerry's new address on it.

She dawdled at McDonald's until one-thirty to drink coffee and get free refills, wanting the morning to wane before traveling to Gerry at his new place in Maywood. He always slept in after his twelve-hour overnight shift.

A female cabbie stopped immediately for her when she signaled at the corner. A woman with a baby (asleep!) would be a good fare.

Gerry would gladly pay the woman once Louise arrived. They would finally be a family.

Louise announced her destination. The cabbie bobbed her head and gestured at the stroller. The woman probably didn't speak English, Louise guessed, but her gesture was clear, so Louise lifted Angel's dead weight from the stroller.

The cabbie held open the door for her—a small luxury—and Louise entered the back seat of the cab and laid the sleeping Angel down. She considered the cab itself a huge luxury after riding filthy buses and trains for the past three days. She could *feel* bugs crawling on her.

A quick fold of the stroller, which the cabbie stowed in the trunk, and they were on their way.

But now she could relax as the cab made its way south on the expressway. Wet flakes piled up in a hurry at the corners of the windshield as the snowfall thickened, and the wipers caked the slush. She would have to talk with Gerry about moving elsewhere, someplace warm, where the baby could play outside all the time without this horrible kind of weather.

54

DANA

9:00 a.m.

I slept in the next morning. When I woke up, I rushed to the bathroom and vomited. After I brushed my teeth, I put on some water for hot chocolate, shunning crappy, metallic-tasting coffee altogether. During my first pregnancy I had no morning sickness at all. Nothing amiss until I miscarried at four months. Jimmy convinced me to quit smoking for our baby. This time was different in both regards.

I sat at my desk, tamped down my nausea with hot chocolate, and smoked a Kool. I was going to pretend the baby wasn't Jimmy's until I could get a DNA test from him to confirm one way or the other. I discovered the test wouldn't be accurate until I was about eight weeks along.

A text from Nuts said he'd be by in an hour for our trip to Gary. I texted back my agreement and asked him to pick up doughnuts for me. He never touches the things. I now had license to eat whatever I wanted—the *eating for two* maxim—and sugar seemed to be a welcome antidote to my nausea and smoking reduced my anxiety. I wasn't going to go through withdrawal unless I decided to carry this pregnancy to term.

I showered and dressed in warm clothes. The windchill again promised a sub-zero temp. I surveyed my face critically in the mirror. I needed to appear presentable for the interview in Gary. Even though I continued to heal, the yellow and green stage of my facial bruises still needed coverage, as did the stubbornly purple welt along my temple. I slapped on Rosie's thick concealer until the remnants of my brutal beating went undercover.

I made my way downstairs to wait in the foyer for Nuts. Bo Sandor was there, retrieving his parents' mail from the metal box embedded in the wall. I waited for him to finish.

"I meant to ask you something last night." When he looked at me, I brandished the invisible weapon Sandor had mimed for me. "What the hell does this mean?"

Bo hesitated only a second and then started laughing. "My father trying to tell you what my name means in Hungarian?"

I grinned. "Yes. I got that your sister's name means *follows God*, but he didn't have the English words for yours."

"Zizi has a deeper meaning, really. More like *dedicated* to God. And she is. Teaching religion in a private school in Hungary."

"And this?" Again, I mimicked Sandor's gesture.

"Mace-wielding warrior." At my puzzled face, Bo pulled out his cell and did a quick search. He showed me a picture of a really lethal-looking weapon, a metal ball about the size of a child's bowling ball, covered in sharp metal spikes. A length of chain attached the ball to a pole.

I could imagine how someone would use the mace, swinging it around to kill someone close by. I could also envision it being swung above the head like a lasso and then released to take out an enemy farther away.

"That's quite a name to stick on a little kid," I said.

Bo blushed. "Yeah. My father's first name is even worse. Sandor means helper and defender of mankind."

"Wait. Isn't Sandor your family's last name?"

Bo nodded. "It is. But it's not uncommon in the old country to have the same name first and last."

"I'm so ignorant of things like this. And it's much more interesting than what Americans do. My father's name is John Josef, but everyone calls him JJ. Pretty simple and without much meaning."

Part of me wanted to tease Botund Sandor about having a first and last name meaning *mace-wielding warrior, helper and defender of mankind.* My god. But I was particularly sensitive to having parents who were different from the majority of American family units, so I wasn't about to act like an asshole about his folks. Besides, I really liked the manager of my building and *Sandor Sandor* fit him.

"Your father gave me a little straw doll along with the soup. The soup was great, by the way."

"You're not supposed to eat that until New Year's Day, you know." He failed at suppressing a smile.

I smiled back. "Yeah, well. Resisting temptation not my strong suit."

"Just means you won't get rich."

"Darn. I like the straw doll tradition, though. She's attached to my car's rearview mirror and I'm going to follow your father's instructions. Definitely want to say goodbye to this shitty year."

Bo said nothing but nodded.

My phone vibrated. A text from Nuts saying he was three minutes away. I waved my phone at Bo. "Getting picked up soon. My ex-partner and I are going to Gary to find out if this woman I told you about took off for her mother's." On my phone I pulled up the picture of baby Melanie from the TV Amber Alert and showed it to Bo, who studied it for a long moment.

He handed back my phone, his face creased with a question. "I thought you were done."

I sighed. "I am, really. This is one last lead we're tracking down. I called the mother and was told the daughter never visits. But that was over a week ago. The daughter might've run out of options and headed for Gary since. This is strictly a last-ditch effort and I doubt it's going to yield anything. After this trip, I'm going to hunker down for a while. No going out on New Year's Eve, I'll let the amateurs get drunk and drive. Done more than my share of that."

"I'm on forty-eight hours at the station starting tomorrow night. Really hoping it's quiet." He gestured at the outdoors. "Especially in this kind of weather."

I glanced out the glass foyer door and saw Nuts's red Prius glide up to the curb.

Bo tracked my glance. "Hope you find her."

"And the baby. Thanks. Me, too." I headed for the door.

"And the baby," Bo echoed.

I slid into the Prius, toasty warm inside after the cold foyer of my apartment building, and greeted Nuts. He thrust his thumb toward the rear seat. "Back there," he said, as he pulled into the street.

Now I could smell the doughnuts. They sat primly on the seat in a pink bag from a local bakery. I snatched it up and peeked inside. Not one, not two, not three, but *four* cake doughnuts, chocolate with chocolate frosting. I downed one before even getting my thanks out.

"You know me so well," I said. I started on the second.

"You're easy. Double chocolate. Doesn't take a genius."

I managed to finish all four on the hour trip to Gary, rationalizing they constituted my absent breakfast and probable missing lunch. True to my experience with this pregnancy so far, my morning sickness nausea vanished with the sugar and carbs combo. I wished I had some coffee, but the mere thought evoked the metallic taste on my tongue. The pink bag also contained a carton of milk—not chocolate —which I guess was Nuts's way of combatting junk food with something healthy. I drank it anyway.

The Skyway traffic wasn't too bad, but Gary's unholy stink greeted us long before we actually arrived. Chicago's air isn't the best, but thank god it ain't Gary. The GPS took us through a few neighborhoods where many homes were boarded up or simply abandoned. Louise's mother lived near Miller Beach on a street with identical square ranch houses repeating on each side. The only visible variation was the different colors people painted their doors.

As we approached Louise Conway's mother's home, Nuts pulled over to the curb and parked.

"You have the number?" Nuts said.

"Yep." I retrieved the mother's phone number from my contacts and had it ready.

We got out of the car and walked to her home, another copycat one-story ranch but sporting a neon green door. Nuts rang the doorbell and after a minute a woman wearing a light pink uniform answered. I assumed this was the caregiver I spoke to when I previously called Louise Conway's mother.

"Yes? Help you?" Her familiar southern accent confirmed my guess.

Nuts held up his badge and introduced himself and me as his partner

—without using my name—and asked if she was Louise Conway's mother.

"No, sir. That would be Mrs. Dryden." She waved her hand over her shoulder. "My name is Grace Harris. I'm a live-in caregiver for Mrs. Dryden."

Nuts asked if we could come in to talk about Louise Conway. I glanced at my phone and pushed the call icon for the home's phone. A moment later came the corresponding ring from inside. The woman got flustered.

"Oh! I gotta get that. Hold on." She started to close the door but then waved us inside. "Too cold to be standin' out there."

I thanked her and we entered a small living room to the left of a long hallway. Ms. Harris told us to wait while she hurried down the hallway toward the back to answer the phone. As soon as she turned away, I followed and glanced into rooms where doors stood open.

On the left, an empty bedroom turned sewing room and next, a bathroom. Across the hall from the bathroom, a flight of stairs led down to the basement. There was one more room with a closed door. Just before I got to the end of the hall where it opened into the kitchen, Ms. Harris answered my call. I disconnected.

I walked into the kitchen, casual and smiling. "Do you mind if I use your bathroom? We had a long drive here from Chicago."

The woman held the receiver of an avocado green landline phone and waved it at me. "They hung up." She shook her head.

"Telemarketers. I can't stand them."

She smiled. "That's the truth." She replaced the receiver. "Oh! Yes. Bathroom's right there." She gestured toward the bathroom I'd just passed.

"Thanks so much. My partner has a few questions, so you can get started with him." I waved at her to follow me back to the living room. As she and Nuts sat down and he began, I murmured *be back in a minute* and again headed down the hallway. A quick trip down the basement stairs yielded one large room holding only a washer and dryer and some boxes stacked up along a wall.

Back upstairs I opened the door to the closed room and peeked in— an elderly woman in bed, asleep. No Louise Conway, no baby Melanie Stuckless. In the bathroom I closed the door, waited a minute, flushed the toilet and washed my hands, and then returned to the living room.

Ms. Harris was saying she'd never met Louise Conway. Louise never visited her mother and wasn't that such a shame. Nuts duly jotted this in his notepad. He glanced at me and I gave my head a slight shake.

"Does Mrs. Dryden ever talk about her daughter?" Nuts asked.

"Mrs. Dryden isn't right in the head anymore. She has that dementia. Sometimes she talks about when she was comin' up, but mostly it's about her childhood. Nothin' about married life or her daughter." She paused, thoughtful. "You know, could be why Louise never visits. Mother doesn't remember her, mostly stays in bed. Maybe it hurts to see her mother like that."

"Could be," I said. "Does Mrs. Dryden have any other children?"

"No. Louise is her only child."

Nuts asked a few more questions and ascertained Louise Conway had no family other than her mother and her husband. Her father walked out one day when she was a young girl and never returned. There were no aunts, uncles, or cousins who might offer her places to hide, which at least made our jobs easier. By not chasing after extended family members we could focus on tracking her down. Unfortunately, even with the APB that challenge loomed almost impossible in Chicago, the third largest city in America.

After we left the house and rode back to the city, I had an unexpected jolt of sympathy for Louise. Hearing the added bit of family information for a second time provided another insight I didn't initially consider. Maybe the kidnapping wasn't only about her inability to have a baby. Maybe she tried to construct a vision of a different kind of family, one unlike her solitary experience growing up.

Her husband Gerry had said something about her childhood loneliness during our interview, but he focused mostly on how Louise's infertility impacted him and caused their break-up. And then Gerry walked out on Louise, surely a haunting reminder of her father's departure. Maybe a tipping point?

Louise's story was an unwelcome reminder of how my drinking affected Jimmy and caused our ultimate break-up. Though our circumstances were different, Louise and I shared a stark truth: our behavior impacted the men we loved and led to dire consequences. My already nauseated gut churned anew. I ordered Nuts to pull over, exiting the car just in time for me to lose all four doughnuts.

I hated my body's clammy feeling right before throwing up, but once it was over I felt better and curiously lighter.

Back inside the car, I scrounged in my backpack for some gum or a lozenge to arrest the sour taste in my mouth but could only come up with a dissolving mouthwash strip. Better than nothing.

Nuts didn't drive on. He peered at me. "Are you sick?"

I lowered the seat-back a few clicks and let the headrest support my neck. I spoke to the windshield. "Depends on who you ask. Actually, I'm pregnant." I didn't want to face him and took in his expression with a sidelong glance.

Puzzled. Then, lightbulb. He shook his head. "Oh. Shit. No."

"Oh. Shit. Yes. Here's the kicker. I don't know who the father is." I straightened up my seat-back and turned to face him. "Could be Jimmy. Could be the fucker who raped me."

Nuts is not demonstrative physically, doesn't hug people—even those he knows—doesn't pat people on the back or shake hands. I even wondered sometimes how his former fiancée and he got along in that department. I chalked it up to Nuts being a germaphobe—COVID scared him witless—or maybe there was some unknown psychological reason.

Anyway, at the mention of how I might be pregnant at the hands of a rapist, Nuts reached out and cupped my cheek with his hand, leaving it there for a long moment and saying nothing. I laid my hand over his and patted it, acknowledging his comforting gesture.

He rubbed his thumb over the place my attacker clouted me. He jerked his hand back. "What the—"

I lowered my sun visor and flipped open the cover to its mirror. His thumb had inadvertently unmasked a slice of my still deep-purple bruise. Using a napkin from the morning doughnuts, I made quick work of revealing the rest of my naked face and then showed him the bruising on my neck. I explained what Fabrizio told me last night, the attack was a message from Carrera.

"But if I hadn't been drunk this never would've happened." Hard to admit, especially to him. I closed the mirror's cover and raised the visor.

Nuts pulled out a handkerchief and rubbed away the transferred makeup on his fingers. I hauled out the sanitizer he kept in the glove compartment and pumped a liberal blob onto his palm, which he slathered around. After waving his hands dry, he settled them on the steering wheel, not looking at me. "Something I always worried about. Drinking—getting drunk—makes you vulnerable."

No comforting words from Nuts like *don't blame yourself,* or, *sorry this happened to you,* just agreement I'm to blame. This time, though, his words came through as a weird kind of affirmation about my recent experiences. I returned the sanitizer to the glove compartment.

He crossed his arms and turned slightly toward me. "What do you want to do?"

Out my window lay a depleted field, bare of last season's harvest, remnants of a few dried corn husks dotting the large expanse. Mounds of gray-black dirt striped the field in long rows, frozen from the subzero weather.

"You're the third person to ask me the same question, Nuts. And you know? Tossing my guts a minute ago finally gave me the answer. I'm giving up. I'm not doing this anymore—"

"But we—"

I held up my hand at his interruption. "Hold on." I swung my arm in a wide gesture. "There's nothing here. We've got nothing. No leads, no idea where Louise is. And I'm not a detective anymore. You are. Go work with Clint, show him how to do what you do so well, and you guys will find Louise and the baby." I motioned for him to put the car back on the road. He didn't.

Nuts crossed his arms over his chest. "I don't want to work with Clint."

"Yeah, well, there are a lot of things on my *don't want* list, too." I held up my hand and started counting in a haphazard order all of the problems bringing me to this point. "Like, Koz Breathalyzing me, suspending me, getting a DUI, Fabrizio blackmailing me, having a miscarriage, Jimmy divorcing me, losing my house, my mom getting attacked," I paused, "...being raped." I flinched, feeling the attacker's roundhouse punch to the side of my head as if it just happened.

"When Koz offered to have CPD pay for inpatient treatment I almost laughed in his face because there was no way I was going to do that. To quote Rameeka, 'stubborn bitch, that's me.' Now the idea of hiding out for thirty days seems like a gift from, I don't know, heaven? God?" Or maybe Koz.

A strong urge surfaced to tell Nuts the news Koz was an alcoholic, something I would have shared without hesitation not so long ago. But Koz's admonition to keep it between the two of us interfered and stifled me, a new signpost of growing apart from my former partner. Keeping secrets from him.

I half-turned in my seat to face Nuts. "I'm gonna go to inpatient, leave all this shit behind, and do whatever they tell me. I give up. I'm done trying to manage my life with booze." What I didn't say was I sure as hell didn't know how I'd manage my life without it.

Nuts took this in without saying anything and we sat for a few minutes in silence.

"Okay," he said. He dropped the car in gear and pulled onto the road back home.

55

DANA

2:30 p.m.

Nuts continued north towards Chicago in silent mode. I think the reality we couldn't deliver on Louise and baby Melanie hurt him somehow. My pointing out we didn't have anything, that we were as bereft of leads as the empty field was of corn, went against every perseverative bone in his body. He never, ever, gives up. And neither do I—at least, not until now—which is why we worked so well together. I had every confidence, though, he would corral Clint and come up with a way to find Louise in a city the size of Chicago.

Admitting I was done, giving up, cashing in my chips, resulted in an unexpected and major dose of relief for me. I again lowered my seat-back a few clicks and closed my eyes. We were about forty minutes from my place, depending on traffic ahead, and all I could think about was lying down on my futon and going to sleep.

A minute later my cell phone buzzed in my pocket. I didn't recognize the number. The area code was Chicago. I was expecting a call back from a new gyne doc to schedule an appointment, so I answered.

"This is Dana Demeter."

"Yes, yes. Hello. This is Gerry. Gerry Conway. Louise's husband? We met a while ago?" He sounded out of breath, like he'd run upstairs to his bleak studio apartment.

"Right. What can—"

He interrupted. "Louise was here. She has a baby!" His panting made it hard to understand him.

"Wait. Catch your breath. Calm down and hold on for one sec." We were approaching the Eisenhower turnoff leading to Maywood. I directed Nuts to Conway's address and put my phone on speaker. "Okay. Louise is there?"

"I don't know how she found me. She has some baby! It's so sick!"

"Okay. We're heading to your place right now. Try to keep her there."

"No! She's gone! I tried to get her to go to the ER but she wouldn't. She kept saying we could be a family. I told her that baby wasn't ours and she got mad. Oh, my god!"

"Where did she go?"

"I don't know! She grabbed my wallet and my keys and ran out with the baby. I ran after her but she got in a taxi waiting outside." His panting slowed.

"Did you get the taxi company's name?" Nuts said.

Conway paused for a moment. "No. The car was white?"

Nuts and I groaned in unison. Many cab companies in Chicago had white taxis. By the time we got an APB out to them Louise would be gone.

"Okay. We're on it. If you see her again, text me where you are. Don't try to engage or talk to her, just text me right away. Got it?"

"I tried to get her to stay." He started to hyperventilate again. "I—I blew it. She just showed up and—and I didn't know. What was I supposed to do?" His question came out in a forlorn voice with a lot of whine thrown in.

"It's okay. Good thing you called." I disconnected.

Nuts put out an APB to all cab companies regarding Louise's pickup point to determine if she could be traveling, or identify her destination if already dropped off.

"It's a long shot," Nuts said, exiting the Ike and taking the overpass to return east to the city.

"Yeah. But it's something."

Nuts grunted his assent, then put in a call for two uniforms to head to Louise and Gerry's condo on the off chance she headed there again. He ordered his phone to call Rokick next, who picked up on the first ring. Nuts ran down what happened and told Rokick to monitor the APB calls if they came in. "Be ready to jump if anything pops."

"Are you coming in? Are we doing this together?" Rokick asked.

Nuts glanced at me. "Yes. To both. Should arrive in thirty."

56

LOUISE

3:00 p.m.

Louise used her arms to pin Angel to her chest, the little girl burning up and unconscious. The cab headed north to the condo. Once she got there, she would be safe. *She could get into their place.* She gripped Gerry's keys. One of them would open the door. Gerry could come a little later, when he had time to understand what she wanted, how hard she worked to make a family for them. He would explain to Bonnie how they adopted the baby.

Gerry's wallet revealed a large amount of cash, relief from the worry she would have to use the credit cards. The woman cabbie—Aleeza, according to the ID on the seat-back—kept glancing at Louise in the rearview mirror. Louise kept Angel draped over her shoulder so Aleeza wouldn't see the baby's face or get any ideas about who she was.

"Boy or girl?" Aleeza asked.

"Never mind! Just drive. Stop looking at me."

The driver shrugged. Louise realized they were almost to the North Side where the cabbie should exit for the condo.

"I have a daughter," Aleeza said. "She's two." She laughed. "And a handful."

Louise couldn't believe this woman and how much she wanted to talk. Louise was sure if Aleeza kept talking, she would figure out who Angel was. But maybe if Louise tried to be nicer to the driver, then she wouldn't report them or call the police.

She forced a smile. "They are a handful, you're right." She shifted Angel's dead weight to her other shoulder. The little girl stirred and made some weird noises. Louise pulled Angel off her shoulder to look at her. The cabbie squinted at them in the rearview mirror. Suddenly Angel arched her back. Louise felt the little body stiffen, and more weird noises erupted.

The cabbie exited the expressway and pulled over to the curb, shifting the car to park. "What's wrong? This looks bad." She reached an arm over the seat toward Angel. The cabbie's other hand held up a cell phone. Louise slapped her.

"Don't touch her! Just drive. Take me home or I won't pay you!" Louise hugged Angel again, who went limp. Then she realized her mistake, calling the baby 'her.' "My son is just tired, that's all. Get us home so he can sleep."

"Look. Let me drive you to the ER. It's not too far from here. I'm not worried about the money. I'm more worried about your...your baby."

Angel arched her back again, her head lolling backward and body stiffening under Louise's hands.

"Oh, my god! She's having seizures!" Aleeza said.

"Take me and my son home!"

The cabbie faced forward and pulled into traffic, shaking her head, and turned east toward the condo.

Out the window Louise saw familiar landmarks, places close to home, but she was afraid the cabbie would ignore her order and drive to a hospital. She needed to be shut of this nosy woman and get Angel inside and safe. She held Angel's body at arm's length to inspect her.

The cab came to rest at a stoplight. Louise caught the cabbie eyeing her again in the mirror. She had to get away from this woman. She laid Angel on the seat for a moment to gather the diaper bag.

In a belabored motion Louise opened the door, stepped out, and turned to remove Angel from the offensive cab.

But the cabbie was quicker. Slinging her arm over the seat, she grabbed the back door handle and pulled it shut as she hit the gas.

Louise dropped her bag and screamed. "My baby! She has my baby!"

People on the sidewalk backed away from her. But as Louise rushed after the cab, now a half block away, she could see it pulling into the driveway of a fire station. She stopped and ducked into the doorway of a convenience store with a clear view of the station.

Even at a distance, Louise heard the cabbie lay on the horn in repeated staccato blasts. A tall man wearing dark pants and a white t-shirt with CFD in large letters on the chest emerged from the station and hustled to the cab.

The cabbie stepped out and gestured at the vehicle. The two of them talked a moment and then the tall man approached the cab's rear door and opened it. Louise pulled her body further into the corner of the store entry. The man leaned into the back seat. For a long minute nothing happened. He straightened, leaving the car door open, and hurried to the station.

A moment later the station's overhead door lifted and a red CFD ambulance pulled onto the driveway right next to the cab. The driver exited and ran around to the back, yanked open the doors, and retrieved a bed on wheels.

Louise held her breath. The man carefully lifted Angel from the cab and placed her on the bed. Why did he have to strap her down? She filled only a tiny portion of the bed. Louise wanted to go to her baby, push the man aside, and take her back. But her little girl's body was not moving.

The man rolled the bed to the back of the red truck, slipped it in, and slammed the doors. He jumped into the driver's seat. The siren pierced the air as the ambulance screamed into traffic and passed by Louise as she shrank into the doorway.

57

DANA

3:15 p.m.

Nuts dropped me off at home and I wished him luck finding Louise and baby Melanie. We made vague plans to have breakfast at the Elite, but I left it to him and his schedule when it would happen. I told him I would be entering treatment soon, so breakfast might have to wait until after the month of January.

I climbed the three flights to my studio and shucked off my winter coat and sloppy wet boots. Outside my window the heavy snow was starting to pile up on the sidewalks, but Sandor would wait until it stopped before doing any shoveling.

On my desk sat the package of long-absent blackout curtains I kept reminding myself to buy. It was time to get them up, which would make my studio dark enough for a nap. The former tenant had left cheap curtain rods in place, so the job was quick, and I closed the new yellow drapery against the outside storm.

I changed into my sweats, pulled on the thickest, warmest socks I owned, and slid under the comforter on my futon. I couldn't recall being so exhausted with my first pregnancy. If anything, I was exuberant Jimmy and I were going to be parents, and physically I felt great. I was one of those pregnant women other pregnant women hated: shiny hair, glowing skin, full of energy.

This time, though, the morning sickness was kicking my ass. Right now, I was hungry because the doughnuts were my only food so far today, but they hadn't stayed put. On top of being hungry I was also quite nauseated, which made anything I wanted to eat about as appetizing as a pile of worms. I got up, drank some ginger ale, nibbled a few soda crackers, and returned to the futon for the oblivion of sleep.

Fifteen minutes into my nap a message dinged on my cell. I'd forgotten to mute the damn thing. I lifted the phone and faced a picture of Louise Conway holding a baby that lay slack over her shoulder. I sat up. Even though the baby's face was hidden, it had to be Melanie Stuckless. The text was from Bo. One word.

Yours?

Yes

Immediately I sent him Nuts's name and phone number as the person to contact, but I thrummed with the urge to jump up, get dressed and rush over to the fire station. My own words to my ex-partner reverberated an unwanted refrain: *I am not a detective anymore.*

My mind served up a vision of Nuts and Rokick storming the fire station and arresting Louise Conway. I couldn't push away my envy, couldn't deny my itch to be an active part of the solution even though I reminded myself: I. Was. Done. I assumed the baby was treated by the paramedics, maybe even Bo, or possibly taken to the hospital.

But what about Louise? She already eluded me twice. I grabbed my coat.

58

DANA

4:00 p.m.

Nuts and I each arrived at Bo's fire station at almost the exact same time, pulling onto the longish driveway leading to the overhead door where a CFD ambulance waited, engine running. Bo stood there talking to an EMT. He turned to us as we exited our cars and rushed toward him.

"Where's Louise?" Nuts shouted.

"The baby's at Masonic," Bo said. He shook hands with the other guy, who jogged around to the driver's side of the wagon and got in. The overhead door to the station rattled open and the ambulance pulled inside. Nuts and I both hustled after the rig and hurried into the station. No Louise. Bo entered a beat later.

"The woman with the baby—where is she?" Nuts again, shouting.

Bo made a shushing motion with his hands and then shrugged, his face creased in puzzlement. "I wasn't worried about her. Just the baby."

"Any idea which way she went? Was she walking? Cab? What?" I spit out my urgent questions.

"She was in the cab with the baby. Cabbie took the pic I sent you. But she was gone when the cabbie got here. We took the baby to Masonic. No idea where the woman went."

Nuts and I grimaced at each other. "Okay," I said to Bo. "If she comes back—like thinking she'll get the baby—hold her here and call us." Bo nodded.

I turned to Nuts. "Get some backup to help us. She can't be far. She's around here somewhere." That might be true only if she walked away.

I gave Bo a thumbs-up and got his okay to leave my car at the station. Nuts and I hurried to his car, got in, and he called for beat patrol to help us scour the neighborhood. I notified the condo manager and Gerry Conway to be on the lookout for Louise, even though it seemed unlikely she would return to either place.

The sun set less than an hour later, making our search almost impossible, but we kept at it for another three hours. Nothing.

59

LOUISE

4:00 p.m.

Louise lumbered east toward the 'L', a COVID mask providing what she hoped was enough camouflage for her face. She was sure they were looking for her. She paused to catch her breath by a metal trash can posted at the foot of the 'L' stairs. The baby's diaper bag weighed heavily on her shoulder. It would be exhausting lugging it up the staircase to the train.

Louise pushed the strap off her shoulder and unceremoniously dumped the entire bag into the trash can. It didn't matter. Her baby was gone.

She caught the Brown Line train heading south toward downtown Chicago. At the Merchandise Mart she got off and descended to street level. The exit from the station led directly to a rusty red bridge over the Chicago River. A survey of the murky water below revealed the semi-frozen river swirled with large chunks of ice floating, bobbing, and bumping into each other.

Louise stood at the railing a long time. Night fell. The hordes of people traipsing to and from the train gradually subsided. She didn't feel the temperature drop below zero. She stayed rooted on the bridge, alone. No one came to arrest her, but she had stopped fearing the police pursuit.

Her mind swarmed with loss, her wishes undone: six months ago she was sure she was pregnant. But her body didn't change, didn't show that truth. She rested her hand on her belly where she had endured countless IVF shots. The doctor was right. Louise was wrong.

Gerry didn't want her anymore. He gave up on having a family, gave up on her. When she tried to bring Angel to him he only got mad and yelled at her about the baby being sick.

Gerry wanting a separation was a lie, he meant to divorce her, she understood that now. He changed the locks on the condo. He put it up for sale. All to get away from her. He would never take her back. They could never be a family.

Most of all, her wish to be like Margot the Monster—no! Not *like* Margot. She wanted to *be* Margot: thin, every physical detail of clothes, hair and makeup attended to. This hapless and unfulfilled wish evaporated as quickly as her hot breath in the cold air.

Angel was her perfect baby. Until she wasn't. Louise sobbed at how poorly she had taken care of Angel in the end. They took her baby away in an ambulance.

She wanted desperately to go into a forest and just lie down, not hear anyone, or see anything, anymore. She had nothing left.

60

DANA

1/1 7:00 a.m.

The baby in the booth next to us fussed at his mother as she tried to keep hold of him squirming in her arms. The man with her—I assumed her husband—glanced up for a moment and then returned to scrolling on his phone. The tussle escalated until the baby let out an ear-piercing wail. More than a few heads swiveled in the direction of the booth.

After my miscarriage earlier this year I would have taken in this scene with a modicum of patience, commenting internally on how I might handle it, and lamenting how unfair it was that women able to carry their babies to term seemed unfit for actual motherhood. Back then, losing my baby only increased my baby hunger. I would've been extremely envious of the woman with the screaming baby. I would've immediately traded places with her.

But now I'm pregnant and in the throes of morning sickness. I just wish the brat would shut up. I can't imagine having to put up with such noise for at least the first two years of the life I carry.

I stuck my fingers in my ears and grimaced at Nuts, who sat across from me sipping his morning tea with equanimity in spite of the high-frequency decibels ringing around us. "How do you stand that?" I nodded in the direction of the offensive booth.

He shrugged. "It's what babies do." More sipping.

The Elite Restaurant was only moderately busy for seven in the morning. Usually, a bustling crowd has already gathered by this hour, a reminder of times past when Nuts and I would corral a booth and dissect our cases. Today, I chalked up the thin crowd to New Year's Day. Lots of people hung over and sleeping in. Not us, though.

Nuts doesn't drink. I do and have. I didn't last night. If I wanted to get wasted one more time, I could do it tonight before reporting for the thirty-day inpatient program tomorrow. I signaled the waiter for a hot chocolate refill, chilled from sitting near the front door, and freed the scarf from my jacket and wound it around my neck for added warmth.

"So how long are you going to make me wait to hear about what happened with Louise Conway?"

Nuts put his cup down abruptly, the clink in the saucer audible even over the baby's squalling. Why the hell doesn't that woman at least check if the kid's diaper is wet? As if she read my mind, she rose, baby still squirming and crying, and grabbed the diaper bag from the booth's seat, then headed for the bathroom near the bar.

Bottles of booze lined up in two tiers along the bar's wall and glittered in the ceiling's canned lights, winking at me. I averted my eyes. The baby's crying diminished as the bathroom door closed.

"She killed herself." Nuts tilted his head to one side and gazed at his folded prayer hands.

"No. Really?" I touched his hand lightly and then pulled back. "My god. I imagined all kinds of things, but not suicide." I assumed after

Nuts and I failed in our search—I truly gave up anything to do with Louise Conway—he and Rokick would take it from there and eventually find her. Then there would then be a competency hearing to decide if she was fit to stand trial. "What happened?"

He told me. Three days of searching for Louise Conway produced no results. Then yesterday a call came in from a conservation-minded citizen clearing trash from the North Branch bank of the Chicago River. A woman's frozen body, mostly hidden beneath an overpass, was wedged between two fallen trees.

I cringed at this information. "Pretty violent way to end it."

"Don't think there was any other way out for her."

What Nuts said rang true. Louise Conway killed a woman, took her baby, and put the baby's life in danger, all in an effort to fashion a life for herself with her estranged husband. Somehow she thought that would satisfy her need to be a family. After her utter failure there was no returning to the quiet life she envisioned. Reality clobbered her delusion. She had nothing left.

"No. No way out," I agreed. "How's the baby doing?"

Nuts see-sawed his hand. "Still touch and go. She should recover but it'll take time. Mac Stuckless is at the hospital with her, now the attentive father."

I raised an eyebrow at this.

Nuts explained. Mac Stuckless would get a lot of money from his wife's death. And probably get a lot more from suing CPD over false arrest and imprisonment. "The media's eating it up and he's starring in his own version of Martyr of the Week."

"Are you tainted?"

"No. Koz seems satisfied to let Rokick take the heat since he was the charging detective. Koz'll probably get some of the fallout, though."

I thought about Koz telling me the one most important fact of his life was not picking up a drink, not his job, not anything else. Sounds like he told me the truth. The urge surfaced again to tell Nuts about Koz, something we would have chewed on for quite a while back when we were partners.

It occurred to me Nuts and Koz would continue to work together. Given Nuts's negativity toward alcoholism, mine especially, I couldn't be the one to color my ex-partner's view of our boss. It also occurred to me I trusted Koz and Nuts to keep my alcoholic status to themselves and not narc on me to others. Even though Koz made what for him was a joke—*I don't care who knows I'm an alcoholic, as long as I don't forget it*—I could and would keep Koz's confidence.

Our food came and we ate in silence, no cases to discuss, no squad gossip to share. The couple with the fussy baby left when we were halfway through eating. Morning sickness edged into my stomach and began its churn, so I put down my fork, pushed away my plate, and ordered another hot chocolate.

Louise's demise, really her entire sad pursuit, highlighted a personal silver lining not apparent to me until now. Since I'm no longer a homicide cop, I won't have to deal with the gruesome messes some people make of their lives. And that realization supports my decision to enter inpatient treatment. I can focus on the mess I've made of *my* life—so far—and maybe turn some things around. Unlike Louise Conway, reality has handed me another chance.

We donned our coats and all the outerwear trappings of winter. Nuts picked up the check and waved it at me. "Merry Christmas, late," he said.

I laughed. This was new. "We never exchanged Christmas presents before."

He pulled at the earflaps secreted in his hat until they lay flat covering his ears.

"We were partners before."

61

DANA

Later that morning

I pitched Rameeka's suitcase next to mine in the Camry's trunk and slammed it shut, then hurried to get in on the driver's side. The bitter wind drove the late morning's temps to below zero. Rameeka sat in the passenger seat, her hair newly refreshed in the standout magenta she favored.

I warmed my hands over the dashboard vent and strapped on my seatbelt. "Warm enough?"

"Nope. Never. I'm always cold." Rameeka crossed her arms over what looked like a new knee-length, puffy down coat. Somehow, the neon green didn't clash with her hair.

"That coat not doing its job?"

Rameeka ran her hands down the front of the coat. "Rhon gave me this. Pretty, ain't it? Oh, it's warm, sure." She wrapped her scarf around her neck, and it pushed up against her short, springy curls, which stuck out in gravity-defying directions. "Don't know why I'm always so damn cold." She gazed out the front windshield. We sat in the parking lot of the treatment center where she'd spent the last twenty-eight days. "Like it's on the inside, you know?"

I leaned across and flipped open the vent on the far side of her seat and was rewarded with a gush of hot air. "There. That should help." As I sat back, my head hit Sandor's straw doll suspended from my rearview mirror. I reached up to stop the doll's sway. Rameeka recoiled a bit in her seat.

"What is that thing, anyway? Kinda spooky."

I laughed and pulled out of the parking lot and headed for Lake Shore Drive. Rameeka's sister Rhonda lived in the 875 N. Michigan Avenue building, otherwise still called the Hancock—its former name—by locals. Rhonda was giving Rameeka a place to live as long as she stayed sober and straight. She also insisted Rameeka give up The Life. After I dropped her off at her sister's, I was heading to a different inpatient program to check myself in.

"The manager of my building gave it to me. Sandor's from Hungary. In his country it's a way to say goodbye to the old year."

"With a *doll*? How people come up with that? What's it supposed to mean?"

I shrugged. "Got me. He also gave me some lentil soup. Eating it's supposed to make me rich."

Rameeka shook her head. "Soup? *Soup*?" This seemed even worse to her than the doll. "Just ignorant what I think, that's all."

I laughed. "Well, it makes a little sense. Lentils are round, coins are round. I guess that was the original idea, you know, a connection. Especially if you're poor, which I'm guessing the people who came up with this idea were. And yeah, like you said, ignorant. At least, hundreds of years ago people probably didn't get much education. So, kind of a way to make sense of life. Or at least to wish for something better."

I filled her in on the water aspect of the Hungarian New Year's tradition and the doll's demise. Intrigued, she reached out and untied the doll, inspecting it as she mulled this over. "Me, I drink on New Year's Eve. Maybe smoke some weed. Well, not this year."

I entered Lake Shore Drive, a breeze to navigate on New Year's Day when there was minimal traffic. Normally at this time rush hour still clogs up the road. I pushed the Camry to the speed limit, which wasn't much faster than the street limit, but the view riding next to Lake Michigan beat the city scenery.

"Yeah, me too," I said. "But I didn't last night. Worried about a urine drop today."

Rameeka made a humming sound of agreement or understanding. "We all had a group this morning, before you came. There's a lady came in who been in and out a lot. She say she don't drink on New Year's Eve, called it amateur night." Her voice turned squeaky. "So *dangerous* to drive the streets with all them people out there drunk." She chuckled.

I lit a Kool. Rameeka waved a hand in front of her face.

"Sorry." I cracked my window and the back window a bit. "You never smoked?"

"Just weed, like I said. Them cigarettes'll kill you."

Rameeka didn't laugh when she said this. I glanced at her. Serious face. Guess she didn't see the irony.

"Last time I saw you," I said, "I chickened out telling you something. It's a good news, bad news, kind of thing about CW."

At the mention of Charles Worthy's nickname, Rameeka muttered what sounded like *muthafucka.*

"That's the one," I said. "The good news is he's being charged with murdering both Toby and your friend Kandy. The bad news is the charge of CW kidnapping you had to be dropped."

Rameeka squawked. "How you figure that, huh? You saw me after the mofo stole me off the street, stuffed me in his car *trunk*. He was gonna kill me!"

"I know. I know. You're right. Thing is, we had to bargain with CW to get him to rat on a dirty cop. No way we were going to drop murder charges, so the only thing we could trade for it was your kidnapping."

She huffed and crossed her puffy arms, but they kept sliding apart.

"Oh. Like that's supposed to make me feel better." Her voice dripped with sarcasm.

"Well, yeah, Rameeka, it is. Girl, you been on the streets hooking, doing drugs. Pretty dangerous stuff right there. You could've died a lot of times, I bet. Just like your friend Kandy."

Rameeka said nothing, her gaze turned away from me and toward the lake. She gripped the straw doll with both hands, one finger stroking the doll's head.

"Never could know what was gonna happen. Trickin' only gave me enough money for one day. All I wanted. One day. Couldn't think about no future 'cause when I did all I saw was more doin' what I was doin' until I was dead."

She pulled up the hood of her puffy coat, which hid her head. Her voice dropped to a whisper. "Drinkin' and druggin' put the future far away so I didn't have to look at it. Or me. I *hated* myself."

I touched her arm. I could say those same words about my own situation. "I'm pregnant."

She turned her gaze toward me.

While we continued north on LSD, I told Rameeka everything that happened to me in the past year, every last shitty detail, ending with the rape and discovery of my current condition. I asked her what she would do in my situation if she was pregnant. Would she keep it or not?

"How I see it? That baby didn't do nothin' to you, it just is. And you got a chance to be a *mother*?" The last word squeaked with excitement. "Who wouldn't jump on that?"

Shades of Father Mik.

"So, I don't know if the father is my ex or the fucker who raped me. And I won't know until another month so I can get a test and find out."

Rameeka hummed a snatch of some tune.

"I lost everything that's meant anything in my life and it's because of drinking. The bitch of it is I can't go on like this *with* booze but I sure as hell don't know how I'll do without it."

"I get it. I do. Like I said, you can't know the future. They talked about it a lot at my program. You'll see. A lotta fear out there." She laughed and I asked her what was funny about fear.

"Oh, nothing's funny. Didn't say *fear* was funny. Counselors kept telling us fear stand for *face everything and recover.* But a junkie from Cicero came and talked to us 'bout his life and gettin' straight. He say fear stand for *fuck everything and run.*" She laughed again.

"Sounds like he has the right idea."

Rameeka quieted. "Now I got thirty days clean and sober, I see he's right."

She was at the end of her program. Mine would start today. But we both had the same problem: What will life afterwards be like? How will we know who to be?

We were getting close to her sister's place. Rameeka held up the straw doll and gave it a light shake. "I like shit like this. Stuff people do to hope. All 'round the world people got some shit like this."

Mickey's tree picture bloomed in my mind. Before, all I saw was a kid's drawing of something outside the apartment where he was trapped. A literal change of scenery. Maybe Rameeka's observation provided a more subtle reading of what Mickey expressed.

As we approached the Ohio Street ramp Rameeka asked me to exit there and directed me to a parking lot by the beach.

"We're not at your sister's."

"Let's go," she said. She waved me on, doll clutched in one hand, and headed toward the beach. I jumped out after her and hurried to catch up. The wind buffeted my ears, and it wouldn't take long for them to numb.

"God! For someone who's always cold, this isn't exactly a day to stroll on the beach."

"Won't take long." As we neared the water Rameeka stopped. "Damn. Lake's frozen. I wanted to send this little bitch flying into the waves."

"Let's see. January first in Chicago. Yep. Lake's frozen. We can't say goodbye that way. But I didn't tell you the other thing you can do with the doll." I dropped to my knees and started digging a small hole in the sand. Rameeka got the idea and joined me, and we made a good-sized hole in a short time.

"Now?" she asked.

"Now."

"In you go, you old-year doll." She plunged the straw figure into the hole and we both pushed at the pile of unearthed sand, filling the grave. We stood.

Rameeka cupped her hands at each side of her mouth and shouted into the wind. "Bye-bye you raggedy-ass year!"

I laughed and repeated her shouted sentiment toward the lake. We started to head back to the Camry, but Rameeka turned around and hustled to the filled-in hole. She beckoned me to join her. We stomped on the sand over and over until the mound was packed flat.

"Make sure she don't get out, right?"

"Right. Hell of a year. Not sorry to see it end."

We fist-bumped over the buried doll.

"Charles Worthy will be convicted for both murders. He'll go to prison and never get out. I promise you, Rameeka."

"If he do get out, he'll wish he stayed in the jail, 'cause I'll be waitin' for the muthafucka."

I busted out laughing and she joined me.

Back in the Camry I jumped onto Lake Shore Drive again and continued north, bypassing Rhonda's building.

"Where we going? Rhon's back there."

"We're going to my treatment program and you're going to take my car while I'm in there. You got a driver's license, right?"

"Sure. Had a old car for a while but it broke down and Rhon wouldn't give me any money to fix it. Had to junk it." She ran her hand over the leather interior covering the door. "This a real nice car. You sure 'bout this?"

"Yep. You gotta get to meetings, right? Driving is better than the 'L' or a bus and a lot easier."

Rameeka nodded. "I know that's right."

"And then after I'm done, *you* can come pick *me* up. Deal?" From the corner of my eye, I caught her staring at me.

She smacked the dashboard with both hands. "Oh, it's a deal all right."

At the treatment center I parked in the lot. We both got out and I retrieved my solo suitcase from the trunk, slammed it shut, and handed the key to Rameeka. "See you in thirty days, hear? You got my phone number and I have yours. Be careful driving. My insurance card is in the glove compartment if you need it. Any problems, you know where I am."

"I do, I do."

I didn't know if her eyes were watering from the cold wind or if she was tearing up for another reason. I held up my fist again and she bumped it with hers. She lowered the hood on her puffy green coat. "See you in thirty," she said, and lifted her hand in a tiny wave, then entered the driver's side.

I waited until she exited the lot and watched my Camry recede in the distance. I've given my car to a slightly reformed hooker who is a newly sober/straight, alcoholic/drug addict. And I don't care. Anyway, I know where she lives—at least, temporarily.

I entered the foyer of the treatment center and settled on a bench near the elevators where it finally hit me this place would be "home" for the next month. I wondered if this inpatient program would be anything like Rameeka's, bad smells and all.

It occurred to me during my time with outpatient I drank an awful lot, and I could have used inpatient treatment instead. Now here I was readying for inpatient and except for Rokick's sabotage, I've been dry for a while. Maybe Koz knew I would fail at outpatient, which would open my eyes to my condition. I'm beginning to appreciate Koz knows a lot more than I ever gave him credit for.

I called Rhonda and explained where I was. I told her Rameeka should be arriving at the Hancock soon and she would have use of my car for the duration of my program. I expected Rhonda to be critical of the decision to loan Rameeka my car, but she surprised me. Before I could explain further, she echoed my hope that having a car would aid Rameeka in attending 12-step meetings and her treatment program's aftercare. She sounded relieved.

"Thank you for helping my sister, Detective."

"We're helping each other. And it's Dana, now. Just Dana."

ACKNOWLEDGMENTS

Although I work in solitude, usually with classical music in the background to mask my tinnitus, I am well aware I do not work alone. Family and friends are the supportive structure upon which I rest in order to continue my creative pursuits. I would like to thank the following people:

Mark Burgess, for yet another amazing cover for the Dana Demeter series. Thank you, Mark, for making my books immediately recognizable by their covers. You're the best!

Bob Carty, for being a beta reader I rely on. Once again your comments pinpoint areas needing improvement that I cannot see on my own. I love discussing books and writing with you, and look forward to seeing your book published!

Karen Graham, a true life-long friend who challenged me from the get-go to keep writing and to pursue publishing. So glad we're trudging the road together.

Patty Whitehouse, a thorough beta reader who knows her stuff. Thanks for taking the time to write out detailed notes and then review them with me in person.

Diane Piron-Gelman, for her excellent editing assistance through some tough personal challenges (for us both!). Diane can be found here: wordnrd.com

Finally, thanks to all of you who have taken the time to read my work. It pleases me that Dana has a fan base!

ABOUT THE AUTHOR

A. F. (Addy) Whitehouse is a writer and a former Sign Language interpreter who hails from Chicago. *Signs of Murder*, her first offering in the Dana Demeter Mysteries, was a finalist (Indie Fiction category) in the 2022 Chicago Writers Association Book of the Year. She lives with her husband, Bob Carty, in Waukesha, Wisconsin.

Please visit my website: afwhitehouse.com

facebook.com/afwhitehouse

amazon.com/author/afw

ALSO BY A. F. WHITEHOUSE

Book I

Signs of Murder, Book one, is titled in blood red. The cover shows a black graphic of two hands against a white background, signing American Sign Language (ASL) for murder: the right hand's index finger (signifying a knife) slides along the left open palm. A red drop of blood drips from the end of the index finger.

Book 2

Signs of the Father, Book Two, is titled in magenta. On the cover is a black graphic of two hands against a white background showing the ASL sign for 'gone' or 'missing', which can also carry the meaning for 'dead'. One hand forms a 'c' handshape, palm facing the signer. The other hand starts above it, palm up, and then drops through to end up underneath the 'c' hand with the tips of fingers and thumb touching. In the bottom right hand corner a smaller graphic of a communion chalice lays on its side emitting a slight stream of blood.